JAYNE FAITH

Blood of Stone

Contents

Chapter 1	1
Chapter 2	12
Chapter 3	23
Chapter 4	31
Chapter 5	41
Chapter 6	50
Chapter 7	60
Chapter 8	73
Chapter 9	80
Chapter 10	92
Chapter 11	102
Chapter 12	112
Chapter 13	119
Chapter 14	126
Chapter 15	133
Chapter 16	140
Chapter 17	150
Chapter 18	156
Chapter 19	164
Chapter 20	177
Chapter 21	183
Chapter 22	196
Chapter 23	208
Chapter 24	219
Chapter 25	231

Chapter 26   239
Chapter 27   242
Chapter 28   251
About the Author   262
Also by Jayne Faith   263

Chapter 1

WITH AN IMPATIENT tug on the cross strap of my broadsword's scabbard, I watched the bouncer, a lanky man of Elvish descent, examine my mercenary credentials. He scanned the I.D. and activated the magical hologram to verify its authenticity. Among other things, the card displayed my name and the Fae ruler to whom I was sworn.

"Petra Maguire," he read from my I.D. in a lilting Irish accent. His shoulder-length orange-blond hair was pulled back in the requisite Elf ponytail, exposing the pointed tips of his ears. "Bit of a runt for a New Gargoyle, ain't ye?"

He peered down at me, his eyes flicking over what little skin I had exposed, looking for outward evidence of my stone blood.

I bit back a smartass retort. My Fae bloodline sometimes aroused some reaction, especially among the Fae races who seldom interacted with my kind. Curiosity was the most common, though revulsion still cropped up occasionally. I reached for my I.D., and he yanked the card back beyond my fingertips.

"You're half a foot shorter than all the New Gargs I know," he pressed.

I seriously doubted he knew any New Gargoyles. For one thing, there weren't that many of us. New Gargs were a new race of Fae spontaneously formed at the Cataclysm, a catastrophic shift in the magical world that occurred a few years before I was born. In a transformation that defied logic, a few hundred Fae abruptly acquired new magic and different features. My father was one of them.

Music pulsed from within the bar, and a line formed behind me. My impatience grew, becoming an itch in my palms, a desire to draw my sword. The Elf, though over six and a half feet tall, wasn't a fighter. He stood back on his heels, and his upper arms and chest had hardly any muscle tone. He wore a light caliber magi-zapper, a magic-powered stun gun holstered on his hip, but it wasn't even turned on. If he actually needed to use it, he'd have to wait several seconds while it warmed up. Amateur.

I could have him on the ground, screaming for his mother with a dislocated shoulder in less time than it would take him to reach for his gun. But I knew I had to behave. I'd save my aggression for my mark, who I hoped was inside the bar.

The Elf was still waiting for me to fulfill his curiosity.

"I'm not full-blooded New Gargoyle," I said, finally relenting.

His mouth widened in satisfaction like a cat who'd just cornered a mouse. He didn't care about my answer so much as the fact that he'd manipulated me into giving one. Elves could be such assholes.

He settled his weight onto one hip. "Your kind is known for fighting. Maybe I shouldn't let you in." He tapped the corner of my I.D. against his lower lip, as if he were going to stand there a while and consider his options.

My temper began to flare in earnest. I needed to get past him before he really tempted me to pull Mortimer on him.

The nightclub I was trying to get into was an establishment on the Faerie side of the hedge, the name for the border between the Faerie world and the Earthly realm where humans and other non-Fae lived. He couldn't bar me from entering based on bloodline alone. In Faerie, you couldn't discriminate based on race.

"That's illegal, and you know it," I growled. "You've wasted enough of my time."

In a blur of movement, I snatched my merc I.D. from his hand and darted around him before he could react. As I passed, I hit the back of one of his knees with my heel. He grunted as his leg buckled, and he scrabbled for the door handle to catch his balance.

A satisfied smile tugged at the corners of my lips. I relished taking people by surprise with my quickness. New Gargoyles were known for being extremely strong, but not swift. My non-Garg blood had diminished my size but also gifted me with reflexes and agility that full-blooded New Gargs didn't possess. Only thing was, I had no idea what made up the rest of my bloodline, because my father refused to tell me who my mother was. Just one of several bones of contention between me and him.

The bouncer didn't come after me, as I knew he wouldn't. I was tempted to pull Mort from my scabbard, sneak back to the entrance, and give the Elf a little parting poke in the ass just for good measure—nothing fatal, of course—but I reined in my focus. I had work to do. A faint zip of energy streaked across my back, the broadsword's response to the possibility of some action.

"Soon, friend," I said under my breath.

The bar, called Druid Circle, had only recently sprung up in this newly-established Faerie territory of the Spriggan kingdom, anchored near the famed Las Vegas Strip. Every Faerie territory had an invisible anchor, or attachment, to a location in the Earthly realm. Up until the Cataclysm, all Faerie territories were anchored in Old World locations—mostly Ireland, Scotland, and England.

Faerie and the Earthly realm were like two parallel worlds. There were points, called doorways, where Fae could pass back and forth between Faerie and the Earthly realm. The doorway outside of Druid Circle was one of the new ones. It was a bit like the normal world versus the realm of Wonderland that Alice found when she fell down the rabbit hole. Two complete worlds that existed separately.

Pausing off to the side of the nightclub's entrance, I reached down and pretended to adjust the zipper of one calf-high boot, allowing myself a moment to get my bearings and let my eyes adjust. I shifted my attention to my magical senses so I could feel out the crowd. The place was full, but not yet packed. Mostly Fae, with a sprinkling of vampires and human magic users who'd come over from the Earthly side of the hedge. Non-Fae could come into Faerie, but only with a Fae escort.

I couldn't imagine how King Sebastian, the ruler of the Spriggan kingdom, had managed to grab a piece of Faerie territory anchored so close to the Las Vegas Strip. It took specialized, extremely expensive magic to carve out new Faerie territories. Plus, the Strip offered the opportunity to easily bring in high rollers from the Earthly realm, so it was valuable territory from a financial standpoint and there would have been competition for this piece of Faerie land. The Spriggan kingdom wasn't particularly large or rich, and I wouldn't have guessed Sebastian had the resources for such a land grab. I'd heard no rumors about the transaction, but that didn't mean much. I usually made it a point to stay as ignorant as possible about Fae kingdom politics and power plays, unless such info might somehow help me catch a mark. My job kept me in the action I preferred: taking out menaces of supernatural society as a bounty hunter for the Earthly realm's Mercenary Guild.

Speaking of marks, I'd gotten a tip that my current target, a reclusive vamp, had been seen here in Druid Circle.

I wove through the milling crowd and tall tables to the bar, where I ordered a seltzer with lime from a curvy Fae woman with impossibly long and feathery eyelashes, a dead giveaway of her Sylph blood. I sipped from my straw and focused my senses, trying to zero in on all the vamps in the bar.

Hunting down criminal vamps was personal work for me, just about the only thing that tied me to the mother I never knew. A vamp had killed her not long after I was born. I was eight years old when my father, Oliver, revealed that my mother had been murdered by a vampire. Usually vamps targeted humans. But my Fae mother, who'd been troubled and vulnerable according to Oliver, had somehow gotten caught up with one and had paid with her life. He'd immediately regretted telling me how she died, because I began having nightmares about fanged, bloodthirsty killers. In my child's mind, all vamps were powerful and monstrous, constantly on the prowl for their next victims. Later I learned that wasn't entirely true; plenty of vampires led normal, peaceful lives. But the mental image of vamps as evil monsters still lingered.

Protecting other innocents from my mother's fate was the best thing I could think to do to honor her. So, after graduation I'd moved out of Faerie into the Earthly realm so I could join the vamp-hunting division of the Mercenary Guild, an organization that came into being after magic went haywire following the Cataclysm. The Guild was formed to deal with the post-Cataclysm criminal activity that the pre-Cataclysm laws weren't doing a good job controlling. Private citizens also sometimes hired the Guild for personal assignments.

Holding my glass, the only purpose of it to help me blend in, I casually turned around and leaned my back against the bar so I could survey the place with more ease. The music was pulsing, but not yet at the volume or tempo that would get the crowd moving. A group of Cait Sidhe girls who looked barely old enough to be out alone were the only ones on the dance floor. They gyrated their lithe bodies with sinuous, feline movements.

One of the girls raised her arms in the air and pitched unsteadily. A couple of her friends caught and righted her before she face-planted.

She raised her arms as if remaining on her feet was a huge victory. "Wooo!" she hollered in an eerily cat-like voice that carried over the noise.

I looked past the Cait Sidhe, refocusing on my assignment.

My mark was a male, one of the new generation of vamps infected by the VAMP3 virus that had spontaneously ripped through the population following the Cataclysm. VAMP3s could be aggressive, but the real danger was their persuasiveness. They could naturally walk in sunlight unharmed, and the Type 3 vamps had glamour abilities that bordered on hypnotism. Unfortunately, supernatural lawmakers in the Earthly realm hadn't figured out how to enforce limits on the use of charm. And so far, vampire rights groups had managed to keep VAMP3s free of the docility implant requirement that befell the naturally bloodthirsty VAMP2s. The Mercenary Guild got a lot of jobs involving VAMP3s.

I knew the gender and name of my mark, but he tended to hide out in Faerie where cell phones and other communication technology didn't work, and no one had managed to capture a photo of him. He'd been selling VAMP3 blood on the black market, touting it as a magical potion that gave the user a soaring high and also imparted some of the legendary VAMP3 powers of charm. Only problem was, after a few doses it was turning users into murderers. One or two highs seemed to be fine, but further exposure somehow flipped a switch, turning users into blood-hungry maniacs.

I distinguished five male vamps in the vicinity, all Type 3. I eyed the male vamp nearest me. His straight blond hair was slicked back from his forehead, and he wore a black leather jacket. He was chatting up the Sylph bartender with his glamour in full effect, but being Fae, she was holding her own against his charm. He didn't appear particularly shady, and my instincts told me he probably wasn't my mark. I could have pulled the bounty card on him, which would have magically identified whether he was the vamp I was after, but if I guessed wrong it would tip off anyone else in the vicinity. I'd check out the rest and come back to him if I didn't get any hits.

The next vamp pinging my senses was above me on the balcony.

6

I scanned the area with a casual glance. Large VIP booth with table service. Money and an entourage—possible signs of a drug dealer. I straightened and set down my glass, looking for the staircase so I could get a closer look.

"Petra Maguire?"

I twisted around at the sound of my name and found myself looking up into the face of Maxen Lothlorien. Full-blooded New Gargoyle. One of the most eligible bachelors in all of Faerie. Son of Marisol, monarch of the Stone Order to which I was sworn.

"Maxen?" I couldn't cover my surprise. "What in the name of Oberon are you doing here?"

He was dressed in the official white and grays of the Stone Order. Usually his diplomatic duties took him to court in the Old World—the castles, palaces, and other strongholds of the Faerie kingdoms. What Order business could he have here in the Las Vegas-anchored territory of the Spriggan kingdom?

A smile broke out over his boyishly handsome face. "I knew it was you, even from a distance," he said warmly.

He leaned against the bar, his blue eyes sparkling in a way that inspired palpitations in the hearts of many Fae women. Some men, too. His easy smile and good looks were disarming, and his warmth unexpected in a New Gargoyle. But underneath the charisma was a shrewd diplomat and a skilled fighter.

His eyes flicked to Mort's grip, which protruded over the top of my right shoulder.

"Here for work, I see," he said.

I gave a half shrug. "When am I not? Guild assignment."

He tsked. "You should be at home, helping your people."

I snorted. "You mean at home, following Marisol's orders and popping out a few New Garg offspring?"

He tilted his head. "Not the phrasing I would use, but if that's what

7

works for you." He leaned in a little and gave me a teasing smile.

We'd been going back and forth like this for years. New Gargoyles were blessed with physical strength and natural fighting skills that were the envy of Faerie, but being a new Fae race, and one even less fertile than the average Fae, we lacked numbers. In Faerie, there was power in numbers. There were several hurdles to overcome to reach Marisol's goal of kingdom status, but the biggest challenge facing the New Gargoyles was population size. It was hard to make a case to the High Court for a kingdom charter with such a small population. Maxen's mother—and likely many New Gargoyles—thought it a disgrace that I was wasting my peak fertility years in the Earthly realm working for the Guild.

But my life outside Faerie gave me some degree of freedom from Fae affairs and politics, which I strongly preferred to avoid. My job in the Earthly realm also gave me space from Marisol. If I'd lived in Faerie, I'd be at her beck and call. Hunting down criminal vamps was more important to me.

Maxen's eyes slipped down over my patched scabbard strap, torn jeans, and worn leather boots. "If you joined the Stone Order's fighting legion, you'd have top-of-the-line equipment. Daily access to the best training facility. You'd be set up with everything you needed, and you wouldn't have to worry about earning a paycheck."

This was our other little ongoing push and pull. When I sidestepped the obligation-to-your-people play, he always tried to persuade me to leave the Guild to join the battle ranks of the Stone Order.

I shook my head. "Placing myself squarely under Marisol's thumb for all eternity? No thanks."

He gave a sad smile that was very much meant to tug at my heart. "You're one of the best fighters in Faerie, Petra. Your skills are wasted with the Guild. The future of the New Gargoyles hangs in the balance. Your people need you."

His plea seemed a bit dramatic, but there was some truth behind the seriousness of it. While Marisol was doing everything she could to strengthen the Stone Order's position, several of the other Faerie rulers were working to oppose her efforts so they could absorb the New Gargs into their own kingdoms. She needed to show strength in every way possible.

"You know what my work means to me," I said. "I vowed a long time ago to get criminal vamps off the streets."

He pressed his lips together, seemingly holding back further attempts at persuasion.

"Your turn to answer questions," I said. "What brings you into a place like this?"

"Business with King Sebastian," he said. His hand moved to rest lightly on the pommel of his sword. The unconscious gesture suggested perhaps the visit wasn't entirely amicable.

My eyebrows rose. "Oh?"

Any remnants of lightheartedness faded from Maxen's face, and his eyes tightened. "Sebastian persuaded a small group of New Gargoyles, ones with some Spriggan blood, to leave the Order and swear fealty to him. I'm here to ask that he allow a Stone Order ambassador to reside in his court, seeing as how we now have this connection."

Maxen was being extremely diplomatic. Even as ignorant of politics as I was, I knew this wasn't truly his aim, or at least not his only one. Marisol would want our people to retract their oath to Sebastian. Not that taking back an oath was a simple matter in Faerie, but it could be done, and I knew Marisol took it as a personal affront when a New Garg pledged to a different leader. It didn't happen often, but as she always said, every New Gargoyle mattered, and our race needed to be united to have any hope of forming our own kingdom.

"And how is the Spriggan king receiving you?" I asked wryly. I didn't envy Maxen one bit. His mother had sent him on an impossible errand.

"Actually, you can see for yourself," he said. He pointed up to a roped-off area in the balcony. I scolded myself silently. How could I have missed those royal guards? I should have been paying better attention. "Sebastian is up there right now, and he sent me to ask you to join us."

I swallowed back a groan. "Can't do it. Busy." I lifted my palms and shrugged in a so-sorry gesture.

The corner of Maxen's mouth quirked a bit. "You know you can't refuse the summons of a Fae king without causing an inter-kingdom uproar. C'mon, Maguire. Buck up."

He grabbed my wrist and began pulling me toward the staircase.

"But I'm not dressed for a royal audience," I protested, dragging my feet. "And he'll blow my cover. My job depends on discretion!"

As Maxen forced me upstairs and across the balcony, I caught a good view of the vamp at the VIP table just as a human kid wearing a ball cap pulled low over his eyes passed a wad of cash into the hand of one of the vamp's entourage. The vamp, a stocky, swarthy guy with dark brown eyes, nodded. Then he stood, pulled on his jacket, and headed for the stairs. As soon as he was clear of the balcony, another of his entourage, a too-thin Fae girl with silver hair down to her waist, slipped a small glass vial of a clear liquid to the kid. Not VAMP3 blood, but it had to be some other drug.

Damn it to Maeve, that vamp was likely my mark, and it looked like he was leaving.

"Your sword, madam," said a deep authoritative voice. It was one of Sebastian's guards. A typical Spriggan, he was built like a muscle-bound oak. He held out one beefy hand and nodded at the grip of my broadsword. I lifted the scabbard strap over my head and reluctantly passed it to him.

"Let me go, Maxen," I hissed. "My mark is getting away."

"Petra Maguire, how delightful to see you here!" called a cultured voice. The guard shifted as he turned to set my sword aside, and I caught sight of Sebastian.

"Too late," Maxen whispered to me. He actually looked contrite.

The Spriggan king beckoned to me. "Not to worry, my man Gerald will keep a watchful eye on your prized shadowsteel spellblade. Please do join us." Sebastian's mouth was relaxed into a pleasant smile, but his eyes were commanding. When I hesitated, his brows rose a fraction.

Maxen was right. I couldn't refuse an invitation of audience with a Fae king. It was just one of those Fae things there was no getting around.

Before I was ushered past the velvet rope, I caught one last glance of the swarthy vamp. He appeared to be speaking to the head bartender or perhaps the owner, a Fae man with a close-cropped salt-and-pepper beard. If my mark got away while I was being forced to dance like a monkey for the king, I was going to wring Maxen's neck.

Irritation buzzed through me like a swarm of hornets. But I tamped it down, mustered up what I hoped passed as a smile, and faced the Spriggan king.

Chapter 2

BEING SEPARATED FROM Mort made me edgy, and it took all of my self-control to keep from glancing over at the spot where my scabbard was propped against the wall. The broadsword was imbued with my blood and therefore my magic, and I got a little twitchy when it was out of reach.

Maxen, in contrast, was allowed to keep his sword and daggers in King Sebastian's presence. Something to do with court protocol for diplomats, most likely. I only knew enough of Faerie court etiquette to keep from getting in too much trouble, but I had never bothered to learn the hundreds of finer points that were second nature for Maxen.

I made an awkward curtsy in front of Sebastian, not an easy thing to do in skin-tight jeans. With no skirt to fan out, I just had to lift my arms at my sides as I put one ankle behind the other, bent my knees, and bowed my head. It was the proper practice for female Fae wearing pants, but there was really no graceful way to do it.

With that little ritual out of the way, the king gestured to a couch, indicating that Maxen and I should both sit there.

Rather than the traditional, showy finery and jewels that many Fae rulers favored, Sebastian was dressed in the human style of a rich businessman: a sleek-looking dark suit with a crisp white shirt and tastefully patterned tie. Only the chunky, bejeweled rings on his fingers gave away his love of sparkly things.

"And how is your father?" the Spriggan king asked as he settled himself on a tall-backed, overstuffed chair that actually looked a bit like a throne.

I blinked. "Oliver? He's well," I said.

I'd been calling my father by his first name since I was about ten years old. He wasn't the warm-and-fuzzy type, and even when I was a child it had felt more natural than calling him "Dad."

My brain chugged as I tried to work out how my father knew Sebastian and guess at how amicable—or not—their relationship was.

"You're surprised we're acquainted?" Sebastian asked.

"A bit, yes," I admitted.

"Ah. Well, I'm making it a point to try to get to know all of your people." He shot me a knowing smile as if we shared a secret, and it made me want to back away.

Okay, at least I had a clue about why he'd called me up here. I decided not to dance around it. I wanted to get back to work before this stupid visit cost me my assignment.

I gave him a tight smile. "I've heard some New Gargoyles have sworn oaths to you. I hope you're not counting on my fealty. I'd hate to cause you disappointment, Your Majesty."

Maxen shifted beside me, my directness obviously making him uneasy.

"Perhaps it might help if you understood why several of your people feel the Spriggan kingdom is their rightful home and I'm their rightful king," Sebastian said. He crossed his legs, visibly muscular even in dress pants.

Fine, I'd bite. "What was their reason, Your Majesty?" I asked.

"The Spriggan's hedges in Ireland house by far the largest population of nesting Old World gargoyles in Faerie. The creatures from which your own people's characteristics were derived." He said it as if he'd made some sort of profound pronouncement that should end any doubt

13

in my mind about swearing fealty to him right then and there.

I snorted a laugh before I could control myself. Sebastian's expression held, but I caught anger flashing in his eyes.

"But Your Majesty, the Old World gargoyles are to us like the great apes are to humans. Or as a housecat is to a lion of the Serengeti," I said. "Yes, there is some connection between those creatures in your hedge and the race of New Gargoyles that spontaneously emerged at the Cataclysm, but only in a vague sense. Those creatures don't even possess sufficient intelligence to be subjects of your kingdom. Are you really implying that I should consider them my ancestors, and because they happen to nest in your hedge I should swear allegiance to the Spriggan kingdom?"

It was beyond ridiculous. And if there were New Gargoyles who had actually bought Sebastian's reasoning, I wanted nothing to do with them. Marisol should let them go as a favor to the Stone Order's gene pool.

But as I took in Sebastian's face, I realized I'd pushed too far. I'd ridiculed him in front of Maxen and the other courtiers sitting nearby. Our corner of the balcony had gone so quiet I could hear the sound of my own pulse in my head. I slid a glance at Maxen, but he refused to look at me. His jaw muscles were bunched, and the tendon on the side of his neck was tight.

I pushed my palms back and forth across the denim fabric that stretched over my thighs, mentally scrambling for some way I could smooth things a little.

Before I could come up with anything useful, movement in my periphery drew my attention upward. Just as I tilted my head back to see what it was, a small person clad in black dropped on a cord from the ceiling like a giant spider from the rafters. Metal flashed.

"Get down!" I shouted at Sebastian.

I sprang to the side, rolling across the floor toward the wall where

Mort was. I snatched the blade from its scabbard, whirled, and charged at the intruder.

As I moved, I connected to Mort and activated the blood magic that made me one with my weapon. Violet-blue fire lit around my arm and surrounded the blade, extending the range of damage I could do with it.

In the second or two I'd spent to grab Mort, two more compact black figures dropped from above, each about four feet tall. All three wore masks that obscured everything but their eyes.

The first intruder hurled a throwing knife at Sebastian. One of Sebastian's men shoved the king to the floor, both of them falling near Maxen's feet. The knife stuck in the guard's shoulder. Maxen had his sword in hand, and his own blue-black magic ignited. He rushed at one of the assassins.

I charged one of the others, jabbing forward at the assassin's torso with deadly intent. He jumped to the side, agile as a cat, and my blade grazed off his ribcage, tearing fabric and drawing blood but inflicting only a superficial wound.

An agonized scream from the ground drew my attention, and a glance revealed that the knife in the guard's shoulder was smoking. He clawed at it desperately, rolling off the king in an effort to stop the pain. His screams turned to foamy gurgles and then silenced.

Just in time, I turned to see my own opponent fling two very short knives at my chest. In less than a blink, I focused on the magic coursing through my blood and drew it to the surface of my skin, where it formed a thin, stony layer. The knives pierced my shirt but pinged off my natural armor.

The assassin tilted his head in confusion. I dropped to one knee, scooped up one of his knives, and flicked it back at him. It sank right into his heart. He clutched at it and then fell to the floor like a bag of rocks. Smoke began to rise around the blade.

The third assassin had seen his opening, with the king exposed, and

15

was going for Sebastian. I charged forward, my arm swinging, and Mort traced an arc that was only slightly interrupted by the would-be assassin's neck. The blade, sharpened by my magic, passed through with hardly any friction. The violet flame instantly cauterized the neck opening, neatly keeping the gore inside. I was particularly proud of that trick—beheadings without the mess.

The assassin's head toppled across the floor and bumped against one leg of the sofa where Maxen and I had been sitting only a few seconds before.

I looked over at him and then down at the body of the remaining assassin, which was face-down and still. Blood pooled from the chest wound and wetted the dark fabric on the back, indicating Maxen's sword had gone clear through. He tapped the head with the toe of his boot and gave me a grim nod.

I scanned the ceiling, and seeing no more attackers lurking, I released my magic. The violet flames around my arm and Mort disappeared. Aching pain bloomed across my torso where I'd activated my stone armor, and fatigue weakened my legs, but I shoved both aside.

I went to Sebastian, who had pushed up on one hip and sat staring in horror at the twisted, tortured face of his dead guard. The knife was still steaming but had started to droop as the flesh around it began to melt away under a powerful poison.

I squatted next to the king, partially blocking his view of the dead man. "Your Majesty?" I asked. "Are you hurt?"

He looked up at me, his mouth open, and then blinked several times and swallowed.

"No," he said weakly. He cleared his throat. "No, I believe I'm unharmed."

Maxen came over and linked elbows with the king, pulling him to his feet. Maxen winced, but not because of the effort of getting Sebastian off the ground. It was the residual pain of having used stone armor, the price we paid for such protective magic.

Sebastian pulled his jacket smooth and brushed a hand down one sleeve. "Gerald!" he called, looking around.

He peered past me and flinched. I twisted around to see Gerald, the head of Sebastian's security detail, slumped over with a smoking knife sticking out of the middle of his back. Another of the king's men was sprawled face-up with a blade in his chest. Only one seemed to be still alive and was just coming to after apparently having been knocked unconscious.

The house music was still pulsing, and no one seemed to have even noticed the attack.

"Stay here and guard him," Maxen said to me. "I'm going outside to move some of the king's guards in here. With your permission, Your Majesty?"

Maxen waited for Sebastian's nod and then took off.

"Any idea who would want to kill you?" I asked Sebastian, still scanning for more attackers.

I glanced at the king just as he pushed his fingers through his short, fashionably spiked hair.

"You mean besides the rulers of most of the Faerie kingdoms?" he said with a humorless little bark of a laugh. He was clearly still shaken. His joke fell flat, anyway, as Sebastian wasn't powerful enough to be the target of all of the rulers in Faerie. He was known for his posturing.

I bent and snatched the mask off the attacker that Maxen had killed. The guy's nearly-white skin marked him Baen Sidhe, colloquially known as banshees. By his small stature and the narrow ears with pointed tips, I guessed he was also at least half dwarf. Odd combination, but not the strangest I'd ever seen in Faerie. I checked the other two and found the same, except that one was a woman.

I straightened. "Pissed off any dwarves or banshees lately?" I asked.

"Not in particular." Sebastian went to his chair and sagged down onto it, his hands propped onto his knees. His mouth hardened, and he cast a look down at the bar below. "My men secured this place. I don't understand how this happened."

I shook my head. "I don't know, but that's some nasty poison magic they used. Probably not banshee or dwarvish. Neither race is handy with potions. I'd have your investigators analyze those knives and the poison, and I bet you'll find who was behind the attack."

He passed a hand over his eyes. "They were very swift. If not for you and Maxen, well . . . I might not still be breathing."

I shifted my feet uncomfortably. What he'd just said was dangerously close to "thank you." In the Fae world, such an utterance was tricky for both the giver and the receiver, and I didn't want that sort of vulnerability opened up between me and the Spriggan king.

To my relief, Maxen charged up the stairs with half a dozen Spriggan guards on his heels, plus the man with the salt-and-pepper beard I'd seen my mark talking to.

Four of the guards took up posts, and the other two set to work moving aside the bodies of the dead guards and assassins, hiding them behind one of the sofas.

The bearded man bowed in front of Sebastian. "Your Majesty, I don't know how this happened."

I figured he must be the owner of the bar.

The king flicked his hand through the air as if waving away a fly. "Assassination attempts are one of the dangers of ruling a kingdom," Sebastian said with a self-important tone. "We'll have a full review of your security procedures, of course."

Sebastian's cool outward confidence had returned full force, but I'd seen how shaken he was only moments before. He was playing it off for the bar owner, and also perhaps for his men who were nearby.

The owner looked somewhat relieved, but not completely. I didn't blame him. It wasn't going to help his business at all once word got out that King Sebastian had nearly been killed in Druid Circle. Or maybe the reverse would be true, and people's morbid fascination would draw them here. Either way, an assassination attempt on a king when he was in his own territory was unusual and sure to cause some ripples through Faerie.

"I'll get someone to help with the bodies, Your Majesty," the owner said with a glance at the sofa that hid the carnage. He bowed low and turned to depart.

I reached out and grabbed his arm as he walked by.

"Hey," I said, my voice low. I made sure I was turned away from the king. "I prevented a royal murder in your club, so now I want something from you."

The man was handsome, his face almost regal, I realized once I saw him up close. Mixed race—too diluted to pick out any bloodlines with certainty, but I thought I detected a hint of Tuatha De Danann in the slant of his cheekbones and the deep set of his eyes. The Tuatha were the ancient Fae gods who had established Faerie eons ago and then disappeared over time, except for some descendants who carried traces of their blood. There was no Tuatha kingdom, and Tuatha blood carried no special magic.

He narrowed his eyes at me but didn't ask what I wanted. That would be too open-ended a question, and one that I could too easily take advantage of. Words could be slippery, binding things in Faerie. Instead, he waited for me to state my request.

"That olive-skinned vamp you talked to earlier, the one who had the VIP table over there?" I asked, and waited for him to nod. "I need to know where I can find him."

He started to shake his head and pull away, but I gripped his arm harder. I let my magic flow from the area around my heart, sending tendrils of stone armor creeping along the surface of my skin, up my neck, and curling in patterns over my face like mineral tattoos. It wasn't possible to fully armor my face, but I knew the effect of the patterned designs on people who had never seen them before.

His eyes popped wide as he took it in. With my stature and in the low light of the club, he clearly hadn't realized until that moment that I was New Gargoyle.

"I can give you the place he frequents," he said. "He has an address in the Millennium Hotel."

I nodded and let my magic go, and the familiar thump of pain took the place of the stone armor patterns I'd drawn across my skin. "Which side of the hedge is that on?" I asked.

"Not here in Faerie," he said quickly. "On the Earthly side, in Las Vegas proper. It's a new resort."

In the Old World, there was an actual hedgerow in many of the places that marked a doorway between Faerie and the Earthly realm, which was how the terminology "hedge" originated. The Cataclysm made it possible to anchor Faerie territories to locations in what we called the New World—the Americas. Here, there was usually no physical hedge to mark the boundary between the Faerie and Earthly realms, but we still used the term "hedge" when we talked about the division between the two realms.

"Good. Any aliases?"

"He goes by Van Zant."

I snorted. Vamps and their pretentious goth names.

I let go of his arm but gave him a stony look. "Were you aware he's passing around VAMP3 blood?"

I could tell by the look on his face that he hadn't known. "I'll make sure he's no longer allowed to patronize Druid Circle."

"Don't do that just yet," I said. "If the address you give me doesn't work out, I may have to come back here to find him."

He looked slightly ill at the prospect of allowing Van Zant back in his club. "Okay."

I was silently cursing the fact that cell phones didn't work on the Faerie side of the hedge. I gave him my number anyway, which he wrote on the palm of his hand, in case he might be able to step out of Faerie to call me if Van Zant returned.

"Anything else you can tell me about Van Zant?" I asked.

The man's brow furrowed. "I've heard he has a gambling problem. He likes the high-stakes poker tables at the Millennium."

"That's helpful. Your name?" I asked.

"Gregory."

I nodded.

Gregory looked like he wanted to disappear, and I didn't blame him—between the assassination attempt and what I'd just told him about VAMP3 blood being sold in his club, his day was really going to shit.

I wanted to slip out but instead forced myself to go bid a proper farewell to King Sebastian.

"You belong in the Spriggan kingdom, Petra," the king said. "It's where your roots are, the seat of your origins. And it would be far better for you if you come willingly. Waiting until your people decide as a group to give me their fealty will put you at a grave disadvantage in terms of where you'll land within the kingdom."

Irritation prickled through me. I'd literally just saved his life, and he was already threatening me. But for the moment, the threats were empty, as Marisol had no intention of subjecting the whole of the Stone Order to someone else's rule. For once, I appreciated her obsessive drive to establish the New Gargoyles with an independent kingdom.

Maxen moved closer to us. "This isn't the first of these attacks in Faerie," he said. "There was a message at the Stone Order today. Something similar happened in the kingdom of the Undine early this morning."

I frowned. The Undine were water elementals. These part-dwarf attackers were completely the wrong choice for taking on water folk. Dwarves typically feared the water. Kelpies—water horse shifters and long-time enemy of the Undine—would have been much more effective assassins against water elementals.

Strange, but I couldn't hang around to investigate. I needed to get back to my assignment.

"I must take my leave," I said, facing the men. "Your Majesty. Maxen."

After gracing King Sebastian with one of my ridiculous curtsies and flipping a parting wave at Maxen, I got the hell out of Druid Circle.

It was time to head back to the Earthly realm on the other side of the hedge. I exited Druid Circle and went to a subtly-designed arch in the side of the building next door. Whispering the magic words and drawing certain sigils in the air with my finger, I stepped forward into what appeared to be solid stone. It gave way to the void of the netherwhere, the space between Faerie doorways.

Chapter 3

AS SOON AS I emerged into the Earthly realm, my cell phone began chirping and vibrating with the messages that had accumulated while I was on the other side of the hedge.

The sigils I'd used took me into a doorway that was situated in the vestibule of a Vegas gym called MonsterFit. The windows on all sides of the space had been treated with Fae magic to keep the people on the inside and the outside of the gym from seeing Fae pass through. It was one of the trickier doorways to use because if anyone was in the vestibule the netherwhere would hold you in the void until it was clear. But the lot outside had free parking, and that was a hard thing to come by this close to the Strip. At this hour, the gym was closed, so I didn't have to worry about cross traffic.

I scanned through the windows as the chill of the netherwhere seeped away, and I headed toward the parking lot where I'd left my scooter, a vintage GTS Vespa I'd named Vincenzo. I had a few texts from my Fae roommate and best friend for years, Lochlyn, about bills and groceries and her plans for later that evening. I'd also missed a call from my father and a voicemail from an unfamiliar number. When I listened to the voice message, I nearly deleted it after a couple of seconds because it was obviously a recording. Then I realized it was a call from the Stone Order.

I let out a groan and started the message from the beginning.

"Hello, this is your official summons to an emergency meeting of the Stone Order scheduled for tomorrow at ten in the morning San Francisco time at the stone fortress. All New Gargoyles sworn to the Order are required to attend. Again, there is an emergency meeting . . ." The recorded voice repeated the date and time.

In spite of the considerable independence my life in the Earthly realm afforded me, I was still a subject of Marisol and the Stone Order. With extremely rare exceptions, all Fae had to be sworn to a Fae leader. It was another of those Faerie things there was no way around. To renounce all fealty would mean that I'd lose my Fae magic and the ability to ever pass into Faerie again. I wanted distance—as much of it as I could get away with—but not to renounce Faerie forever.

I shoved my phone back into the pouch sewn to my scabbard, pulled the faded hand towel off the seat of my scooter, and stuffed it into one of the saddlebags. It was dark out, but when I'd parked, the evening Vegas sun was still blazing, and out of habit I'd covered the seat.

I was just about to hop on when there was a petulant yowl behind me. I turned to see a skinny striped tabby sitting on the sidewalk and looking up at me with big yellow eyes.

"Hey, Lemony, I thought you'd left me," I said, digging in another pouch on my scabbard strap for a piece of jerky. I bent to give the treat to the stray who often lurked near this doorway. He took the offering, and I gave his head a pat before straightening.

For reasons unknown to me, I'd been a stray magnet since childhood. Usually cats, but occasionally dogs. Even a rabbit and a turtle once. I used to try to shoo them away, but years ago I gave in and began carrying treats with me. My roommate Lochlyn said it was good luck to show kindness to stray animals. I wasn't so sure about that, but the animals seemed to appreciate the handouts.

I looked up the Millennium's location on my phone and then hopped on my scooter and headed around to the other end of the Strip, taking roads that would keep me out of the thickest traffic. Van Zant's hotel was in an area of second-tier luxury hotels.

At the Millennium, I left Vincenzo in one of the motorcycle spots, went inside, and headed toward the nearest restroom. In the privacy of a stall, I drew transformation magic to change my clothes. My jeans shrank into a micro-mini denim skirt, my boots turned to shiny leather with stiletto heels, and my long-sleeved navy henley transformed into a crop-top that fell off one shoulder and displayed a gold silkscreened couture logo on the front. I tied my hair up into a messy bun. Using slightly different illusion magic, I added the appearance of heavy black eyeliner around my eyes, mascara on my lashes, and glossy pink lipstick to my lips.

All Fae have magic called glamour, but it's different than vamp glamour. Ours was primarily for changing the way we looked to non-Fae. Usually we use it to mask features that didn't look entirely human, so we blend in better when in the Earthly realm. I could pass for human without any glamour, but I liked to use it to disguise myself at times.

After pumping up the spell that obscured my scabbard and sword from human eyes—more Faerie glamour-type magic—I emerged. Letting my hips swing as I walked slowly on the plush carpet in the spike heels, I headed toward the elevator that went up to the residences. There was a female concierge at a podium and a beefy man in black guarding the elevator. The man wore sunglasses and an earpiece. He was Fae, but she was full human with no magical ability, which should make this easy.

I gave the concierge—Brittany, by her nametag—a sultry smile.

"Hello," I said. "Van Zant invited me up tonight. I should be on his list."

She gave me a tight stretch of her lips that said she doubted it. "Your name?"

"Penelope," I said, using the pseudonym I adopted when I had to use the sort of getup I was wearing at the moment.

I glanced down at the tablet on the podium as Brittany began tapping the device's screen, and when she paused, I pushed a tendril of illusion magic to make it look as if my name appeared there.

"Well, *Penelope*," she said. "Mr. Van Zant must have forgotten to tell you that he left town an hour ago."

She quickly lifted the tablet, and it flashed in my face as she snapped my picture.

"But rest assured that I'll tell him you were here," she continued. "And now I've got your picture, so you'll be in our system. Have a lovely evening."

She cast a look at the guard, and he casually strolled a few steps closer to the podium.

I ground my teeth. Dammit. I'd missed my mark, and it looked like my usual illusions wouldn't get me past the desk.

I forced a disappointed pout. "Oh, silly me, I must have gotten our times mixed up. Thanks anyway!"

I turned and speed-walked away, not wanting a run-in with the guard.

As I passed through the exterior door, I dropped my cosmetic illusions and transformed my clothes back as they were. The transformation happened in a fraction of a second, banking on the chance that anyone who might have seen the change wasn't sober enough to question it.

I headed back to the MonsterFit doorway, taking my scooter inside with me. Instead of using the doorway to pass into Faerie, I whispered different words and traced a sigil in the air with my index finger. Then I closed my eyes, sucked in a deep breath, and held it, bracing myself in anticipation of the frigid blast that came with using a doorway.

All Fae were born with the magic that allowed us to use doorways and helped us blend in with humans in the Earthly realm, as well as specialized magic that was based on the race or races of the individual.

Our magic literally runs through our blood. To call on it, we only need to turn within and focus on the sensation of our own hearts beating and the magic-infused blood coursing through us.

The darkness and freezing cold of the netherwhere engulfed me, and I lost all sense of up or down. Seconds ticked by, and I held my breath until the chill began to thaw. Allowing myself to breathe again, I cracked open my eyelids.

I was standing in a corner of a condemned parking garage on the edge of Boise, Idaho, the city where I lived with my roommate, Lochlyn.

Faerie doorways had limited capabilities to transport us between various locations in the Earthly realm. Any doorway could theoretically connect to any other doorway in Faerie, if you knew the right sigils to trace. But in the Earthly realm, the connections were scarcer. For instance, there was only one doorway in the San Francisco area, where the Stone Order's fortress was located, that could take me here to Boise.

I straddled my scooter, started it up, and zipped toward home, located on a slightly raised plateau known as The Bench, which was situated behind the train depot that was still in operation.

It was after two in the morning, and weariness pulled at me. I parked Vincenzo in his assigned spot and went up to the second-floor apartment. The place was dark and silent, and the door to Lochlyn's bedroom stood open, indicating she was still out for the night. Part of me was disappointed she wasn't there. It had been a few days since we'd been able to catch up with each other. But the other part was too tired for a late-night chat.

In my sparse bedroom, furnished with only a frameless twin mattress and a second-hand dresser I'd bought for nine bucks, I propped my scabbard against the wall next to the bed, shed my jacket and boots, and then collapsed across the mattress. As my eyelids drooped, I tried to muster the will to take a quick shower but fell asleep before I could force myself up.

When I awoke, morning light slanted through the cheap blinds. I sat up and could feel by the stillness that Lochlyn was still gone. I reached for my phone, thinking to text her to see if she'd be home in time to grab coffee together. But then suddenly remembering the summons to the Stone Order, I scrambled to power on my phone and check the time.

I had exactly an hour to get there, and the drive from the Bay Area doorway to the stone fortress would take at least half that.

"Shit!"

I sprang off the bed, shed my clothes in a heap, and scooted to the bathroom for the fastest shower in history. Oliver, my father, would kill me if I showed up at the Order wearing yesterday's sweat-wrinkled clothes.

Back in my room, I put on the least-torn pair of jeans I owned, my worn boots, and a faded but clean tank top with a light jacket. Throwing my scabbard on over my head and adjusting it to settle in its usual place over my shoulder and across my chest, I was out the door.

Dammit. I was probably going to be late. Oh well. It was only by pure luck that I didn't sleep through the whole thing. I always slept more deeply after using my stone armor, and I'd done that twice the previous day. It would be a small miracle if I made it to the fortress close to the start at all, considering the time change between here and San Francisco, where the fortress was located. Not that Oliver or Marisol would see it that way.

I zipped down the road that skirted the train depot and weaved around cars to get to the downtown parking garage that hid the Faerie doorway I had to use to get to San Francisco.

The netherwhere swept away all sense of my mortal form. I emerged with a shiver in Crosson Hall, an abandoned naval base located on Treasure Island in the San Francisco Bay Area. Walking Vincenzo through the graffiti-covered corridors and weeds that had encroached into the structure, I exited the base, shoved my sunglasses onto my face, hopped on my bike, and took off down the road. The scooter's engine echoed loudly off the walls as I gunned it.

I got on I-80 to 580 toward San Rafael. Lucky for me, it was the tail end of the morning commute traffic, and vehicles were moving along. I took advantage of California's road rules that allowed motorcycles to pass between lanes, and got into the rhythm of weaving between cars on the freeway.

It was a beautiful sunny Bay Area morning, and a relief from the summer scorch of Vegas and the lesser but still toasty heat of Boise. I inhaled the salt-tinged air, enjoying the rush of the wind past my skin. My chest and face still pulsed with a vague ache in the places where my stone armor had been the night before.

Remembering how my mark had eluded me, my mood soured. I'd taken that assignment, which had an unusually high payout, because I really needed the cash. Recent repairs on Vincenzo had eaten next month's rent money. My irritation turned toward the Stone Order. If it weren't for this damned meeting, I could be hunting down Van Zant right now. I wouldn't receive another Guild assignment until this one was resolved.

The Stone Order's fortress was located in the facility that was formerly the San Quentin prison. It was a formidable concrete structure located on a point overlooking the water. Much of the exterior had been left as it was to mask the fact that it led into Faerie. The non-Fae of the Earthly realm knew of Fae and Faerie, but generally Fae preferred to keep our secrets to the extent possible. Many humans looked upon Fae with suspicion, mostly due to the lore about us stealing human babies away into Faerie. It was a silly story—we Fae had no use for magicless human children who technically couldn't swear fealty to any Fae ruler.

Marisol had converted much of the old prison into living quarters for the hundreds of New Gargs who lived there and official headquarters for the Order. One of the residents was my father, Oliver.

The interior of the facility had also been transmuted through the hedge to Faerie, so technically it was no longer part of the Earthly realm. Once you stepped through the doors to the fortress, you entered Faerie. It was a strange concept if it was something you were not accustomed to. I admit, it still twisted my mind up a little if I thought about it too hard. Mostly, it meant that the fortress was impenetrable to non-Fae folk unless they were granted passage. Even a very nosy and curious non-Fae would simply find it was a completely inaccessible building. From the outside, the windows appeared to have been sealed over with concrete, and the doors barred.

When I arrived, the place of course looked deserted. I rode around the corner. There was no one else in sight, probably because they'd all been on time. I walked the scooter up to what appeared to be an alcove. I pressed lightly on a lopsided star that looked almost like a random scratch in the concrete and whispered magic words. The wall shimmered like water, and I stepped through the arch and into the interior of the New Garg fortress in Faerie.

Leaving my scooter parked near the entrance—and knowing it would piss off Marisol to no end that I was using the Order's grand marble entry as my own personal parking lot—I hurried toward the auditorium.

Chapter 4

MOST FAE ARE to some degree obsessed with pretty things, usually the more gold and sparkly the better. The Stone Order's fortress reflected the slightly different tastes of the New Gargoyles. As a people, we tended to prefer, unsurprisingly, stone in all its forms. Everything from marble to semi-precious crystals.

The Order was decorated with geometric patterns of all manner of stones. As I raced by, I recognized in the wall designs inlaid turquoise, obsidian, quartz, tourmaline, and half a dozen others. The place practically resonated with the vibrational frequencies of various crystalline materials. New Gargoyles also had an affinity for geometry. We liked everything to be at neat angles.

Usually, Marisol had a few courtiers and pages out in the marble entry, acting as sort of butlers and concierges. The empty entry I'd encountered meant that even the greeters had abandoned their posts to attend the meeting.

I could hear Marisol's voice from within the auditorium. Grasping the metal handle of one door, I held my breath and pulled.

Inside, the concentric circles of stadium seating appeared completely full. The lights were up on the stage, and the audience area was darkened.

I let out some air. It seemed I'd snuck in. I stood with my back to the wall, letting my eyes adjust. There were only around seven hundred Fae with proven New Gargoyle blood that made them eligible to swear to the Stone Order—demonstrated by forming rock armor—and it seemed all of them were here. Others stood at the wall as I did.

I flicked my eyes left and right, and then did a double-take to my left. My father was one person away, and he was peering at me.

"Nice of you to grace us with your presence, Petra," he said over the head of the teenage New Gargoyle girl who stood between us. Sarcasm was about as close as stone-faced Oliver Maguire ever got to showing actual emotion.

I gave him a saccharine smile and tilted my head innocently. "Hey, Dad."

He whispered in the girl's ear and they switched places. I held in a groan and turned my attention to Marisol.

New Gargoyles generally didn't go for the fluff and finery typical of the Fae courts. Marisol looked understated but regal in a simple, floor-length dress the color of storm clouds. Strands of semi-precious stones had been woven into her intricately braided ash-blond hair, and a wide mother-of-pearl belt was cinched around her slim waist. She looked like a Greek goddess.

" . . . the Spriggan kingdom has already stolen a dozen of us," Marisol was saying from the dais that was the focal point of the curved bench seating. Her son, Maxen, stood just off to one side of the dais, his weight eased over to one hip and his hand resting on the pommel of his sword. His attention was fixed on her. "But Sebastian's isn't the only kingdom vying for New Gargoyles. King Periclase of the Unseelie Duergar has just made an appeal to King Oberon, arguing that his kingdom has the right to absorb the Stone Order."

I suddenly felt a little sick to my stomach. The possibility of ending up under the rule of an Unseelie kingdom such as the Duergar had never entered my mind. A Seelie King like Sebastian would be bad enough, but being forced into the Unseelie world would be my own personal nightmare. Whereas the Seelie kingdoms were defined by oaths and honor, the Unseelie kingdoms were known more for deception. And with the Unseelie, the manipulation and political intrigue was ten times worse. The Duergar's petition to Oberon, a near-god in Faerie and the current king of the High Court, was only a step less serious than a declaration of war.

I blinked and turned a sharp gaze up at my father. "Is she saying what I think she's saying?"

Personally, I'd always hoped that if Marisol did succeed in forming a Stone Court, she would establish it as an independent kingdom, subjected to neither Seelie nor Unseelie. Such kingdoms were very rare and there were none currently, but then again, we New Gargoyles were an unusual bunch.

Before Oliver could respond to me, Marisol continued.

"One of Periclase's main arguments is that the Stone Order is much too small and our rate of reproduction much too low to ever gain the numbers needed to formalize into our own kingdom. So, the time has come to strengthen our ranks." Marisol paused dramatically. "We must begin to show our true strength. First, we will bring the hidden ones into the fold."

The audience seemed to inhale and murmur all at once. Not quite a gasp, but a collective sound of surprise.

"It's true." She raised her chin and looked out solemnly. "There are over a hundred more New Gargoyles. I received a prophecy twenty-five years ago, not long after establishing the Stone Order, that directed me to keep some of our numbers concealed."

Did I mention that Marisol had prophetic visions? One of her many talents. It wasn't the sort of thing I'd normally put much stock in, but her prophecies were the real deal.

"For obvious reasons, only a few of us have known about the changelings and other hidden ones," Marisol said. "Yesterday, I received a sign that it was time for us to seek them out. Only hours later, I got word of the Duergar King Periclase's formal bid for our fealty."

Changelings were a fact of Faerie life and always had been. Infidelity was rife in Faerie, and Fae sometimes had need to hide illegitimate babies among the humans in the Earthly realm. This was especially true in earlier eras, when Fae were considerably more brutal and bloody, and infanticide for reasons of jealousy and power wasn't uncommon. There were other reasons to hide Fae in the Earthly realm, but the myth of the reverse—Fae stealing human babies off to Faerie—was entirely false. No one really knew how or why the rumor began, but Fae had no use for human children. Fae changelings were usually placed in human households after crib deaths. There was an entire race of Fae responsible for executing the placements.

"I tried to get a hold of you last night," Oliver whispered in my ear.

"What?" I glanced at him distractedly but then returned my attention to Marisol. "Oh, uh, I was on assignment in Faerie and missed your call."

"We need to talk," he said.

His tone, which sounded just this side of worried, snagged my attention. Apprehension snaked through me as I looked up at him. My father was one of the most formidable Fae alive. Physically, he was as tall as a full-blood Elf, but with twice the shoulder span, and he was pure, solid muscle. As a fighter, he was almost unbeatable. He'd always been more soldier than father figure, and he was about as touchy-feely as a sandstone cliff. I didn't resent him for it—he'd made sure I had what I needed when I was growing up—and frankly when he did show anything hinting at emotion, it set me on edge.

He clamped a steel paw around my elbow and pushed me toward the door.

"Let's go into the hallway," he said.

"But she's still talking," I protested, gesturing at the lit dais. "Isn't this pretty important?"

"The rest is just wind-down from the big announcement," he said brusquely.

My brows shot up. Oliver had sworn fealty to Marisol before the Stone Order was even official, and his loyalty to her ran deep and in all directions. This was about as close to disrespectful as I'd ever heard him in regard to her.

I wasn't sure what the hell was going on, but I was fairly certain I wasn't going to like it.

Oliver faced me, holding my shoulders in his huge hands. "Petra, King Periclase has taken a New Gargoyle changeling. A very important one. He kidnapped her."

I looked at him in confusion, my head pulled back as if he'd shouted at me. "What in Oberon's name are you talking about?"

"We need you to get the changeling before Periclase tricks her into swearing fealty to him," he said. "This is important, Petra."

I shook my head and crossed my arms. "I'm not doing anything until all my questions are answered."

Oliver's eyes seemed to plead with me, but only for a split second before they hardened into a glare I knew all too well—it was a look that sliced right through you. But I stood my ground.

"You're the one who taught me to question until all of my questions are answered and I'm satisfied with the answers. You always said it's the best way to protect myself against—"

"—the manipulative tendencies of the Fae," he finished for me. "I'll give you as much as I can, but you're going to have to trust me. This is crucial, Petra. Someone has to go get that girl, but it can't be me. I'm too high profile. It should be you because—"

He cut off abruptly as his gaze flicked over my shoulder to something down the hallway. He stepped to the side and reached up for the grip of the sword he wore on a cross-body scabbard similar to mine.

I twisted to look for whatever had caught his attention. "What is it?"

But even as I said the words, black-swathed figures about four feet high had begun to appear as if out of thin air—dropping from the ceiling and materializing from the walls like a swarm of stealthy insects. Metal glinted in their hands. They looked exactly like the ninja wannabes who'd tried to take out the Spriggan King Sebastian at Druid Circle.

"Assassins!" I hissed needlessly, as Oliver was charging them before I finished saying the word.

Mortimer was already in my hand, engulfed in the violet fire of my magic. I pushed more magic across my skin to activate my stone armor. Pain gripped me as thin plates of stone formed over my body under my clothes. Just in time, as three blades flashed through the air right at me. I leaned right to avoid the one coming at my head and let the other two harmlessly ping off my armor.

"Watch the knives. They're poisoned," I called to Oliver, remembering what had happened to Sebastian's guards.

My father was mowing down the assassins with his sword, a handful of the short-statured figures already lying still on the ground.

Distracted by the knives flashing through the air at me, I didn't notice the attack from above until it was too late. The surprise of a person's full weight dropping onto my shoulders pulled me off balance. I stumbled and dropped Mort. Hands curled around my neck as the ninja rode me piggy-back. The sharp edge of a blade slid across the armor at my throat. It caused no injury, but if the blade were slim enough and found one of the hairline spaces between rock plates, I'd be in serious trouble.

I clamped one hand around the attacker's elbow and yanked sharply. I felt the arm dislocate from the shoulder. A male scream of pain came from under the black fabric mask as I hurled him to the floor. I left him there, writhing. No one was badass enough to keep fighting well with a dislocated shoulder, except maybe Oliver.

The assassins came after us with daggers, having spent their throwing knives. Another ninja flew at me with a murderous yell. I dove and scooped up Mort, then went up to one knee, and pivoted just in time to slash at the glinting metal the attacker wanted to drive into me. The diminutive assassin parried with unexpected skill, lunging and stabbing at my abdomen. He was quick enough to get past my defenses, but the point of his dagger slid off my armor, leaving only a gash in my tank top.

Rather than go for a kill, I used the flat side of my broadsword to whack him on the side of the head. He crumpled to the floor.

I stood up, watching as Oliver finished off the last attacker. My father was breathing through his mouth but had barely broken a sweat.

Something wasn't adding up here.

The ninja whose arm I'd yanked out of its socket was still on the ground and groaning in agony with his eyes pinched closed. I went to the decorative linen curtains that hung to one side of the door leading into the auditorium and pulled off the length of silvery rope that held them back. Kneeling next to the wounded ninja, I snapped my fingers in front of his face.

"Hey!" I said over his loud moans. "Shut up a second."

He opened his eyes.

"Put your arm out straight, and I'll pop it back in," I said.

He did as I commanded, letting out a screech when I gripped his arm and shoulder and snapped everything back to where it was supposed to be. Before he could get any bright ideas, I flipped him to his stomach, and with my knee pressed into his lower back, I pulled his arms around behind him and tied his wrists together.

Oliver had gone to the auditorium door and pushed it open just a crack to look inside.

"Looks like they're none the wiser," he said over his shoulder. He let the door close softly and came to me, a baffled look twisting his face.

I stood. "These are the same guys who attacked yesterday when I was with King Sebastian," I said.

He beckoned me away from my prisoner.

"They tried to kill the Spriggan king?" Oliver asked, his voice low enough that the tied-up ninja wouldn't overhear.

"Yeah. I was on an assignment in a nightclub in the new Spriggan territory on the Las Vegas Strip. Sebastian was there meeting with Maxen, and the king invited me for audience. The ninjas attacked and killed a few of Sebastian's men."

"Did any of the attackers get away?"

"I don't think so, but I couldn't say for sure." I glanced at the bodies and throwing knives scattered around the hallway, remembering how the bodies at Druid Circle had been quickly piled behind a sofa by Sebastian's men. "This doesn't make sense. If it was an assassination attempt, they would have gone after Marisol, but they wouldn't have done it when she was surrounded by so many who could defend her. And it was like they knew nothing about New Gargoyles. Throwing knives and daggers are all but useless against us, unless one of them gets a lucky stab."

"I agree." My father looked grim. "They're all wrong. Wrong weapons, and too small to be a match physically. I'm much more concerned about how they got in."

"Oh. Yeah." Suddenly, I felt a little stupid. The fortress was protected by magic that only allowed New Gargoyles to enter the premises. The doorways literally wouldn't form for anyone who wasn't a member of the Stone Order, unless the visitor had explicit permission to enter, and that didn't happen often.

Oliver stalked over to the ninja I'd tied up and rolled him over, squatting to pull off the attacker's mask. He looked similar to the one I'd unmasked at Druid Circle—ghostly pallid skin and narrow, pointed ears.

"The others looked banshee-dwarf, too," I said.

Oliver peered down into the captive's face, and to his credit, he stared right back.

"Who sent you?" Oliver asked, his voice deadly calm, his tone almost conversational.

A shiver raised goosebumps over my arms. When Oliver used that voice, it meant you were in deep shit. Like, waist-deep. Too much shit to try to turn and run. I remembered it well from my teenage years.

The pallid ninja just stared, his face hard.

Oliver shifted and placed a hand at the ninja's throat.

"Who sent you?" Oliver repeated. His fingers flexed as he gave a squeeze.

The ninja's eyes bugged a little, but he pressed his lips into a firm line. Oliver applied more pressure. One of the banshee-dwarf's eyelids began to twitch. The twitch seemed to spread, and within a couple of seconds his entire body was making tiny jerking movements.

I lunged forward and grabbed my father's shoulder, pulling him back just as dark purple liquid began to leak from the corner of the banshee-dwarf's mouth. It sent up a wisp of black vapor. Oliver and I both scrambled backward to avoid inhaling it. The ninja's jerks grew more pronounced, and then he went still, his head rolling to one side and his dead eyes slanting blankly up at the ceiling.

"Damn," Oliver muttered. He moved toward the body and nudged the dead ninja with the toe of his boot.

"I knocked out another one," I said, going over to the assassin I'd whacked with my sword. "Maybe he'll talk."

He was on his side, so I pushed him over to his back. Just as he rolled, the same dark curl of vapor rose from the liquid that dripped from his mouth. I jumped back and watched the vapor rise to the ceiling and then dissipate.

"Well, shit," I muttered. "So much for questioning them. What should we do with the bodies? Think we can get them out of the way before Marisol's done talking?"

I turned to find my father looking down the hallway, his head tilted. "There were more," he said.

"More what?" I walked over to stand next to him. My gaze followed his, searching for what had caught his attention.

"There were more of them." Oliver took a step forward, peering at the still figures scattered like dolls down the hallway. "I killed eight. Now there are only seven."

One of the bodies shimmered, as if we were looking at it through the heat waves rising from hot asphalt. And then the body disappeared.

I squinted, not quite believing my eyes. "What the—"

Two more ninjas winked out—there and then not. The knives on the floor began to disappear, too. Within the next ten seconds, the rest of the bodies were gone.

Oliver turned to me, his mouth agape. I'd never seen him look so openly baffled.

I shook my head in confusion. The violet flames around Mort sputtered and then extinguished as I let go of my magic. "What in the name of Oberon just happened?"

Chapter 5

MY FATHER AND I were still staring at each other in shock when people began pouring out of the auditorium. I took one last look at the floor, which wasn't even marred with a drop of ninja blood as evidence of the battle that had just occurred, before my view of the hallway was obscured by the entire population of New Gargoyles.

Well, not quite the entire population. As Marisol had said, a handful of New Gargoyles had sworn fealty to the Spriggan king, and as subjects of Sebastian, they were no longer members of the Stone Order.

Oliver's face shifted from confused to grim. He flipped his fingers at me, beckoning me to follow him back into the auditorium. I quickly sheathed Mort before the press of people made it too dangerous to be waving a sword around. My father went ahead of me, and I caught a glimpse of his expression before he turned away. I wasn't surprised that the crowd parted to allow him to move upstream with me in his wake.

As we made our way toward the dais where Marisol stood with Maxen and two of her advisors, I tried to reason out who had sent the ineffectual assassins. The attacks were odd for so many reasons.

Oliver went up to Marisol and spoke in her ear. Her blue sapphire eyes widened and her mouth flattened into a tight line. When Maxen spotted me waiting just off the dais, he lifted his chin in acknowledgement, stepped off the platform, and strode over.

41

"We meet again," he said, with the tiniest arch of one brow and a slow grin.

Ignoring the slightly sultry look in his eyes, which were the exact blue of his mother's, I leaned in and spoke in a low voice, my words rapid. "Remember those ninja guys at Druid Circle? Oliver and I just killed a dozen of them out in the hallway. Then their bodies disappeared. Poof, there one second and gone the next."

Maxen opened his mouth but didn't have a chance to reply.

"Petra. Maxen." Marisol called to us as if we were still seven years old, errant children giggling in the corner. "I need more details about both incidents with the shrouded attackers. But not until we can speak in private."

She turned to Raleigh, the head of the Stone Order's security and the only New Gargoyle larger than my father, and spoke a few words to him. He hurried off, as fast as a man of that size can hurry. Then she curled her hand at me, Oliver, and Maxen, indicating we should follow her.

We left the auditorium through the back with her personal bodyguard, a stocky expert swordsman named Jaquard, in the lead. I'd trained with him for a few years when I was a teenager. My father brought up the rear of our little procession.

We moved quickly through the hallways of the fortress until we reached Marisol's circular office, a sort of Stone Order equivalent of the Oval Office of the United States president. The floors were inlaid with lines of opal that cut concentric circle designs through the square marble tiles. Linen curtains and wall hangings softened the stucco walls.

Jaquard closed both interior office doors and went to the door that led to a private courtyard to peer outside. Satisfied, he turned to Marisol and gave her a slight nod.

With urgency straining her face, Marisol faced us.

"Did the assassins' corpses disappear after the attack in Spriggan territory?" she asked Maxen.

He nodded and slid a quick glance at me. "It was after Petra left, and I didn't get a chance to tell her what happened."

She turned her intense blue gaze on me. "And you think they were part banshee and part dwarf?"

"Lack of pigment in the skin like banshees, and narrow ears with peaked cartilage like dwarves," I confirmed. I held my hand out flat about four feet above the floor. "Diminutive size, about this tall."

I was substantially shorter than the average New Gargoyle, as that Elf bouncer at Druid Circle had so helpfully pointed out, and the shortest person in the room by a solid half foot. I was used to it, though, as I'd grown up around full-blooded New Gargoyles. Once I began training as a fighter when I was a child, I discovered I was ten times stealthier and quicker than any full-blood New Garg could ever dream of. Once I developed strength, too, I was almost unbeatable by my peers. That took care of any self-consciousness I might have had about my height.

Oliver shifted. "Petra's right. I would have guessed the same. I assume we can rule out King Sebastian?"

Marisol nodded, but frowned at the same time. "It appears so. By Maxen's account, the assassins were genuinely trying to kill Sebastian."

It had certainly seemed so. The knife that had stuck in the shoulder of Sebastian's guard had started sizzling and smoking, killing him almost instantly. And that blade had definitely been intended for the king.

"Then who?" Oliver asked.

"Someone with the power to create and command a large number of servitors," Marisol said.

I stared at her. Servitors were made of very complicated illusion magic, but I'd always thought they were more like apparitions. Not solid-bodied figures who wielded knives that could kill. "You mean those ninjas weren't real?"

"They were real, just not quite in the same sense as you and me," she said. "They were created to serve a single purpose and then disappear. This is where the oddity comes in. In both attacks, no one of great importance was killed, yet the servitors dissolved."

I wasn't so sure the dead guards would agree with her assessment, but I tried to focus on the salient point.

"If that's true, in the attack at Druid Circle their main purpose wasn't to kill King Sebastian," Maxen said. "And in the attack here, again they weren't sent to kill a ruler."

Marisol let out a tiny breath, not quite a sigh. "I believe the assassination attempt was just a distraction. Whatever their purpose was, they achieved it and then returned to their master. More reports of similar attacks are filtering in from smaller kingdoms."

She and Oliver exchanged a long look. I could tell by their intent expressions that they were following the same thought train, perhaps something they'd whispered about back on the dais. But by their silence they weren't in the mood to share.

"Petra, Maxen, I need to speak to Oliver privately for a moment," Marisol said.

The two of them moved off to the far side of the office, behind her great oak desk. Maxen and I wandered over to the fireplace, which had a small fire lit. Even though it was summer in Faerie, the day was cool.

"What do you think they're saying?" I asked, eyeing my father as he stood just a bit closer to Marisol than any of her other advisors ever did.

Oliver had sworn his allegiance to Marisol before I was born, and I'd always assumed he'd also shared her bed regularly. He wasn't Maxen's father, though. Except for Maxen's sapphire blue eyes, he was the spitting image of Marisol's deceased husband. I couldn't help wondering if Oliver's relationship with Marisol had preceded even the time he was with my mother. He refused to tell me who my mother was but had implied that their relationship was intermittent. She'd died when I was still a baby, so I had no conscious memory of her.

"She's most worried about the breach," Maxen said.

"Oliver was, too. Has anyone ever breached the fortress before?" I was fairly certain it hadn't happened in my lifetime, or I surely would have known about it. But I wasn't well-versed in fortress history. Growing up, I'd paid little attention to the lessons that didn't involve some sort of combat or weapons training.

"No breach since we staked claim to this territory and sealed the doorways," Maxen said.

Marisol had claimed the prison for our people when she was only eighteen. I did remember that. First, she'd had to acquire it from the State of California, which I imagined took some considerable persuasion, especially considering she had always resided in Faerie. Then, she had to come up with the funds for the very expensive magic that transmuted the interior of the prison into Faerie and formed the outer doorways into the fortress and additional interior doorways. She, like Oliver, was a first-generation New Gargoyle, meaning that both of them had started life as a different race of Fae. At the Cataclysm, the disruption in magic sent out a ripple, causing the spontaneous formation of our race. Magic is strange like that, occasionally causing sudden shifts that defy logical explanation.

Initially it was thought the features of New Gargoyles were a disease, like the VAMP viruses, and that attitude still existed in some circles even though it had long been proven false.

Marisol was sixteen when the Cataclysm hit, and Oliver was twenty-six, just a year younger than my current age. They'd both been born into a minor Seelie kingdom that had since been absorbed by larger kingdoms. Like most first-generation New Gargs, Marisol and Oliver said very little about their lives before the Cataclysm. I suspected my mother might have been a subject of a small Seelie kingdom as well, maybe even the same one as Marisol and my father, but of course Oliver wouldn't confirm my guess. The only thing I knew about her for sure was that the Cataclysm caused only part of a change in her. She'd been part-New Gargoyle and part mystery Fae when she had me. She'd died in the tumultuous couple of years after the Cataclysm, just before it was determined that New Gargoyles were a legitimate Fae race and not diseased, and Marisol subsequently claimed the fortress.

Marisol and Oliver finished their whispering, and they rejoined me and Maxen.

"If you remember any other details of the attacks, you'll inform me immediately," she said to all three of us. "And of course you will report any word of these servitors appearing again."

With that, she turned and strode over to her desk, dismissing us. One thing I appreciated about Marisol was her tendency to get straight to the point. Many found her too brusque, but I thought it was refreshing.

Jaquard stayed behind while Maxen, Oliver, and I headed to one of the interior doors to make our exit.

"Oh, Petra," Marisol called.

I cringed internally at her voice as my boots squeaked to a halt on the tiles.

Maxen pulled the door closed behind him, a little smirking smile on his face.

Grudgingly, I turned and went to stand in front of the wide desk, feeling oddly like I was facing a judge even though I hadn't done anything wrong.

I settled my weight on one hip, trying not to look as if I couldn't wait to spring for the door. "Yes, My Lady?"

"The invitation to join the Stone Order's fighting ranks still stands," she said. She'd set a postcard-sized piece of stationery in front of her. Without internet, cell phones, or phone lines that stretched between kingdoms, communication in Fae was still fairly archaic, and much of it had to be hand-written and then transported by ravens. She put down the pen and folded her hands on the desk. "Your father would welcome you into the legion, and you'd be a great asset to your people if you served here in the fortress."

"I'm fine with my position in the Guild," I said evenly. It was a considerable compliment to be invited to the fighting ranks outright, but flattery wouldn't draw me in.

She regarded me for a moment. "Once the Stone Order becomes the Stone Court, you won't have the freedom to work and reside on the other side of the hedge. Your people will need you here. You'd best get used to the idea sooner than later."

I ground my teeth in annoyance. The implication that I'd be totally under her control and would regret not cooperating with her demands echoed King Sebastian's threat, and it made me want to pick up something breakable and toss it against the wall.

"I understand that," I said tightly. I waited to see if she had anything more to say.

Her nostrils flared slightly, but she lowered her lids and waved me away, dismissing me.

"Oh, and Petra," she called after me. I turned. "Stop parking your damn scooter on the marble."

I saluted and quickly slipped out. I wasn't sure how she'd even known Vincenzo was out there in the lobby of the fortress.

I had to hand it to Marisol. Her conviction and confidence when it came to establishing a Stone Court was admirable. Or maybe it was blind stubbornness. Either way, she clearly didn't put any stock in the assumptions of the rest of Faerie that New Gargoyles would eventually succumb to a larger kingdom.

I wasted no time leaving her office, and I found Oliver waiting for me in the hallway.

"I didn't get a chance to finish before," he said.

I blinked up at him, at first unsure what he meant. "Oh yeah, the changeling you were telling me about. The one King Periclase took."

He glanced at the closed door and flicked his eyes down the hall, signaling that we should walk. He wanted to get away from Marisol's office, and that meant he had something to tell me that she didn't know.

I walked beside him down the hallway, expecting him to pause and fill me in on this secret changeling. But he continued through the administrative wing, and we crossed over into the residential quarters. As we moved through the fortress, people skirted glances at us, some of them wary but most of them respectful. Oliver was Marisol's champion and her first sworn follower. But aside from all that, he was pure badass from head to toe. He looked like an ancient warrior, with almost impossibly broad shoulders, cropped hair with horizontal stripes shaved into the sides, and searing intensity that never dropped from his aventurine-green eyes.

We finally reached his apartment, and the door opened automatically under his touch, having been charmed to recognize him. His quarters were sparse, not unlike my own apartment. He didn't ask me to sit down or offer me anything.

I crossed my arms, waiting for him to do a sweep of the place. This check wasn't just about the ninja breach. He did it every time he came home. Oliver wasn't a trusting man.

After he finished, he rejoined me in the tiny living room that was furnished with only an easy chair, ottoman, side table, and floor lamp. Not only did he tend to not trust others, he also wasn't interested in playing host.

He pulled out his phone and held it so I could see the screen. On it was a photo of an attractive, smiling girl with blond hair pulled up into a sleek bun. It was a tight shot, one that had probably included other people but had been cropped down to her face. In it, I could clearly see the tawny yellow-flecked brown eyes that were strangely similar to mine.

He was watching my face. "The changeling's name is Nicole. She's your sister."

Chapter 6

I PEERED AT him out of the corners of my eyes, at first thinking it must be a joke. Then I remembered I'd never heard Oliver tell a joke in my life.

Still, I waited for a moment on the off chance there might be a punch line coming.

After several seconds of silence, I blinked. "Come again?"

"She was placed as a baby right after the two of you were born. She's your twin."

My arms were crossed over my chest but suddenly seemed to lose the tension necessary to hold them there. My hands slipped down to my sides as I stared at my father.

I shook my head. "I have a *twin*?" I blinked again.

"Marisol knows of the changeling, but not that she's your sister," he said.

My brows rose halfway up my forehead.

He looked off to the side, his jaw muscles flexing and releasing, flexing and releasing. He looked uncomfortable. That made me twitchy. I preferred stoic Oliver.

"I swore to your mother that I'd keep her secret, and the only loophole was if there came a time one of you was in danger," he said finally. He heaved a sigh, and just when I thought he was going to refuse to say more, he continued. "Right after the Cataclysm, Marisol had a prophetic vision. She saw herself ruling a Fae kingdom, her throne built upon the bloodied bodies of a set of New Gargoyle twin girls who were conceived exactly a year after the Cataclysm. One was fair and the other dark haired. She named them the 'sisters of sacrifice.' Marisol told me of the prophecy, and I repeated it to your mother. I shouldn't have broken Marisol's confidence that way, but . . . I did. When your mother had you and Nicole, she panicked. She was sure the sisters in the vision were her daughters. I tried to tell her that sometimes visions are symbolic, not literal, but this one was too specific. Your mother was already quite unstable by then, and she nearly went mad with fear. She *was* mad for a time, threatening to kill one of you to keep Marisol from killing both of you. I convinced her to let me hide Nicole."

A soft breeze could have knocked me over. I'd never heard Oliver speak so many words at once. I'd never heard him admit to a mistake in judgment. I'd never, ever considered that I had a sibling somewhere out there. What in the name of Oberon was happening to the world?

"But if I go get her, Marisol will find out," I said.

"You're not identical," Oliver said. "And with care, we'll be able to keep the secret. Just in case your mother's concerns had any merit."

I slowly shook my head. I really, really didn't like that Oliver seemed to think there might actually be some stock in my mother's mad fears for her daughters.

"Prophecies aren't for certain," he said. "And the Stone Order may never become the Stone Court. But if it does, I won't take the chance."

In theory, he was right. Generally speaking, prophecies didn't always bear out. But all of Marisol's prophecies—the ones that were made public, anyway—had come to pass. And as for the formation of the Stone Court, it was her sole obsession in life. If there was any possibility of making it happen, she would find a way. I didn't doubt she'd do it at the cost of blood.

"Marisol is determined to get Nicole away from King Periclase," he said. "Nicole is New Gargoyle, and Marisol won't let a single New Garg slip through her fingers if she can help it. Besides, Nicole is our family."

Family. Oliver had been my only family for my entire life.

"How did anyone even discover that Nicole is part New Garg?" I asked. "Her magic surely hasn't come in yet."

"Periclase had her blood divined," Oliver said. "And Marisol acquired the information that Nicole has New Gargoyle blood."

Blood divining was a special type of Fae magic. It didn't tell you who your parents were, but it revealed the races that ran through your blood.

"I'm surprised Marisol doesn't want to send you," I said.

"I'm too high profile. Everyone knows I'm one of Marisol's closest advisors, but I don't go on diplomatic trips. My position is military, and it wouldn't help discussions to send a high-ranking military man on a diplomatic mission. It would look aggressive."

"But won't it raise suspicion if I go? I'm not exactly the first on board when it comes to forwarding the interests of the Stone Order." I knew it sounded cold, as if I were begrudging his request to go to the aid of my own blood, but that wasn't it. I still had questions. And I really needed to know whether there was anything else Oliver was holding back. I had the uneasy feeling that there was.

"I wanted you to go," he said. "I suggested you."

I regarded him for a moment. This was his daughter we were talking about. I could understand why he wanted to send me after her. If he couldn't go himself, I was the next best thing.

"Does King Periclase know who Nicole is? He couldn't, I guess."

"I can't imagine he does."

My brow furrowed with sudden worry. "But I'll have to bring her here to the fortress. She'll be right under Marisol's nose. Doesn't that seem, I don't know, dangerous in light of that bloody-ass prophecy?"

I felt itchy. Edgy. Like I needed to sprint a mile or punch something. I wasn't good with big revelations that had the potential to jump-kick me right in the emotions.

Oliver's mouth twitched, a subtle sign I'd said something that amused him.

"Aren't you full of questions," he said mildly. "Yes, we'll have to put her up here. We can't let her go back to the Earthly realm. Periclase will just take her again. The fortress will be her home for now. Hopefully for the long term. She is, after all, as much New Gargoyle as you are. We can't abandon her to Periclase."

The word "abandon" sent a pang through my heart. New Gargs were protective of our own because there weren't a whole lot of us.

"We can't let that happen." I pressed my lips together and then blew out a slow breath. "I can't imagine what's going through her mind right now."

"She was raised by humans with magical aptitude, but having been on the Earthly side of the hedge her entire life, she won't even know she has her own magic."

Changelings' magic was always suppressed, on account of not having spent their childhood in Faerie. Since Nicole was here, things were probably starting to get very weird for her.

I shoved my fingers into my dark hair, pushing it back from my face.

"I'll do it," I said. I was still in the middle of my Guild assignment, but I'd just have to find a way to accomplish both missions. "But this doesn't mean I'm quitting the Guild."

He lowered his lids a fraction, an Oliver version of a withering look.

"Just join the damn battle ranks already, Petra."

I took half a step backward toward the door, my mind on escape. I was starting to have flashbacks to the epic power struggles we'd fought when I was a teenager. I'd been kind of a rebellious little asshole. Even though I was now twenty-seven, we sometimes still slipped back into those roles, and I wasn't in the mood to replay those days. I edged a little closer to the exit.

He shifted his weight, his stance easing slightly.

"Wait," he said. "You're going to need some help getting in and out of Periclase's palace."

I halted my getaway. "You've got a plan in mind?"

"Maxen is taking a group of dignitaries to the Duergar kingdom. He was already scheduled to go on a week-long ambassadorial visit. Due to arrive there tomorrow night."

My eyes popped wide. "Wait, Maxen knows about Nicole?"

"No, Marisol hasn't told him yet. She will before he leaves, but she doesn't want him involved in any way." His gray-green eyes grew more serious. "I know you know this, but I'm going to say it anyway. You must take care, Petra. You'll be in the kingdom of a potential enemy, and an Unseelie territory at that. The Unseelie can be ruthless in ways others aren't."

"Right. Get the girl and sneak her out without pissing off anyone or starting a war. And do it all around my day job."

Oliver gave a low chuckle. "Smart ass. Oh, and don't forget that you can't reveal Nicole's true identity to Maxen."

It was going to be a fricking mine field, and he knew it. But Oliver wouldn't send me in if he didn't believe I could pull it off. An eager little part of me was already getting psyched at the challenge—another quirk of the father-daughter dynamic. No matter how hard I might have railed against his authority when I was a kid, there was—and still remained—a desire for his approval that seemed threaded through my DNA. I'd spent my childhood trying to fight it, but at some point in the past few years, I'd finally accepted that it wasn't going away.

Ah, family.

Speaking of, my known blood relations had just doubled. Somewhere out there in King Periclase's kingdom, I had a sister.

A little surge of anticipation spurred me through the fortress in search of Maxen. I spotted an Order page, identifiable by her blue vest, and jogged to catch up with her.

"I need to find Maxen," I said to the startled girl. "Official business, Oliver Maguire's orders."

She blinked a couple of times and then tapped the tablet on top of the folders she carried. Cell phones didn't work in Fae, but electronics had become fundamental tools in the kingdoms decades ago. The only snag was that there was no Wi-Fi. Like cell phone signals, it didn't work on this side of the hedge. Tablets had to be frequently plugged into the fortress's hard-wired lines to update data, and there were ports all around the building.

"Mr. Lothlorien's schedule, current as of an hour ago, says he's in training right now," she said.

I nearly shuddered. I couldn't imagine a life where dozens of people knew where I was and what I was doing from one hour to the next.

I nodded and continued through the hallways of the fortress toward the training yard. I passed more pages, advisors, and people performing more menial tasks such as cleaning and moving supplies around. New Gargoyles were built for fighting, but it didn't mean that all of them wanted to pursue the training necessary to become skilled at it.

I reached the workout room, an open-concept modern gym outfitted with weights and treadmills. I waved at a few New Gargs I'd trained with when I was younger but didn't stop to chat. On the other side of the gym, wide glass double-doors led to the training yard, where trainees and full members of the battle ranks worked with weapons of all kinds and practiced hand-to-hand combat.

Some of the instructors were younger than me. I'd had many teachers, but the most significant was my father, though he'd never officially been an Order instructor. He was the one who'd taught me that my smaller size could be an advantage. He'd also trained me in the mental discipline of pain tolerance. People would make assumptions when they saw me, about my strength and abilities. Others wouldn't expect a small female to be mentally tough. He made me see that with the right training and hard work, I could be a match for any opponent. Under his guidance, I'd transformed from a scrappy little New Garg girl who just wanted to swing swords around into a formidable fighter who could best nearly anyone in the fortress.

I spotted Maxen training with a short sword. A V of sweat on the back of his gray t-shirt showed he was well into his workout. He and his partner both had their rock armor fully activated and were going full intensity at each other using real weapons. When it came to strength, New Gargoyles reigned above the other Fae races. The Spriggans were the only other race that came close in terms of physical stature and strength, but they didn't have our stone armor and as a race didn't tend to put much stock in battle training because they formed one of the smaller kingdoms. If a larger kingdom really wanted to take the Spriggan by force, it wouldn't be that hard simply due to numbers.

I watched appreciatively as Maxen and his sparring partner, a guy named Shane who'd graduated a few years after us, slashed and jabbed at each other, each of their weapons engulfed in their respective wielders' magic. Maxen's was like deep indigo smoke dancing around his arm and sword. His brow was lined with concentration, his teeth gritted.

I felt a zip of recognition across my back, Mort waking up in the proximity of other weapons. My hand itched to grab my broadsword and a partner. While I appreciated the sheer strength Maxen and his opponent displayed, I was much quicker than the full-bloods, and I loved fighting them. Skilled quickness beat brute strength nine times out of ten. At least, when it was *my* quickness in the fight.

Two short beeps sounded, and Maxen and Shane lowered their swords, let their rock armor dissolve, and went to the towels and jars of water they'd left near where I was standing.

Maxen caught sight of me, and the tension of the fight eased from his face, replaced by a boyish grin.

"Hey, Petra. You next?" He playfully tossed his short sword from one hand to the other and assumed an exaggerated fencing pose.

"With you already tuckered out? Nah, I'd probably hurt you. I'll fight you when you're fresh, Lothlorien."

"So, you just wanted to watch me, then," he said.

I rolled my eyes and shot Shane a long-suffering look. I'd sparred with him plenty of times growing up. I'd always envied the fact that he could fight equally well with either hand. True ambidexterity was rare. He gave a good-natured smile, nodded, and walked off toward the locker room with his towel draped around his neck.

"Got a minute?" I asked when Shane was out of earshot.

"For you? I've got five." Maxen's tone was teasing, but his eyes had sharpened with interest.

"I need to get into the Duergar Court, and I know you've got official business there," I said.

He peered at me out of the corners of his eyes. "Work?"

"Sort of." I glanced around, considering how much to say. Remembering the urgency in Oliver's eyes, I decided to keep as much to myself as possible. Channeling my more seductive alter ego, Penelope, I leaned in and flicked my eyes down to Maxen's lips before giving him a direct, unblinking look. "So, think you can get me in? C'mon, it'll be fun."

He tipped his head back and let out a short laugh. Merriment danced in his sapphire eyes. "Considering your little tirade at King Sebastian, I have serious doubts about taking you on a diplomatic trip."

"Yeah, I probably went a bit too far." I tilted my head to one side. "But then the assassins showed up. You can't tell me *that* wasn't fun."

"Adrenaline junkie," he accused, but he was grinning.

I knew I had him.

"You leave tomorrow night, right?" I asked. "What time should I come back here?"

"Noon tomorrow," he said.

"Isn't that a little early for an evening arrival?"

He gave me a droll look from under his brows. "You don't just saunter through a doorway into another Fae palace. There are preparations. Pageantry. Protocol."

I tried not to grimace. "That's a lot of P words. Okay, noon it is. See you then."

I didn't even make it a full step.

"Petra."

"What?" I asked innocently.

"You haven't told me why you need to go to the Duergar court."

I bit my lip for a second. I had to tell him something. Besides, Marisol would inform him soon, anyway. "Periclase is holding a New Garg changeling against her will. I need to get her out."

He regarded me for a long moment. I could see the confusion on his face. Marisol hadn't told him about Nicole yet. Part of me wanted to tell him that Nicole was my sister, but I remembered Oliver's warning. My mother had apparently feared for my life and Nicole's life at the hands of Marisol. I trusted Maxen, but if Oliver didn't want Marisol to know about my twin, he certainly wouldn't want Maxen to know.

"Periclase is holding a New Garg changeling," he repeated.

I reached up to rub at the back of my neck. I really wished Marisol would have briefed him already. "Yeah. I just found out."

"Why you?"

I shrugged. "You'd have to ask Oliver," I said, skirting around the real reason. Fae can't lie to each other, but we can be evasive.

"Okay," he said finally.

I flipped my braid over my shoulder and let out a quiet breath of relief.

He pulled his sweaty t-shirt up and over his head and then balled it up in his hands and used it to wipe his forehead. "But this isn't going to come for free."

My gaze slid from his muscled shoulders and down across his chest to his cut abs. Just because I wasn't interested in Maxen's overtures didn't mean I couldn't appreciate what he had to offer.

I nodded once and then turned and strode away. Even that little acknowledgement was too close to agreeing that I'd owe him a favor. I needed to get out before I accidentally said something more binding.

A glance at the clock in the training yard told me that Order business had already eaten up a good portion of my work day. I still had to find that drug-dealing vamp, Van Zant.

Chapter 7

THERE WAS A huge payout for apprehending Van Zant, and I sorely needed it. My roommate had to cover my part of the current month's rent, we had a handful of bills that were overdue, I hadn't paid off all of Vincenzo's last round of repairs, and my account balance had dwindled to double-digits. Not to mention the fact that Van Zant was a menace to society and his black market VAMP3 blood would cause deaths of innocents, if it hadn't already.

When I stepped through the doorway and back into the Earthly realm outside the fortress, my phone buzzed and bleeped. I scanned through my messages to make sure there was nothing urgent—there wasn't. But there was the picture of Nicole that Oliver had shown me on his phone. He must have stepped outside of Faerie to send it to me while I'd been in the training yard.

I gazed at it for a long moment, looking for any other resemblance between me and my twin besides our eyes. Our skin tone was similar, except mine was a tanner version. She looked like she wore sunscreen a lot, or maybe just didn't spend much time outside. Her makeup was heavy, almost like stage makeup and much more than a girl with her sunny good looks needed.

I tucked my phone away, started up Vincenzo, and drove back toward the city and the doorway in the abandoned naval base on Treasure Island that I'd used to come from Boise to San Francisco. The ache from using my rock armor was more pronounced than it had been when I made the drive in to the Stone Order's fortress, and my entire front torso was tender. I was drained from having conjured armor three times in less than twenty-four hours, and I'd need to do something about it soon. I wanted to find Van Zant before I had to travel to the Duergar palace on the sister-rescue mission and really hoped that errand wouldn't require more armor.

On the drive, my mind buzzed around Nicole. Her name and the headshot were all I really had, and her face hovered in my thoughts. My hair was a medium neutral walnut and my face defined by my jawline and cheekbones, whereas she was honey-haired with a softer, heart-shaped face. Nicole had the face of a prom queen, and I looked like I played lead guitar for an all-girl ska band. We didn't even look related. I wasn't sure if I felt surprised, disappointed, or relieved about it.

I couldn't see her build in the photo, but imagined from her slim, graceful neck that she was more petite than I was. They said that changelings often had a sense of separateness, of never quite feeling like they fit into their human world. Nicole looked happy in the picture, but that was just a brief second in time. Perhaps she'd had moments when she'd felt that inexplicable aloneness or glimpsed a vision of a different world in a dream. I wondered what kind of life she'd had, growing up with a human family. Nicole was old for a changeling coming home to Faerie—usually it happened in the teenage years or sometimes younger—and I suspected it was going to make it that much harder for her.

I couldn't imagine living twenty-seven years without knowing I was a New Gargoyle. I made every effort to steer clear of Marisol and Faerie politics, but still. I was Fae, and I'd always known it. The thought of getting thrust into some strange alternate world was so foreign to me it was hard to wrap my head around it. I'd been raised in Faerie, but from a young age I'd spent some time here and there on the other side of the hedge. Oliver had thought it important that I understood the Earthly realm and its people. I always suspected he felt that way because of what happened to my mother, maybe thinking that if she'd been less naïve about vampires and other workings of the Earthly realm she might not have died. He'd taken me on many excursions to sightsee around the San Francisco Bay Area. Later, he'd allowed me to go through the hedge with friends, on occasion. When I decided to move out of Faerie altogether, perhaps he'd felt that encouraging my familiarity with the Earthly realm had backfired. He'd never voiced that regret specifically, but he'd made it clear he would prefer to have me permanently in the fortress.

I wheeled my ride into the doorway in the naval base, and a moment later the obliterating cold of the netherwhere swept away all thought.

I emerged in the MonsterFit vestibule in Las Vegas and quickly pushed Vincenzo out into the searing midday heat. I briefly wondered if the gym owners ever wondered about the faint tire tracks I sometimes left on the linoleum. Leaving my scooter in one of the free parking spots associated with the strip mall, I turned back to the doorway.

Out of the corner of my eye, I caught movement. Lemony, the yellow-eyed stray, came over and nuzzled my shin with the top of his head. He must be lonely to turn on the affection like this. He was usually more aloof.

"Lemon-cat, what are you doing out in this heat?" I asked, reaching for a treat. I squatted to offer it and then scratched him between the ears. "Must have missed me, huh?"

When I straightened, Lemony scampered away, probably seeking shade.

I went back into the vestibule, where I used the doorway to hop to the Strip, emerging next to Druid Circle, the club where King Sebastian had been attacked.

I walked the short distance to the nightclub's entrance. The door to the club was cracked open and unguarded, which gave me a tiny zing of disappointment. I would've enjoyed harassing that jerky Elf bouncer.

Inside, I breathed a grateful sigh for the darkness and AC. The place was nearly empty. I went up to the bar and asked the bartender—not the Sylph girl, but a petite, busty redheaded Fae of too many races to be distinguished—to summon the owner, Gregory.

"Tell him it's the New Garg who kept King Sebastian from getting knifed on the balcony last night," I said to her.

When Gregory appeared in the doorway next to the bar, his dark eyes were guarded.

"Seen Van Zant around?" I asked, skipping the pleasantries. "The tip about the Millennium didn't pan out."

"Hold on a second," he said, glancing around even though there was barely anybody in the place, let alone within earshot. He tipped his head toward the doorway where he'd emerged and then led me about ten feet into the hallway.

"He hasn't come back here," Gregory said in a low voice. "But I heard he's in Faerie."

I frowned. A vamp couldn't just wander around in Faerie at will. Non-Fae required escorts, someone from this side of the hedge to act as a sort of guide and sponsor. Non-Fae couldn't even physically pass through doorways without an escort.

"Who's he with?"

Gregory shrugged. "Someone with Unseelie ties."

I narrowed my eyes. "And?"

His gaze slanted down at an angle, and his mouth tightened into a line.

"C'mon, Gregory. He's passing VAMP3 blood in your club. That's a huge liability to you. One of his customers might go rogue. Can you imagine what a massacre it would be when it's shoulder-to-shoulder in here and everyone's drunk off their asses? It'd be a bloodbath."

His shoulders sagged, and he passed a hand over his weary eyes. "I don't know if it's true, but some are saying there's a Spriggan-Duergar woman with him."

My frown deepened. Huh, a mixed Seelie-Unseelie was escorting Van Zant around Faerie.

"First, you said it was someone with Unseelie ties, so if it's a Spriggan-Duergar woman that means she could be sworn to the Duergar kingdom," I said.

He lifted a palm. "Maybe."

He was right to be uncertain. Just because Van Zant's escort was part Duergar by birth didn't mean she was sworn to the Duergar kingdom. Gregory called her Spriggan-Duergar likely because those were the bloodlines that were obvious from her appearance. But it didn't mean those were her *only* Fae bloodlines. She might have additional Unseelie blood in her lineage that allowed her to align with some other Unseelie kingdom. Every kingdom has its own rules about who can swear fealty. With the Stone Order, you had to be able to demonstrate rock armor as a sign that you had sufficient New Garg blood. Some kingdoms were fairly lax in their requirements because they cared more about numbers than purity of blood, but with very few exceptions you had to offer at least something supporting your blood ties. Without knowing the woman's name or any other details about her, it would be hard to ask around to find out more.

I stepped out of Druid Circle, but instead of going back to MonsterFit, I intended to use the doorway in the alcove to hop to another location in Faerie. It was a neutral area, not part of the realm of any kingdom, that was simply known as the Carnival. It was a place known for shady business and illegal trade, and I thought I might be able to glean something more about the VAMP3 blood trade.

The oblivion of the netherwhere folded me into its welcome coolness. But a second later, I realized something wasn't right. The empty void didn't feel as empty as it usually did.

I automatically tried to reach for Mort, but there was no hand to move, no sword to grasp. Physical form didn't exist in the netherwhere the way it did in the world. Yet, something began winding around me, curling like tentacles. My mind strained to fight, but it was like being tied up while paralyzed in the black vacuum of space.

Something had followed me into the void, and it was holding me there. Too long, and I'd never return to the world. My mind thrashed again, trying to command phantom limbs to battle my attacker, but nothing happened.

I was drowning . . . suffocating . . . dissolving into the void.

No.

I wasn't going to die this way.

My thoughts raced, trying to conjure in my mind the sigils for a doorway—any doorway. It was the only thing I could think to try. If I could concentrate hard enough on them, maybe it would be enough to draw me out of the netherwhere.

A symbol appeared in my mind, and in my panic I wasn't even sure which doorway it belonged to. I focused on it, grasping at it with all the energy I could muster, and it lit into lines of flame in my imagination.

The doorway spilled me out of the netherwhere, and I fell to my hands and knees, panting as if I'd been held under water.

I stayed there for several seconds, drinking in gulps of air and reveling in the pounding of my own heart. I was still alive. There was a muffled noise nearby. I raised my head. There was a glass door in front of me, and Lemony was on the other side. He rose to his back feet, placing his front paws on the door as if scratching to be let in. I was back in the vestibule of MonsterFit.

A strange smell clung to my clothes—metal and blood and decay. My entire body seemed to throb and itch, the sensation intensifying as the chill of the netherwhere wore off. I raised my arm and pulled back my sleeve to find red welts striping my skin.

I stared at them as my heart skipped a beat. I'd felt this before, once during training when we were learning strategies to fight magical vulnerabilities. Cold iron burns. If not for my New Gargoyle blood, those welts would be terrible, agonizing burns. For reasons unknown to us, New Gargs were a bit more resistant to iron than other races of Fae. But the longer the exposure, the worse the burns. Eventually cold iron would eat right through a Fae body.

My stomach turned. Somebody really didn't want me to come out of the netherwhere alive. I swept my gaze side to side, suddenly paranoid. Maybe it wasn't the best idea to hang out right in front of a doorway. Who knew what might come through.

Just as I reached for the door handle to pull myself up, my phone began exploding with bleeps. I got to my feet and then pulled out the device, absently whispering the Faerie magic words that allowed me to pass out of the locked vestibule as if the walls were air.

The Vegas heat hit me like a furnace blast. Lemony began weaving around my legs while I scanned through my messages. There were half a dozen from Maxen. I read the first one.

Petra, are you okay? The club owner at Druid Circle was murdered by a wraith. He wrote your name in blood before he died.

I swallowed hard. Gregory was dead? Damn. Anger began to harden in the pit of my stomach. I'd just been with him at Druid Circle. He'd tried to help me, and now he was gone.

My breath died. That was what the dead smell was, the tendrils that had tried to squeeze the life out of me. A wraith had come after me in the netherwhere.

Each subsequent message was more urgent. I dialed Maxen, but his phone went to voicemail. I left a quick message to let him know I was alive.

I scrolled through the messages again, confused.

"I *just* saw Gregory," I muttered. The wraith must have attacked him literally the second after I left and then come straight for me.

I looked up, shaking my head. Then I noticed the low angle of the sun. I looked down at my phone again to check the time and just stared. It couldn't be right. Again, I looked at the sky and then at the digital clock readout.

In spite of the heat, my blood chilled. I'd been in the netherwhere for almost four hours.

I dialed Maxen again, and this time he answered.

"Petra?"

"Yeah, I'm okay," I said. "But I think the same wraith that killed Gregory tried to kill me in the netherwhere. It held me there for hours."

"Thank Oberon you're in one piece." He let out a whoosh of a breath. "A wraith in the netherwhere? Damn it to Maeve. I've been searching for you in Faerie. No wonder no one's heard from you in a while. Are you sure you're all right?"

"I've got iron burns, but they're not bad. Otherwise I'm fine." I sounded a little calmer than I felt.

"Why would the owner of Druid Circle give the wraith your name?"

"It's connected to my Guild assignment. I went to speak to the deceased right before I went into the doorway."

"You can't screw with wraiths, Petra," Maxen said. "This is high-level. Way beyond merc work."

I used my fingers to comb my hair back from my forehead.

"Don't worry about it, Maxen. I'll be fine."

I forced a level tone, but inside I was pissed. Not at Maxen, but at whoever had sent the wraith to kill Gregory and then come after me. You had to be either desperate or extremely stupid to go after someone in the netherwhere. The doorways were made by ancient, intricate magic, and the netherwhere was a profound magical achievement. Trying to attack someone there was a real asshole move.

Yet, someone had done just that.

"Do you want me to tell Oliver?" Maxen demanded.

"No, Maxen," I said, irritation edging my voice. "Please do not go tell my daddy."

He sighed heavily. "Fine. But if you don't show up at noon tomorrow, I go straight to Oliver."

I echoed his sigh. "All right." I knew he was just trying to look out for me.

"Be careful."

"I will." I hung up.

Letting out a long breath that ended in a grumble, I looked down at Lemony, who was sitting at my feet and flicking his tail. I reached for a treat and then tossed it to him.

The sensation of the wraith trying to squeeze the life out of me crowded into my mind again, and my heart thumped at the memory. I swallowed sourly and brushed my fingers across the front of my neck, still feeling the choking sensation.

Wraiths were disembodied spirits that on their own were harmless and invisible to the living. But if a living person caught a wraith and imbued it with magical power, it became a problem. The one who gifted the power also commanded the wraith.

Maxen was right about wraiths. They were nothing to screw around with.

"Not good, Lemony," I muttered, bending to scratch the cat under his chin. "Even I'm willing to admit that."

I straightened and looked off to the west, where the sun was balancing atop the high rises.

It was time to turn the screws on Van Zant. The wraith had to have come from someone who was associated with him. It was too big a coincidence that it had gotten my name out of Gregory, killed the club owner, and then come after me in the netherwhere. Gregory and I had only spoken twice and both times it was about Van Zant. That was our only connection.

Van Zant wasn't the one actually commanding the wraith—that had to be a Fae—but I was certain it linked to him somehow.

I went back into the MonsterFit vestibule and traced certain sigils in the air with my index finger and whispered the magic words that opened doorways.

My destination wasn't Carnival as I'd intended before. Instead, I used the doorway to travel to a pub in the Duergar realm. While I would need Maxen's help to get into the Duergar palace where Nicole was being held, there were plenty of other places within the territory I could go without a bureaucratic chaperone.

The Aberdeen Inn was a pub in a Duergar-held realm in Scotland. Yep, as long as I knew the right sigils to draw, I could step through a doorway and go from a Vegas-anchored Faerie realm to a Scotland-anchored Faerie realm in a matter of seconds. Who said being Fae didn't have its perks?

My destination doorway took me directly into the pub. I arrived in a corner that was roped off to keep anyone from loitering or moving a table there that would trip up visitors coming in from the netherwhere. The wooden planks under my feet were worn and bowed from thousands of years of countless Fae who had stood in this spot when they'd come and gone through the Aberdeen doorway.

The light was dingy and the aromas of beer, fried food, and sweat hung like a mist in the air that held a pleasant humidity compared to bone-dry Las Vegas. The pub was filled with a rainbow of Fae races, all showing their true forms. There was no need for any humanoid-illusion glamour in a place where non-Fae weren't allowed. Every race of Fae could let their freak flags fly in places like the Aberdeen.

I flipped a wave to a couple of Fae Guild mercs who were obviously off-duty, but I wasn't there to socialize. My time to track down Van

Zant before I had to join Maxen for the trip to the Duergar palace was dwindling, and I had to find out who was behind the wraith. I needed to talk to the owner of the Aberdeen Inn.

Morven was a rare Ghillie Dubh, the only race of Fae allowed to remain independent from any kingdom. He stood behind the bar with his hand on a tap, looking like Santa Claus if old Saint Nick lost fifty pounds, started a serious weightlifting regimen, and trimmed his white facial hair to a neat quarter-inch of stubble.

No one save Oberon really knew how old Morven was or exactly where he'd grown up. He seemed like one of those institutions who spontaneously sprang to life just as he was now—gently wizened, sharp-eyed, and one of the most well-connected people in Faerie.

Aside from lack of kingdom affiliation, the other curious thing about Ghillie Dubh was that they had no qualms about coming to the aid of others. I could ask Morven for help without risk of the usual obligation that other Fae would normally incur. But a favor from a Ghillie Dubh wasn't without a price. It was a price paid right away, and it wasn't one that everyone could afford. You had to be very strong in magic, preferably with some unique quality, and possess nerves of steel. I had the first, my New Gargoyle blood gifted me the second, and my training and background provided me with nerve.

Morven's gaze slid to me as I approached.

"Ah, Petra Maguire," he said in his thick, rolling Scottish brogue. The way he pronounced my name always sent a little thrill up my spine. It somehow made me feel connected to the Old World. Even though I'd been raised in a realm anchored in the New World of the United States, Faerie began as territories anchored to the Old World—mostly Scotland, Ireland, and England. All of our roots were there, even mine.

"Hi, Morven."

I leaned on the bar and watched as he finished filling the mug he held, stopped the tap to pour off some of the foam, and then added another half-inch of beer. He pushed the frosty, thick glass mug across the bar to the waiting hand of a tall Elf. He gave Morven a respectful nod and then moved away from the bar and looked for an empty seat at a table, even though the barstools were all unoccupied. The stools along the bar of the Aberdeen were almost always empty. Fae were generally a bit wary of Morven, keeping their distance as if they feared he would reach out and take a piece of them. He wouldn't do that, of course. Not unless you asked him for help.

Morven lifted the corner of his dirty apron and wiped his hands on it. "So, you need the help of the Ghillie Dubh?"

"I do," I said.

I appreciated the way Morven cut straight to the point when it came to requests. And somehow, he always knew when I was there to drink and when I was there for help.

"Why don't we step upstairs?" He curled his hand, beckoning me to follow.

I walked behind him up a claustrophobic wooden staircase. It was so narrow Morven's broad shoulders brushed the walls on either side. There was a smooth, smudged line at his shoulder height, evidence of decades, maybe centuries, of his passage up and down.

The stairs let out into a loft with a peaked ceiling overhead that revealed the roofline. Partitions partially divided the space, but there were no visible doors. The smells of the bar below had drifted up and gone somewhat stale in the stuffy space. We stood in an area set up as a little sitting room, with a thick but worn woven rug underfoot, a small coffee table, and three large, matching, high-backed wooden chairs that looked as if they'd come from a dining set.

"Please, make yourself comfortable." He gestured to one of the chairs, waited until I sat, and then lowered himself to the chair angled toward mine.

He crossed one ankle over the other knee and leaned on the armrest with a jolly Santa Claus smile on his face. His posture was easy, as if he had all the time in the world and not a care in his heart. But his twinkling eyes had turned intent with a faintly predatory gleam.

I swallowed and pushed my palms down the thighs of my jeans. I'd done this before and knew what to expect, but that didn't make it easier. I couldn't do this often—I didn't *want* to—but sometimes it was the fastest route to something I needed.

"Now, what can I do for you?" he asked.

For one crazy second, I could almost imagine that I was a little human kid, ready to go sit on Santa's lap and whisper my Christmas wishes in his ear.

"There's a vampire, third generation. He goes by the name Van Zant," I said. I saw a flicker of recognition in Morven's eyes at the vamp's name. That was good. It meant Morven had heard of him and might have information. "I need to know who's escorting him around Faerie. And if you happen to know where he is right now, that would be helpful, too."

Morven's eyelids lowered a bit, as if he suddenly felt sleepy.

"I have the information you seek," he said. Faint, brownish magic, like wisps of smoke, began to leak from his mouth.

Watching as his eyes darkened, I gripped the armrests of my chair, bracing myself for what Morven was about to do to me.

Chapter 8

A SILENT, UNSEEN vacuum seemed to pull the breathable air from the room. It wasn't like the void of the netherwhere. It was much worse. There, I had no sense of my own lungs or need for oxygen, so the lack of it wasn't bothersome. But here, sitting in the loft of an ancient Duergar pub, I was acutely aware of the sense of suffocation.

Morven's grayish-brown magic filled the space like thick pipe smoke. I felt it creep into my ears, nostrils, and I swear it even went in through my tear ducts. And yes, you can bet your ass I was sitting there with my legs tightly crossed.

It was like having every orifice and pore invaded by tendrils of something awful and irritating. Steel wool. Pieces of fiberglass. Barbed toothpicks.

I ground my teeth and tried to stay as still as possible and ignore the sensation of a million probes and pricks. Any disturbance would just prolong the agony. But the full-body probing wasn't the worst part.

Just as I was sure I'd keel over from lack of oxygen, the swirling sensation in my chest began. It was like my torso was a blender and Morven had just pressed "liquefy." It literally felt as if my organs were being ripped from their cozy little pockets and churned into pulp.

I let out the tiniest of groans, more of a low hum in my throat, and a bead of sweat rolled down the center of my forehead and off the tip of my nose.

Then all at once the tiny probes receded and air flooded into my lungs. Dark blotches blotted out my field of vision. I slouched over, too weak to keep my spine straight. With my chin on my chest and my eyes squeezed closed, I focused on breathing and not vomiting. A sheen of sweat slicked my skin.

When I finally looked up, Morven had moved a bucket near my chair. I averted my eyes, refusing to look at it, while I waited for the nausea to subside. The muscle weakness and lightheaded feeling would take longer to go away.

Finally, I swallowed hard, faced forward, and looked him in the eyes. Every muscle in my body was trembling with the effort of staying upright.

"And the information?" I asked calmly.

I wasn't angry or resentful that he'd just taken a bit of my magic. It creeped me out, sure, and it was extremely unpleasant. But it was a transaction I'd willingly agreed to, and I would survive. In a way, it was a bit like donating blood. It depleted you temporarily, but then you recovered.

He tipped his head down, looking at me from under his bushy brows. "You're a tough one, Petra Maguire," he said. "I've seen men twice your size writhe and scream and then lose their lunch for their trouble."

The corners of my mouth twitched slightly at the compliment. I decided to ignore the familiar irritation that came when someone was surprised by my strength—either physical or mental.

"So," he said, drawing out the word in his brogue. "You're looking for Van Zant and his Fae companion."

I nodded. No point trying to rush him, as I already knew Morven wouldn't be rushed. I needed to sit there for a few minutes before I'd be able to stand, anyway.

"Bryna is her name. Duergar-Spriggan girl," he said. I hadn't specifically asked him to tell me her lineage, but one didn't speak of

Fae without mentioning such things. It confirmed what the nightclub owner had told me.

"Sworn to the Duergar kingdom?" I asked.

"That wasn't part of your original request, but I'll give you that as a wee bonus since you guessed it right."

"How generous," I said wryly.

"As for the vampire's location, I got wind he's lodging at the Cockburn with the girl Bryna."

"Lodging there tonight?"

"Aye."

My pulse bumped up a notch. The Cockburn was a hotel in an old Duergar mansion, and it wasn't far from the Aberdeen.

"She's the owner of the wraith," he said.

My brows lifted. Now I knew for sure that the wraith was connected to Van Zant. And I knew who to thank for sending it to kill me in the netherwhere.

Morven rose. "Always a pleasure doing business with you."

He gave me a little salute and then turned toward the staircase, leaving me alone in the loft.

I tipped my head back and closed my eyes, letting my full body weight sag into the chair while I mentally took stock of my condition. I'd managed to hold my shit together in front of Morven, but it had taken all my willpower to keep my spine straight. I was still sweating, though the chill from having a bit of magic torn from me was starting to set in, along with a pounding in my temples.

It was basically like an epic hangover, but without the fun part that comes before.

After another minute of deep breathing, I used the armrests to heave myself up, straightening gradually once on my feet. By the time I made it to the stairs, I was fairly sure I wasn't going to throw up.

Down in the pub, several people eyed me with knowing looks. I lifted my hand at Morven as I walked gingerly past, and he returned my wave with his signature Santa Claus smile.

Outside, the night air was the perfect summer's eve temperature. A deep breath of Faerie air, and I almost felt decent. I had a short walk ahead of me to the Cockburn, which frankly I needed to make sure my legs were in working order. The streets in this Duergar township were narrow, having been designed long before the advent of cars.

Everything here was very old, and as in the Aberdeen, all manner of Fae creatures roamed the streets. It was like walking through a Disneyland set or a fantasy-themed Vegas hotel complete with costumed characters. As I drew closer to the Cockburn, I skirted glances at the faces I passed, looking for Van Zant. I had no idea what his Fae companion, Bryna, looked like—maybe stocky, based on her Spriggan blood, but with mixed Fae races you never knew for sure.

It had been early evening in Las Vegas when I'd stepped through the MonsterFit doorway, but in this Scotland-anchored territory of the Faerie realm, it was just past midnight. The only people out and about seemed to be those who were pub hopping or heading home for the night. A raucous group of Cait Sidhe men was coming my direction on the other side of the street, and one of them tipped his head back and yowled up at the sky with an eerily perfect alley-cat call. The Cait Sidhe were felines at heart, even in their humanoid forms, but those noises coming from a person always set my nerves on edge.

I was reminded of my roommate, Lochlyn, who was part Cait Sidhe. Thank Oberon, she hardly ever made cat sounds. But being also part Baen Sidhe, or banshee, she could scream to make a person go insane. Whenever she brought a guy home, I did my best to find another place to be.

I turned a corner onto a block away from the main strip that was lined with pubs. This street was empty. I frowned, a tingle of apprehension spiraling up my spine. Just as something in the air seemed to shift,

I drew Mort and whirled around, shifting my weight to my toes and taking a fighting stance.

But no one was there.

Thin violet flames of magic ignited, activating the spellblade to extend the reach of its damage, but it was a mere wisp of what I could usually do. My temples throbbed with blinding pain from drawing magic, and I nearly reeled with nausea. Compared to my usual power, I was weak as a lamb from my session with Morven.

I glanced up, remembering the ninja attackers. While my gaze was averted, the wraith attacked.

Even if I'd been looking right at it, I probably wouldn't have seen it coming. Wraiths could sometimes be sighted out of the corners of your eyes, but they were as elusive as smoke. As in the netherwhere, a dozen appendages seemed to wrap around me—neck, shoulders, waist—pinning my arms to my sides. They looked like something in between old bone and rotted wood. I could smell its deathly rotting breath wafting over my left shoulder. It squeezed with vise-like strength, forcing the air from my lungs.

It aimed to make me lose consciousness, so it could then use one of its needle-sharp appendages to pierce my skull and drink the fluid from my brain. There'd been no corporeal skull to jab in the netherwhere, but here I was in real danger. The thing had somehow been imbued with cold iron, and the burn was starting to set in. She must have had a human helping her. Or maybe the vamp.

Stars began to dance around in my vision. I couldn't pass out. I groaned and drew more magic to form rock armor around my torso to keep the creature from squeezing more air from my body. Pain ripped over my skin where the armor plates sprang forth, but I had just enough juice to keep them in place.

Mort was useless in such close combat, but I held the grip hard to keep my sword in my hand. I'd need it in a second.

The wraith had to take solid form to hold me like this, which meant it was vulnerable. I flexed the bicep of my sword arm and felt the wraith's appendage give just a little. It was strong, but so was I. Clenching my teeth, I forced a flash of magic around my arm, forming a layer of stone. The sudden change broke the wraith's hold, and it squealed in protest. My sword arm was free.

I jerked Mort up and back over my left shoulder and felt the blade hit something hard but brittle. It gave way with the sickening crack of a bone breaking. An other-worldly scream filled the night, and all the limbs holding me went limp. I kicked back with one heel and spun away, using my momentum to pull Mort free.

Lightning fast, I whirled and stabbed at what appeared to be a hollow-eyed hooded face carved of rotted wood. There were cracks radiating from one of the eye sockets, indicating where my first hit had landed. My second stab was straight into the thing's awful yawning mouth, through greasy-looking strands of some unknown substance that strung between top and bottom jaws.

The wraith's scream rose in pitch until I thought my eardrums might implode. I held Mort's grip with both hands and sharply shoved the blade several inches deeper into the creature's throat.

Like something out of a horror film, long, bony branch appendages that sprouted from its shoulders began to curl up and shrivel. A moment later, the wraith exploded into a decay-scented puff of ashy dust.

I stood there gripping Mort, my chest heaving as if I'd just sprinted a mile. Magic drained away, and as it did the pain in my head and where my armor had been intensified so swiftly my limbs lost strength. The new iron burns screamed. Mort slipped from my hand, and I went heavily down to one knee.

I needed to stand, to be ready for whomever had sent the wraith, but I was on the edge of losing consciousness. If not for Morven sucking out some of my magic and leaving me weakened, I could have ended that wraith and a dozen more in three seconds flat.

Grimacing, I felt around for Mort and shifted so I was sitting on the cool cobblestones. Just as the spots in my vision cleared, the dark alcove of a nearby shop entrance began to shift. Out of the shadows stepped Van Zant.

My brain tried to command my muscles to pick me up off the ground, but my limbs weren't interested.

The vampire came forward to loom over me, and there was just enough light to see his upper incisors extending.

"Oh, shit," I groaned.

Chapter 9

I WISHED I could look around for Van Zant's Fae companion, Bryna, who'd been driving the wraith. I wouldn't have minded introducing her to Mort. But alas, I had to avoid the fangs bearing down on me.

Van Zant sprang at me in that creepy, animal way that vamps move. I rolled to my back and kicked out with my feet, nailing him in the stomach with one boot and the groin with the other. The blows catapulted him over me. He landed with a grunt and skidded along the ground.

He must have been high on his own power and adrenaline because he sprang to his feet almost immediately, and seemed none the worse for wear from the crotch kick.

I forced myself to rise and mirror his crouch. I growled, not because of amped-up aggression but because I felt like a re-heated carcass that had already taken all the abuse it could handle for one twenty-four-hour period, and I was pissed. Van Zant and I had started circling each other, and he kept flicking glances at Mort. I was pretty sure my sword was the only thing keeping the vamp at bay. I reached for magic, and searing pain and sparks exploded through my head.

"Damn it to Maeve," I muttered.

All I needed was sufficient magic to incapacitate Van Zant long enough to flash the bounty card in his face, and he'd be magically identified and cuffed. Then I could haul him in, and there'd be one less vamp hazard on the loose, and the fat payday would be mine. But vamps were preternaturally strong, and this one clearly wanted to end me.

My quads were shaking with the effort of holding the crouched ready stance, and my sword arm was already aching. If he came at me, I was done. I sneered, trying to look menacing enough to disguise the fact that I was about to keel over.

"Come at me, bloodsucker," I snarled, changing my grip so I held Mort in both hands.

I really didn't want to kill him. The assignment was to bring him in alive so he could stand trial. A dead mark only paid out ten percent of a full live capture—the Guild's way of discouraging mercs from becoming legal paid assassins. Plus, the thought of the paperwork that ensued from a kill on the job sent fresh nausea spinning through me. Oberon's balls, the damn *paperwork*. It would bury me for a week.

Van Zant lunged and swiped with his claw-like nails. Only my years of training saved me with a reflexive twitch of my sword that blocked him. He pulled back, again looking warily at Mort.

"Aw, is that all you got?" I waved my sword, which helped to mask the shaking of my arms. "Try again, leech."

Van Zant answered my taunt by springing up from the ground with blurring speed. I twisted, struggling to keep up with his movement. He rebounded off the building we were next to. My mind barely had time to process his trajectory. He was going to land on my shoulders and take me down backward.

I couldn't raise my arms in time, so I threw my weight forward and allowed gravity to assist my fall. I dropped hard onto my knees, spun to face him with one knee up, and slashed wildly. Even in this position, I could barely hold myself up, but it was enough and he scored only a glancing blow to my head from one of his boots as he tried to jump clear of my blade.

He shrieked, the sound echoing down the empty street. When he curled up on the ground, writhing, I saw it: the vamp's severed hand.

I crawled forward and snatched the dripping chunk of vampire flesh, and then used Mort as a crutch to push me up to my feet.

"Regenerate *that*, you bastard," I said. With a new surge of strength, I kicked him in the back of the head.

I reached for the bounty card and managed to pull it out. But when I crouched to try to flash it in his face so the certificate could identify the mark, Van Zant sent up a sharp kick that caught me on the wrist. I dropped the card. He snatched it up with his remaining hand and let out a screech of fury. He tore at the card with his teeth as if it were a chunk of jerky. It sparked and then disintegrated to dust, the charm that was supposed to ID and cuff the mark destroyed.

Shit!

Without a functioning card, I had no way to apprehend him. And I was running on fumes. I wouldn't be able to apprehend him without the card, and I didn't have the strength left to kill him. If I stuck around, he'd end me.

Cursing as I went, I hightailed it away from the vamp as fast as my shaky legs could shamble. I had to get away before he managed to attack me again. At least since he knew he was a Guild target, he would go into hiding and stop passing VAMP3 blood around to avoid attention. Temporarily, anyway.

A severed hand certainly wouldn't kill Van Zant, but I honestly wasn't sure whether a vamp could grow back a limb. I didn't really give a shit. I was just happy I'd managed to inflict enough damage to get away alive.

By some miracle, I remembered that there was a little town square nearby and, in the center of it, an ancient oak that served as a doorway.

When I arrived in the MonsterFit vestibule, I'd never been so happy to smell the stale-sweat aroma of the gym. It was dark out in Las Vegas, but the enclosure was still about a gazillion degrees after being bombarded with the western sun. I passed through the doorway and stood outside, Mort in one hand and bloody vampire fingers clutched in the other. It was almost like I was holding hands with Van Zant.

Ewww.

I dropped the hand, and it landed with a faint, fleshy plop, and I went to pull the towel off Vincenzo's seat. I wiped the vamp ick off Mort, sheathed the sword, and then used the towel to pick up Van Zant's hand. I wrapped the worn terrycloth around the severed appendage and stuffed it in one of Vincenzo's side cases.

Then I wheeled my scooter into the vestibule and used the doorway to travel home to Boise.

At the foot of the stairs leading up to my floor, a stray I'd named Emerald sat primly. All I could do was groan and drag myself past her. She let out a plaintive meow at my back, obviously affronted that I hadn't offered her a treat.

"Next time, Emmy," I grumbled. Cats were so demanding.

When I opened my apartment door, it was only eight at night local time, but I felt like I'd been awake for about three days straight.

Lochlyn looked up from where she was curled into one corner of the sofa with her tablet in one slim hand and a cup of coffee in the other. She quickly set the mug down on the side table.

"You look like hell," she said, rising.

"Uhh." I couldn't do more than groan in response. I dropped my keys on the floor, took a couple more steps, and dropped the towel-wrapped hand.

She squinted at me. "You're hurt."

I shook my head, pulled off my scabbard, and let it fall to the ground, too. I knew I was leaving a trail of junk across the floor, but I couldn't work up the energy to care.

"Well, *something* got you," she said. "Bath?"

I collapsed on the sofa and stuffed my face against a pillow.

"That would be fantastic," I said, my words all but unintelligible.

Lochlyn understood, though, because a moment later I heard water pouring into the tub. I wasn't the bubble-bath type, not by a long shot, but one of the only things that helped New Gargoyle magical exhaustion was a soak in a mineral salt bath. My roommate and I had specifically chosen this apartment because it was one of the few in our price range that had a proper bathtub.

"I poured the rest of your bag of salts in," came Lochlyn's voice. "You're gonna need to buy more."

I turned my head so I could peer at her with one eye. "Sure. I'll do that with all the extra cash I have lying around."

The salts I needed weren't your run-of-the-mill Epsom salts that only cost a couple of dollars a pound at the drugstore. Oh, no, of course not. The optimum soak was a mix of salts from ancient sea beds all over the world that had been enhanced with a bit of magic from witches specializing in healing. Each dose was about a hundred bucks. I only used it when I was really hurting.

Lochlyn went back to her corner of the sofa and pulled her feet up. She sank into the pillows and curled up in a decidedly feline posture.

"Didn't catch your mark, I take it?" she asked, blinking wide, almond-shaped eyes that appeared to be the color and texture of marbled jasper.

"No, I didn't," I grumbled. "But I daresay he'll think twice before attacking me again."

I gestured at the bundle I'd dropped on the floor.

Lochlyn looked at it, her elbow-length, straight pink-streaked platinum-blond hair swinging around her face, and then back at me. "Do I even want to know what it is?"

"It's a vampire hand."

She covered her mouth and giggled. That was what I loved about Lochlyn. Most people would be grossed out, but not my roommate. She found a severed vamp hand amusing. Not for the first time, I considered

84

whether she might be slightly insane. I didn't really care if she was. We meshed, and that was an extremely rare thing for me. We'd met when I was chasing down a vampire mark in the Nashville, Tennessee, bar scene. At the time, she was trying to get a record deal. She'd used her stage skills to stall my mark, ultimately helping me catch the young vamp woman. When I learned Lochlyn had recently lost her lease and was living out of her car, on a rare impulse I invited her to crash with me a while in Boise until she'd saved enough to return to Nashville. Not long after, we were looking for a two-bedroom place and became permanent roommates.

"What are you going to do with it?" she asked.

"Dehydrate it and wear it as a necklace."

She snorted. "Please, *please* do that. And then let me borrow it." Unfolding her long, slim legs, she rose. "C'mon, the bath is just about ready."

She stood at my end of the sofa and held out both hands.

I painfully sat up and waved her away. "I'm okay."

"Bullshit." She grasped my hands and leaned back, straining to pull me to my feet.

Lochlyn was taller than me, but whereas she was all lithe ethereal legginess, I was solid muscle and outweighed her by at least twenty-five pounds. After she got me upright, she grabbed her phone and went to get mine out of my scabbard. I trudged into the bathroom, and she waited outside the door until I'd undressed, lowered myself into the tub, and pulled the shower curtain across before coming in and sitting on the toilet. Her hand appeared, holding my phone, which she set on the edge of the bathtub.

I let out a long groan as I sank up to my chin in the lukewarm water. My skin tingled with a prickling, electric sensation in the places where I'd used rock armor in the past couple of days. The feeling was strong enough to make me want to claw at it, but I clenched my fists and waited for it to pass.

Lochlyn snapped her gum, blowing bubbles and popping them loudly. Her phone was blipping and vibrating with messages and notifications. She was as social as I was solitary. It was rare to come home and find her as I had, alone and reading quietly. I suspected she might have been waiting for me, since we hadn't crossed paths in a few days.

"So, what happened with the vamp?" she asked. "Start at the beginning."

I told her about the visit to Morven. I started to recount the wrestle with the wraith, but she cut me off by whipping the curtain aside several inches to stare at me.

"A fricking *wraith*?" she asked, her cat-eyes huge and tense with alarm.

"Yeah. It was actually my second run-in with it. Earlier, it tried to kill me in the netherwhere."

"Petra. This vamp's so-called Fae companion has gone off the rails, commanding a wraith to murder you. You need to tell someone."

"Who? The Faerie cops?" I asked sarcastically. There were no police in Faerie.

"Oh, I don't know, Oberon? The High Court?" She shot back. She gave me a pointed side-eye and then let the curtain fall back into place.

She was right—I probably should have gone to the High Court and submitted my accusation to Oberon—but I really didn't want to deal with it. I'd killed the wraith, after all. It wasn't a problem anymore. Bryna needed to answer for sending it to kill me, sure, but the approach Lochlyn was suggesting would involve getting mixed up in court protocol and inter-kingdom drama. I preferred to deal with the offender directly.

"We're putting a pin in this Bryna business," Lochlyn said. "Now, tell me about how the vamp lost his hand."

I raised an arm out of the water and waved it around dismissively.

"Eh, fangs, sword, blah, blah. I have something more interesting to tell you."

She snorted a laugh. "Okay?"

"I'm going with Maxen into the Duergar kingdom tomorrow to jail break my—" I cut off. My father had said to keep the secret, but I told Lochlyn everything. She was my only confidant in the world, loyal to a fault, and I knew I could trust her.

"Jail break your . . ." she prompted.

"My changeling twin sister from King Periclase's clutches."

There was a clatter that sounded like her phone hitting the tiled floor.

"You . . . your . . . *what*? You waited until NOW TO TELL ME THIS?" she thundered.

I was pretty sure she'd jumped to her feet and was trying to pace around the small bathroom.

"Uh, sorry," I said. "I was getting to it, I swear."

"You have a sister? A twin sister? A *changeling* twin sister?"

"Apparently," I said.

I picked up my phone and flipped to the picture of Nicole that Oliver had given me. I shoved the phone around the side of the curtain so Lochlyn could see. She snatched the device from me.

I let my arm sink back into the salt water. "We're not identical, obviously."

"I'm going," she said.

"Huh?"

"I'm going to the Duergar palace with you. This is huge, Petra. You need moral support."

I smiled. I didn't really need moral support, but I appreciated her sentiment, and I wasn't at all surprised at her insistence. "I don't think Maxen will—"

"Aw, you can persuade him," she cut in. "Flirt a little. Make him think you want to clank rocks or whatever you New Gargs do when you have sex."

I burst out laughing. It kind of hurt because it contracted muscles that weren't really in the mood to do any work yet. But at the same time, it felt good to laugh.

"Clank rocks?" I asked, laughing harder.

"Whatever! That's not the important point, here, Petra. You're going after your *sister*. I want to be there to help if I can, and that's all there is to it. You'll just have to figure it out with Maxen. When do we leave for Faerie?" she asked, all business.

"I'm supposed to meet Maxen at the fortress at noon. I guess we have to do a bunch of nonsense to get ready, because we're not actually slated to arrive at the Duergar palace until evening. Wait, don't you need to work tomorrow night?"

"Uh, no."

"Lochlyn?" I drew out her name in a low voice.

She sighed dramatically. "I may have . . ." She trailed off into mumbles.

"May have what?"

"Gotten fired."

I groaned. "For the love of Oberon, what did you do?"

Remember how I said Lochlyn could scream like the half-banshee she was? Well, there was something about the cat-banshee combo that gave her a voice that was downright legendary. Think Fae skinny-model blond with the pipes of Etta James. Lochlyn's voice had a rich, soulful, throwback quality that no one with her looks deserved. She'd recently scored a regular gig singing on a rotation in a very upscale chain of steakhouses sprinkled around the Pacific Northwest and northern California. She could pull off the geographical spread and cut the cost of travel by using the Faerie doorways to get to each location. Her agent, Rodney, had gone to great pains to set it up for her, and it was the highest paying gig she'd ever had. After only a few months, she'd even started chiseling away at her insane amount of credit card debt.

"I, um, may have missed my set," she said. "Three nights in a row."

"Lochlyn!" I sounded like a disapproving mother scolding her child for getting in trouble at school, but I couldn't help it. I'd hoped she'd finally started to leave some of her flighty ways behind. She had an amazing talent that deserved recognition.

"I know," she said, sounding genuinely miserable.

"What the hell were you doing when you should have been at work?"

The water was starting to cool, so I turned the faucet on to heat it up a little. The salts and magic were working. My skin no longer hurt, and the pounding in my head had dulled to a low throb. I'd still be weak for a while, but the minerals would help me be able to generate rock armor without too much pain in hours rather than days.

"I met this guy, this billionaire auto industry guy who'd bought up a bunch of super high-end nightclubs around the world. One thing led to another, and he invited me and like twenty other people to go with him to Ibiza. Then we decided to go to Italy to see this DJ he knows," she said nonchalantly, as if this sort of thing happened to most people on the regular. "I just, I don't know, lost track of time."

Here was one area where Lochlyn and I were glaringly different. She loved to party. It wasn't the partying that primarily attracted her, but the music. Live music was like a drug to her. As soon as she said "Ibiza," which was known for its insanely awesome club scene, I knew there'd been no hope.

"Was it worth it?" I asked.

"When I woke up this morning, I would have said yes. Now I'm not totally sure. That was a really, really good gig I lost."

"Any way Rodney can beg for another chance?"

"Maybe," she said. "But right now, he's still pissed. Pretty sure he's not in the mood to do me any favors."

I flipped the switch on the bathtub's drain, and water began glugging down.

"Well, at least now you've got something to do tomorrow," I said.

"Yay, court!" She made a few little claps. "And, thunder of Oberon, Petra. You have a twin sister."

"Yeah." I shook my head, still not quite believing it.

"What's going through your mind?" she asked carefully. She knew better than to ask me directly about my feelings.

I let out a slow breath, stalling a little. "I don't know her, so I can't say I feel any connection to her at this point. But I think I feel . . . I don't know, sorry for her?"

"Why's that?"

"She must be so confused and alone right now," I said. I hesitated. "But I pity her for having grown up in a mundane world thinking she was just an ordinary human. Even though I got my ass out of Faerie as fast as I could after graduation, I can't imagine a different upbringing than I had. Being raised by Oliver, in the fortress, in Faerie . . . I wouldn't have given that up for anything."

"I get that," she said softly. "I feel the same way about my child-hood."

My father's warning about the secret pinged in my mind. "Lochlyn, I know I can trust you, and I hate to ask, but no one can know that Nicole is my sister."

Lochlyn might have been flighty when it came to employment and her social life, but she was as loyal as they came. Still, I felt the need to seal her secrecy.

"An oath, of course," she said. "I promise to you, Petra Maguire, that I will never reveal to anyone that Nicole the changeling is your sister unless you release me from this binding oath."

A tingle of magic formed in the air like a fine mist, settling over us and marking the promise, and then dissipated.

I stood up in the tub and rolled my shoulders, marveling at how the movement didn't hurt my muscles or pull at tender skin. I reached a hand around the curtain to pull my towel off the bar and inhaled deeply. The minerals and magic had given me a new lease on life, and I had a feeling I was going to need it to get Nicole out of the Duergar palace.

Chapter 10

THE NEXT MORNING, I had to stop by the Guild headquarters in Boise to pick up a duplicate bounty card, after Van Zant had destroyed the original.

My supervisor, Gus, used to be a merc but for the past ten years had ridden a desk at the Guild. I'd seen pictures of him when he was still an active bounty hunter and guessed he'd put on about sixty pounds since he left the field for his current position. I couldn't imagine transitioning to administration, but he'd seemed to settle into it. He wasn't so bad, as long as I made my deadlines.

I sat in his office while we waited for a magi-technician—a human with decent magical abilities—to imbue the card with the spell that would be able to ID my mark.

Gus waved a chewed-up ballpoint pen admonishingly. "You're really pushing the timeline on this assignment, Petra. The Guild has already given you one extension on this one. You're not going to get another. If you don't bring the vamp in by the deadline, you'll be—"

"Suspended from Guild work for at least a month," I cut in. "I know, I know."

He stuck the pen in his mouth and began gnawing on it as he straightened the piles of folders on his desk.

"I just don't know what's gotten into you with this one," he said with a sad shake of his head. "Usually you're out there kicking ass.

Extensions make us all look bad."

I sighed in the back of my throat, trying not to show my irritation. I hated it when Gus got patronizing.

"This one's slippery," I said.

The tech showed up with the duplicate card, saving me from any more supervisory disapproval. I stuffed it in my pocket and got the hell out of the Guild building.

I made my way to the New Gargoyle fortress the next morning without Lochlyn. Fae not sworn to the Stone Order weren't allowed in the fortress without Marisol's permission, and that usually meant it had to be for something important. But no one had to worry about Lochlyn being properly prepared for court. Despite living outside of Faerie since she was seventeen, she was well-versed in all the proper customs. Her mother was a courtesan in the Cait Sidhe palace, and Lochlyn had spent her youth deep in court life with the other children of courtesans.

I arrived at the fortress with a lot of time to spare, and it was by design. I wanted to sit in the mineral sauna, a treatment room where magic and the energy of stone permeated the air like thick steam. A half hour in there—the maximum anyone was allowed—should get me most of the way healed. The rest would just take time.

I went directly to the sauna, but as luck would have it, the door was locked, indicating it was occupied. At least no one else was waiting to get in. I sat down on the wooden bench to wait. The sauna was located within the gym and training area of the fortress, and I could hear the clangs of swords in the yard and the clunks of weights in the lifting room. I eased my head back against the wall, crossed my arms, and closed my eyes, lulled by the sounds. I wasn't tired, exactly. I'd slept deeply the night before. But a weariness from my payment to Morven, cold iron burns, and use of my rock armor still lingered.

"Looking for me, Petra?" asked a smooth voice right next to me.

I jumped guiltily, not realizing I'd dozed off a little. Maxen stood in front of me, shirtless and in long gym shorts, glistening with the dewy condensation from the mineral sauna. The smell of mountain streams and wet sandstone hung around him.

I looked him up and down, but I wasn't checking him out. "What's wrong?" I asked, looking for evidence of a recent injury.

New Gargs didn't use up their precious mineral sessions for no reason. And it wasn't just the limited allotment given to each of us. It was even more a matter of pride. We were fighters, and we were tough as granite. We normally didn't use such treatment unless there was true need.

"Nothing," he said. He plucked his shirt from the hook next to the door and flashed me a smile. He pulled the t-shirt down over his head. "Good as new."

I arched a brow at him. "Care to prove it after I'm done in there?" I tipped my head at the mineral sauna's door.

He licked his lips. "Absolutely. See you in the yard."

He walked backward a couple of steps and then flipped me a little wave.

"Hey, Maxen?" I called, suddenly remembering I had a plus-one for the trip to the Duergar court. He stopped and came partway back. "My roommate, Lochlyn, wants to come with us today. She, uh, really likes court."

It was a pretty lame reason, but I couldn't lie outright about why she wanted to come and I wasn't supposed to tell Maxen that the changeling was actually my sister and Lochlyn wanted to be there for moral support.

He narrowed his eyes for a minute, and I couldn't help thinking of Lochlyn's command to flirt with him. *Make him think you want to clank rocks.* I nearly snorted a laugh but managed to control it and turn it into a broad smile. I tilted my head, channeling Penelope, my sex kitten alter-ego.

Maxen shrugged a shoulder. "Why not?" He turned to go but then paused. "Only if you beat me in the yard."

I let out a laugh that echoed down the hallway. Since we were kids in training, I'd defeated him nine times out of ten, at least.

I pushed open the door of the mineral sauna. The small space wasn't much bigger than a closet, with just a wooden bench by way of décor. The walls were made of slabs of shimmering opalescent stone from deep in the earth of the Old World. It was said the stone combined all the minerals and precious stones that existed on both sides of the hedge. Fae called it Brigitstone after Brigit, the Celtic Saint of healing and blacksmithing.

I took off my scabbard and set it against the wall, settled on the bench, inhaled deeply, and let my body drink in the magical nourishment.

When I emerged, my skin slicked from the mist of magic and minerals, I felt like a god reborn. I wasn't fully healed yet, but the moments after time in the mineral sauna were always filled with a surge of energy and vitality. It was like a triple espresso after the best night's sleep you've ever had.

I put on my scabbard and rolled my neck as I made my way to the gym, letting the mist of the mineral room dry on my skin. Poor Maxen. I was going to kick his ass all over the training yard.

When I got outside, I squinted and shaded my eyes against the bright sunshine, automatically looking toward the flash of metal and clangs of swords. Maxen was sparring with Shane again, who was the current general weapons teacher for the youngest class of New Gargoyles. Maxen's eyes flicked to me, but he somehow kept his focus on the fight at the same time. He slashed at Shane with a complicated sequence of strokes, but the teacher was faster—Shane fought back and slipped his blade under Maxen's elbow, where it slid off the rock armor protecting Maxen's ribs.

Shane spoke a few words to Maxen, the two men shook hands, and the teacher departed.

"Sure you want to do this?" I called to Maxen. With a languorous stretch of my arm, I reached for Mort. "Maybe you need to rest first?"

"Nope," he said, working his blade in a figure-eight warm-up pattern. "Let's go, Maguire."

We faced off, and when our eyes met, I flashed a grin. But I waited, wanting Maxen to make the first move. He feinted a lunge and slashed upward. I sidestepped and parried. It all happened in barely a blink.

"Not even going to use your armor?" Maxen asked as we circled each other.

"Nah," I said. "So far I see no need for it."

He laughed good-naturedly. I attacked with an overhand swing, and Maxen barely blocked it. I came in for a jab at his midsection and hit his armor. He was stronger than me, but I was faster, and my sword was a bit lighter and shorter than his. Size wasn't everything.

I tsked. "You still keep your elbow too high. How many times did Jaquard give you that correction when you were a kid?"

"About a million."

We traded blows, our swords clanking in a rhythm that almost sounded deliberate, for several minutes. I got completely absorbed in the enjoyment of the dance.

Maxen came in for a complex attack, trying to use his size and strength to overpower me, and managing to drive me back several steps.

I was running out of room. I dropped to one knee in an attempt to make him think he'd gained the upper hand. When he telegraphed a too-large overhead slash downward, I spun on my knees, darted under his arm, and sprang up three feet away from where I'd been. The end of Maxen's heavy sword jammed into the grass, and I flicked Mort out and tapped the side of his neck.

"Mine!" I shouted. It was our tradition—whoever won got to crow about it. Jaquard always told us it was a crass and immature habit. That was half the reason Maxen and I had kept doing it.

I lowered Mort and backed away.

"Again?" I asked.

We were both breathing hard. Sweat beaded on Maxen's forehead and darkened his hairline.

"I'd like to, but it's time to get ready for court," he said, sheathing his sword. He glanced off to the side of the training field. I followed his gaze to where a blue-vested page was waiting with his hands folded and a tablet tucked under his arm.

I groaned and let my head drop back.

He arched a brow at me. "You're the one who wanted to go."

"I know. I just don't want to go through the ridiculousness of all the pomp. It's just so . . . *archaic*." I wrinkled my nose.

"You should have more respect for Fae traditions," he said in a lecturing tone.

"You sound like your mother," I shot back.

Side by side, we headed inside.

"Why did you need the mineral sauna?" I asked.

"I just want to be at full strength for the trip," Maxen said absently. "After your shower, there will be a page waiting to take you to your dressing room. They'll have something frilly and lovely waiting for you, I'm sure."

I shot him a sour look over my shoulder as I pushed the door to the women's locker room. But his comment about being at full strength snagged in my mind. Things with the Duergar were contentious. I wondered if Maxen truly feared that the situation could turn violent.

After showering and dressing, I stood in front of the mirror and tried to finger-comb my hair into some semblance of neatness but soon gave up. A stylist would most likely be in my dressing room to work out the knots and make sure I looked proper and presentable.

"Lady Maguire?"

I turned to see who the hell thought I was a lady. It was my page, a girl of about seventeen.

"Please, call me Petra," I said.

She smiled politely, but I saw a brief flash of amusement in her fluorite-lavender eyes. She'd probably seen me fruitlessly fiddling with my hair.

"If you're ready, I'll take you to your dressing room now," she said.

I strapped on my scabbard and held out my arm, indicating she should lead the way out of the locker room.

"How long have you been a page?" I asked her once we were out in the corridor and walking side by side.

"Just six months," she said. She slid a look at me. "When I turn eighteen, I want to leave the fortress and live on the other side of the hedge. Get a job as a mercenary."

I lifted my brows. "Really? What a coincidence you got assigned to me." I gave her a wry look.

She shrugged a shoulder in a very teenage gesture. "Not the only reason, but yeah."

"I bet you're a handful for your father," I said. "Let me guess. You and he butt heads about a dozen times a day."

She let out a tinkling laugh. "How did you know?"

"Personal experience." Poor Oliver. "Are you a good fighter?"

"Top three in my class, combat all forms, combined," she replied automatically but with pride.

I gave her a nod. "Impressive."

She smiled with delight at the compliment, revealing a dimple. Her eyes flicked to Mort on my back.

"Got a sword?" I asked.

She shook her head, her shoulder-length brown hair swinging a little. "Father wouldn't buy me one. He thinks if I don't have a weapon I won't try to go into a dangerous line of work. That's why I'm working as a page. I want my own blade by the time I turn eighteen."

"Ah, a girl after my own heart," I said approvingly. "What's your name, anyway?"

"Emmaline."

"Pretty," I said.

She groaned. "I know. I hate it. I wish my parents had named me something more bad ass." She glanced at me quickly. Cursing on the job—even mild swearing—was against the page's code of conduct.

I snorted. "Don't worry, I won't tattle on you."

She steered me through the corridors in a way that was almost like leading me, but without walking ahead. Despite her little slip, I could tell she was good at her job.

"When you get out of the academy, look me up," I said. "I'll give you an intro at the Guild."

Her mouth dropped open, and her pale purple-gray eyes widened. For a moment, she dropped both her professional façade and her teenage pretense of nonchalance.

"Really?" She blinked at me. "You'd do that?"

I nodded. "Sure, I'd be glad to."

"I—oh my gosh!"

Rather than respond, I brushed off her gratitude, not wanting to make a big deal of it. "Please tell me you're coming to the Duergar palace," I said. "I'm not built for courtly nonsense, and I'm going to need all the help I can get. Plus, it would be nice to know there's another fighter in the group."

She nodded eagerly. "Oh, yes. Lord Lothlorien assigned me to you for the duration of the trip."

I snorted a laugh. "Lord Lothlorien," I mumbled to myself.

"Yes, Maxen?" Her brow creased in confusion. "I thought the two of you were long-time friends."

"Yeah, we go way back," I confirmed. "I just have a hard time thinking of him as 'Lord Lothlorien.' It sounds funny. Makes him seem so high and mighty."

"Oh," she said, carefully neutral and clearly not sure what the proper response was.

I cleared my throat. I shouldn't have spoken so casually about Maxen, regardless of my personal history and friendship with him. He was the equivalent of a Fae prince. He *would* be prince if Marisol got her wish and succeeded in forming a Stone Court. Marisol and Maxen were the closest things New Gargoyles had to royalty. And in any case, I needed to shift into a more reserved mindset and conduct. I couldn't get around the ridiculousness of formal courtly etiquette, but it served a person well to stay tight-lipped while at court. Gossip spread faster than balefire, and one wrong word or sidelong look could set off a cascade of whispers and backlash. I didn't have the patience or personality to succeed at courtly games, so I'd just have to keep my trap shut to get through it.

"Hey, Emmaline," I said. "Could you do me a favor? If I start running at the mouth when we're in the Duergar palace, clear your throat. That'll be the signal that I need to zip it."

She squashed a look of amusement before it could fully develop. "I'm sure that won't be necessary, Lady—uh, Petra."

"Don't bet on that."

She pointed to a door with a plaque holder next to it. "Here we are," she said, artfully avoiding having to respond.

The temporary plaque was printed with my name. She pushed the door open and gestured at me to go in first.

If Emmaline hadn't been standing directly behind me and blocking the door, I might have turned around and left.

The room was a nightmare of pretty, girlie things. Racks of dresses, a styling station with a bazillion curling irons, makeup, and other tools of torture. And mirrors *everywhere.*

A very polished, made-up woman floated across the room at me, gracefully extending her hand.

"Lady Maguire, I'm so pleased to be working with you today," she said in a rich, cultured voice. "I'm Vera, your head stylist."

For a split second, I just stared stupidly. I'd never seen a New Gargoyle woman who seemed so thoroughly frilly, curvy, and feminine. But then I noticed her crazy-long eyelashes and realized she wasn't full-blood. Probably at least a quarter Sylph.

I stuck my hand out and shook hers. "Pleased to meet you. And good luck with this." I waved my other hand down my body.

She smiled at me out of the corners of her eyes. "Challenge accepted," she said, already reaching for my scabbard. I stepped back and removed it before she could put her hands on it.

"I'll be waiting outside," Emmaline said, and backed out the door. I shot her a look of desperation, but she just smiled demurely as she closed the door.

Two more women appeared from an adjoining room, and then hands were everywhere, undressing me, arranging me, pushing clothes at me.

"Help me, Oberon," I whimpered.

The ladies just laughed.

Chapter 11

THE LAST TIME I'd been to court, I was a teenager and no one had made a fuss beyond forcing me to wear a dress.

"Really, there's no need to go to such effort," I said, my words muffled as one of the ladies pulled a horrible, crinkly, pale orange dress over my head. "I'm just tagging along. I'm not one of the important guests. No one is even going to care I'm there."

"Every New Gargoyle who visits a foreign court is a reflection on her people," Vera said. "As such, it's our duty to ensure you make the proper impression."

I snorted. They could dress me up like a doll, but making a proper impression? There wasn't a lacy frock in the world that would guarantee that.

After much yanking and manipulation, they pulled the dress down into place. It was sleeveless, and the arm openings were so tight they bit into my skin.

"She's very muscular. Look at her arms," one of the assistants remarked, speaking about me as if I weren't standing right there. A slight crease of worry formed across her forehead. "Lord Lothlorien failed to mention it."

I scowled. I had no shame about my body, but it irritated me that Maxen hadn't told them I was fit.

Vera had stepped back and was squinting at me, one arm wrapped around her narrow waist and the other index finger pressed to her lips.

"The color is all wrong, anyway," she said crisply. "Take it off. We need to try a cooler palette."

"Thank Oberon," I grumbled.

Off came the orange sherbet dress, and I let out a sigh of relief. Not even my sexy alter-ego, Penelope, would want to wear that mess. Penelope was more ripped micro-minis and off-shoulder tops, not ice-cream-colored taffeta.

One of the assistants rifled through a rack of gowns and pulled out an aquamarine one. It was simple, with a wraparound design that created a V neckline. The hem was higher in the front and cascaded to floor-length in the back. It completely lacked any frilly nonsense.

They worked me into it, and when I faced the mirror, I found the color perfectly complemented my sand-toned skin and tawny eyes.

All the stylists were nodding.

"There's a similar one in brown," one of the assistants said. "I'll pull that one, too, and also pack some riding pants and blouses."

In court, women were expected to wear dresses at all times, with the one exception of riding pants. The riding pants were intended, of course, for horseback activities. Regardless of the intent of the rule, I planned to take a very liberal interpretation of the pants allowance and make good use of the loophole.

Off came the dress and over my underwear went a bathrobe. Under the direction of the ladies, I sat down in the chair at the styling station while a new trio came in—a man and two women this time—and set to work filing my fingernails, doing various manipulations on my hair, smearing things on my skin, and brushing makeup over my face. After a while, I just closed my eyes and tried to send my mind to a more pleasant place.

Thoughts of my sister, Nicole, crept in. I couldn't help thinking of my mother, too, with two newborn girls and terrified that they would be killed to fulfill a prophecy. Oliver had told me she'd been unstable long before I was born, but had there been any merit to her fear? Apparently, there could be, if Oliver didn't want Marisol to know about Nicole.

Another large question loomed in my mind: Why had the Duergar King Periclase taken Nicole?

I had no idea why Nicole was valuable to him. At twenty-seven, she was very old for a changeling to be brought back to the Faerie side of the hedge. Usually it happened well before the seventeenth birthday, sometimes quite young, because a person was still malleable in the right ways at that age. Much older than that, and it was too hard on the mind to try to integrate into Faerie, not to mention almost impossible to effectively learn to use and control magic. And a Fae without magic would never be fully accepted on this side of the hedge.

I honestly couldn't even imagine what was going through Nicole's mind. Humans were aware of the Fae, but knowing about something was very different than being yanked from your life and into a world you'd never seen and didn't know how to navigate. And who knew what Periclase's people were filling her head with. At their worst, the Unseelie were ruthless manipulators with grudges and jealousies that ran deep and sometimes spanned generations. And King Periclase . . . he was on an altogether different level. He actually cared less for the usual Unseelie manipulations than he did for calculated power plays. I'd met him once when I was a child, and the memory was enough to send a little shiver down my spine, even twenty years later.

"Yes, I believe she's ready," the male stylist said. I opened my eyes as he reached out to touch my hair, arranging it over my shoulder.

After what had seemed like hours of primpage, the team of stylists stepped back to scrutinize me. As they shifted, making small adjustments, I caught a look at myself in the mirror. I let out a surprised laugh, I couldn't help it. Leaning forward, I turned my face from side to side.

They'd managed to curl my long, stubbornly straight hair into gentle waves that somehow looked polished and natural at the same time. A simple off-center part and a silver clip held back my long bangs, which were swept to the side. My makeup was expertly done to emphasize my eyes, cheekbones, and lips, but thankfully in neutral shades. They'd stuck a bit of false lash on the outer upper corners of my lids. It remained to be seen if I could manage to get through the evening without accidentally pulling them off.

I didn't like getting all made up, and within the hour I'd probably be itching to wash my face and throw my hair into a ponytail, but I could appreciate anyone who excelled at their chosen craft, regardless of what that craft was.

"Wow," I said appreciatively. "You people are magicians."

The stylists left, and the wardrobe ladies returned to get me into my blue dress, some matching shoes with heels that were only about two inches, thank Oberon, and some opal jewelry that complemented the dress.

When one of the assistants came at me with a mister bottle of perfume, I held up a hand to stop her.

"Sorry, I have to draw the line there," I said. "I can't stand the smell of that stuff."

She inclined her head, giving in. "I'll add it to your trunk in case you change your mind later."

As if he'd been waiting for a signal, a young page came in from a side doorway with a large piece of luggage, which he set down near the main door. When the stylist tipped back the lid of the trunk to add the perfume bottle to the toiletry tray that sat on top, I caught a glimpse of the clothing carefully folded within it.

"At least one pair of riding pants in there?" I asked, craning my neck.

"Khaki and navy," Vera confirmed.

"Boots?"

Vera nodded. "Riding boots to match."

As I took a few steps to test out the high heels, I tried to console myself with the prospect of being able to change clothes and shoes later.

I got the sense the ladies were waiting for me to dismiss them.

"Your services were performed with skill," I said. I winked at Vera. "I'm sure my impression in court will be a worthy one."

I didn't even want to think about how much the services that had just been performed and the items packed in the trunk had cost, but as part of Maxen's royal contingent, I wouldn't have to foot the bill.

The ladies filed out through one of the doorways into one of the side rooms, and the page opened the door that led into the hallway.

"My lady." He swept out one arm, indicating I should go ahead, and he bent to lift the trunk.

I retrieved Mort and put the scabbard on over my dress, not caring at all how it looked with my outfit.

Emmaline was waiting for me. She'd changed into a simple silver-gray gown, but still wore her navy page's vest over it, and her auburn hair was pulled back into a businesslike bun at the nape of her neck. Her eyes popped, and her mouth fell open when she saw me.

"You look incredible!" she said. "Like royalty."

"Very kind of you to say so." I gave her a wry side-eye with one brow raised. "Okay, what torture awaits next?"

"We join the rest of the traveling party in one of the reception halls for cocktails and hors d'oeuvres."

"A party before the dinner that will be followed by another party," I said under my breath, followed by a tortured sigh and a look skyward.

She gave a small smile. "I'll take you to the hall now."

She led me to one of the upper floors of the fortress, to a large room I'd been to before. But last time, it was to be honored along with my class for our graduation from advanced weapons training. My clothes had been a hell of a lot more sensible for that event.

The walls of the reception hall were decorated with enormous geode slices that served as natural artwork. There were granite pillars interrupting the marble floor at evenly-spaced intervals. Swoops of velvet softened the right angles where the walls met the ceiling—decorative touches that were cleverly disguised echo dampeners.

There were already about two dozen guests gathered, and at least that many servers and attendants like Emmaline. Pages in black serving attire and white aprons circulated with trays of some pinkish bubbly cocktail in tall glasses. My stomach grumbled loudly, and I looked past the drink servers for any with food platters.

"I'll bring you a small plate," Emmaline said. She lifted her chin, her eyes cast across the room. "It looks like you're being summoned."

I followed her gaze to find Marisol with her arm lifted toward me. She flicked her fingers, beckoning me in a way that set my teeth on edge. There was nothing specifically condescending in her gesture—it was inviting, if anything—but standing around at a formal reception making polite talk with the New Gargoyle matriarch was not my idea of a good time. I just wanted to get to the Duergar palace and on with my mission.

Fat chance of that. This was only the beginning of the night's painful formalities. My best hope was to slip away after dinner. It should be easy to sneak out once everyone had been drinking a while and the dancing started.

But at the moment, duty was literally calling to me, so I strode across the marble floor to join Marisol. As I approached, people shifted, revealing Maxen standing in the small crowd surrounding his mother. In a split-second, he took me in from head to foot. One corner of his mouth crooked up almost imperceptibly, and he gave me a subtle nod. I knew he was trying to play the stoic New Gargoyle prince. But I also knew him well enough to read his small changes in expression, and he was quite pleased by what he saw. I channeled Penelope and shot him a sultry little smile while Marisol's attention was elsewhere. The quirk of his lips bloomed into a full grin, and he gave a tiny shake of his head. He knew I was just playing with him.

"Lady Lothlorien," I said with a deferential inclination of my head as I approached Marisol and dredged up what I could remember of formal etiquette. "Lord Lothlorien. Ladies, gentlemen."

I couldn't look directly at Maxen, or I would have busted up laughing. I knew it was juvenile of me, but calling him "Lord" gave me a case of the giggles.

I recognized a few of the New Gargoyle political figures milling around Marisol and Maxen, if not by name at least by face. Seeming to sense that Marisol wanted to speak to me without an audience, they all drifted away except Maxen.

"I wanted to express my appreciation for your willingness to accompany the attaché to the Duergar palace," Marisol said. "I know it's not your usual scene. But we need our changeling to come home."

Ah, Marisol and her dependable bluntness. She wore it easily, like an invisible crown she'd been born to. The leader of the New Gargoyles was the very definition of regal, standing rod-straight in a crystal-white dress that somehow made her sapphire eyes even more blue.

Maxen shifted his weight next to her, outside her field of vision. I knew he was confused about why Marisol hadn't told him about Nicole earlier and probably wondered why I was being sent after the changeling. I was barely a member of the Stone Order, and my involvement had to seem strange.

"I can't say I'm disappointed you'll be by Maxen's side," Marisol said. "He's extremely capable, of course, but backup never hurts."

I pulled back slightly in surprise before I could control my reaction. Marisol had to be aware of her son's long-standing interest in me, and we all knew she had absolutely no intention of letting him make such an un-strategic match. That she'd admit she was glad I was traipsing off to court with Maxen was a bit of a shock. She must have been more worried about King Periclase than she let on.

Emmaline appeared at my side, offering me a little plate piled with finger foods, which saved me from having to come up with a suitable reply to Marisol and gave the New Gargoyle ruler an easy out. She excused herself to speak to some new arrivals.

I glanced at Maxen before stuffing two cubes of cheese and an olive in my mouth. I was amped up, antsy from standing around and thinking of the mission ahead, and with no means to expend my energy, I just wanted to eat. He was drilling me with his blue eyes.

"I want to know why you're really going," he said, tipping his head down to look at me from under his brows. "You of all possible people."

I shrugged. "Did you ask Marisol?"

His blue eyes remained intent on me. "Must be something dire if you're willing to put on a dress and go to court," he said, ignoring my question.

I gave a short laugh.

"I'm glad you'll be there."

"You don't really think you'll need backup, like Marisol said?"

"The thought crossed my mind. It's often occurred to me to ask you to join in some of our missions. But I never would have expected you to say yes to an invitation," he said.

I looked away again. I knew what he was implying—that I wasn't likely to be a dutiful New Gargoyle. He didn't expect he could depend on me for things such as backup in a foreign kingdom. I had to admit, it stung a little. It wasn't that I didn't care about him or the Stone Order—I did. But my work kept me mostly outside of Faerie and almost completely isolated from the matters of the Order. I couldn't do both—be fully active in the Order's affairs and hunt down vamps.

"I guess you never know what the answer will be if you never ask," I said mildly, my gaze still fixed across the room. I was trying not to sound defensive, but he probably saw through it.

"On that, you are correct," he said, his voice soft.

I shifted my weight and shoved a few grapes in my mouth. I didn't like what was hanging in the air between us—some vague sense of disappointment on his part but confusingly mixed with what almost seemed like a hint of apology.

I swallowed and wiped my lips with the little napkin Emmaline had tucked into my hand when she'd brought the plate.

"Well, I somehow ended up with Marisol's approval," I said with a light tone. "Temporary, I'm sure, but still, this is an historic occasion."

I swiped a glass from a passing server, clinked it against Maxen's, and took a long drink of the pink liquid. I recognized fizzy, flowery rose amrita. He chuckled and sipped, too, allowing the tension to dissipate.

The rest of the reception passed relatively painlessly, despite the fact that I only allowed myself the single glass of bubbly. Soon Marisol and the others who weren't going to the Duergar palace departed, and Emmaline was coming at me holding a jacket that was really more of a cape.

"Seriously?" I said as she settled the garment around my shoulders.

"It's tradition and protocol to cover the shoulders when you arrive in a foreign court," was all she replied.

The envoy, including Maxen, began moving out of the reception hall. Emmaline walked beside me with her ever-present tablet.

"So how do we travel there?" I asked. "Horse-drawn carriage?"

She snorted a laugh at my sarcasm. "You haven't been part of many diplomatic parties, have you?"

"That obvious, huh?"

"We'll be traveling by doorway," she said. "In fact, the porters have already gone through with all of the luggage."

She told me the sigils to trace to go to the destination doorway, which she said was near a road leading to the Duergar palace. I'd been in the Duergar kingdom before, of course—Morven's pub was located there—but never to the palace.

A little sliver of ice crept up my spine as I remembered the wraith trying to kill me in the netherwhere. I shook it off. That wraith was dust. It still irked me that my mark was at large, but I'd told Oliver I'd rescue Nicole, and of course I had to. Even if she weren't my sister, I couldn't leave a New Gargoyle changeling in Duergar hands—in spite of what Maxen believed about my lack of duty to my people.

Emmaline and I followed the others through the corridors of the fortress and out into a small, circular courtyard that was ringed with what appeared to be a solid wall. But in the sculpture of the wall were several arches, designs that would catch any Fae eye. Doorways.

The man who seemed to be the head attendant, the one who was personal servant to Maxen, was leading the party. He took us to one of the arches that looked the same as the rest, until the page began drawing sigils in the air. The area under the arch shimmered, as if inviting us through.

I waited my turn while others entered the doorway, and then I stepped into the void of the netherwhere.

It was time to find my twin.

Chapter 12

COMING OUT OF the netherwhere, the first thing to greet me was the bright, upbeat music of the Duergar royal buglers. The second was Lochlyn.

Because she wasn't New Garg, she'd had to take a different doorway and meet us here rather than travel with the official party from the fortress. Dressed in a blue gown so pale it was nearly white, the bodice and hem embellished with crystals, she looked like a fairy-tale princess. She skipped up to me, clapping her hands under her chin.

"You look like royalty," she said with a pleased little giggle.

"That's what my assistant said," I groused. "Where did you get that dress?"

"Oh, this old thing? One of my gig dresses." She swished the skirts and then twirled, letting them flare gently.

"I'm glad you're here," I said, letting my mood warm a little under the influence of Lochlyn's excitement.

I drew a slow breath and looked around, taking in the pomp and the setting. We stood in a clearing of a wooded area and overhead the branches of very old trees had interwoven to form a natural canopy. Wildflowers edged the clearing, and birds chirped and swooped overhead, competing with the trumpet flourishes. A hard-packed dirt road bordered by ancient hawthorn trees led away from our gathering place toward the Duergar palace, just visible in the distance. Performers dressed in leotards and body paint of Duergar colors—pine green and pale orange—danced around the spot where the clearing turned into the road, ready to lead the party. Even my crusty, court-hating heart recognized that the scene was quite beautiful.

King Periclase himself stood to one side with his hands clasped in front of him, flanked by six hulking guards dressed in full body armor and outfitted with a sword and two daggers each. On one side of the king stood a man I recognized as his brother—Darion, a formidable Duergar soldier. On Periclase's other side was his wife, Queen Courtney, casting her chalcedony-blue eyes aloofly over the heads of the crowd.

I tilted my gaze upward and spotted a few crossbowmen and women among the trees surrounding the clearing, and if that many were visible, I'd have bet there were at least twofold more out of sight.

In contrast to the festive atmosphere, the Duergar king's face was hard enough to rival my stoic father's. Periclase was an oddity of the Cataclysm. He'd spontaneously become part-New Gargoyle, but something had gone wrong with the transformation. Periclase's change had left him with a face that was stone across the temple next to his left eye, over the cheekbone, and along the jawline on that side. He also had one hand that was curled into an immobile stone fist. It was as if stone armor had permanently taken over those areas of his face and body. In a strange twist of the Cataclysm, despite the areas of stone skin he couldn't summon full rock armor. But even if he'd been able to prove sufficient New Garg blood, he'd have had no real reason to join up with Marisol. The Duergar kingdom was one of the larger Unseelie realms, and he'd been in line to rule it since the day he was born.

I'd heard that Periclase was a formidable-looking figure even before his transformation. With his half-stone face and stone fist, he was downright fearsome.

Maxen was striding across the clearing toward the Duergar king with half a dozen New Garg politicos following him. They stopped and bowed before the king, and Periclase gave them a slight nod of acknowledgement. Maxen straightened and spoke a few words to Periclase, who responded briefly. I wasn't near enough to hear any of it.

Maxen took a position opposite Periclase, so he and the Duergar king each stood to one side of the road. The rest of the New Garg party formed a loose line to pay their respects to Periclase and Courtney. Lochlyn and I joined the queue with Emmaline behind us. When it was our turn, Lochlyn and I stood side by side before the King and Queen.

"Petra Maguire," I said.

"Lochlyn Tisdale," my roommate said.

In unison, Lochlyn and I curtsied deeply, with Emmaline doing the same a few feet back. Protocol dictated that attendants did not announce their names.

I lifted my head and found Periclase's eyes boring into mine. The Duergar king's jaw flexed, though the bunching of muscles was only visible on the fleshy side of his face. His eyes flicked to Mort's handle, visible over my right shoulder.

"Oliver's daughter," he said, his voice almost unnaturally deep.

I blinked, automatically guarded at the recognition. "Yes, Your Majesty."

He dipped his chin almost imperceptibly. The calculating look in his hard eyes made my stomach tighten.

Not knowing what else to say and wanting to avoid drawing any further attention from Periclase, I gave another, smaller curtsy, and then scooted away with Lochlyn and Emmaline.

When I glanced back, the next diplomats in line were bowing, but Periclase's eyes were still on me.

"He's kind of hot in an evil overlord way," Lochlyn said in my ear, drawing my attention away from the Duergar king. "I mean, that stone. It's badass."

I shot her a warning look. "He's dangerous, Lochlyn. Don't let his stoicism fool you."

"Oh, I don't doubt it," she said sincerely. "But he only had eyes for you."

I snorted, finally cracking a smile. "Trust me, he's not interested in that way."

"Don't be so sure. He doesn't come off as passionate, but I've heard he *really* makes the rounds," Lochlyn said, but she jabbed me in the ribs with her elbow, and I knew she was mostly teasing.

"I'm glad you're here," I said. "But we're in Unseelie territory. Please be careful."

She linked her arm with mine in a gesture that I probably wouldn't indulge from anyone else in the world.

"I will," she said.

We walked slowly to the loose queue of people gathering at the head of the road that led deeper into the Duergar realm. While we were waiting, Emmaline briefed me on what would come next. After the procession to the palace, we'd be shown to our rooms for a brief freshen-up period before we'd be expected at the welcome reception. The reception would lead directly into a four-course dinner, which as I'd expected would be followed by dessert, drinking, music, and dancing.

This was all an opportunity for the Duergar to show off their riches and power under the guise of merry social events. The diplomatic discussions would formally begin in the morning, and I had no doubt that those would involve very little merriment. But that was Maxen's department. Marisol had sent him and the others to try to talk Periclase into dropping his bid for absorbing the Stone Order into his kingdom.

I looked around, taking in the faces of the Duergar guards—what little of their faces I could see behind the armored masks—the dancers, and the other attendants. Any of the Duergar surrounding us could be spies. Knowing the Unseelie, maybe all of them were. I sobered as I considered my mission and just how difficult it was going to be to slip through the Duergar palace to search for Nicole. There would be even more people around later that evening, when I planned to break away from the party.

It might be necessary to reconsider my tactics. I wasn't among fighters and blunt talkers like I was used to with my own people, or with the Guild mercs. Here, everyone was part of some scheme or intrigue, dealing in information and trading secrets.

"Spent much time in Unseelie courts?" Emmaline asked.

"No," I said. "Is it that obvious?"

She gave a tiny shrug. "I'd guessed," she said.

"How about you?"

"Yes, actually, that's one of the reasons I was granted this assignment. From the age of thirteen, my mother made me spend a month every summer vacation at court, both Seelie and Unseelie. I had to bust butt to be ready for training each fall after missing out on summer sessions." She rolled her lavender eyes, obviously still frustrated at the memory.

My brows rose, and I looked at her with new respect. She'd made it clear she wanted to go into a line of work that involved a weapon, but her parents had made sure she was well-rounded. It wasn't unusual for young people in Faerie to spend time in foreign courts, but it was less common among New Gargoyles, and it was something Oliver had probably known better than to try to force on me. Or maybe it hadn't ever occurred to him in the first place. Emmaline didn't appreciate it yet, but her experiences would serve her well. And perhaps on this particular trip, they'd serve me well, too.

I leaned close to my page. "If you'll help me out, I'll make it worth your while when it comes time to apply to the Guild," I said to her.

Emmaline's eyes gleamed, but she managed to keep her professional veneer. "It's my duty to help you, my lady," she said, her words formal but careful.

In spite of what she'd said, I knew by her deliberate look that she'd accepted—we had an agreement. Now I just had to figure out what I needed her to do.

We didn't have time to discuss it, though. Maxen had broken away from his post and was sauntering up. Emmaline stepped away, almost seeming to melt into the background of people.

He nodded at Lochlyn. "Lady Tisdale. So nice to see you."

"I'm honored to be allowed to join your party, my lord." She gave him a coquettish little smile before lowering her head in a deep, graceful curtsy.

He bowed with a flowery twirl of one hand, and she curtsied again.

I groaned loudly. "Could the two of you stop enjoying all of this quite so much?"

"In case anyone asks why I'm along, you could just tell them I'm a gift of entertainment," Lochlyn said. She fluffed her hair. "Say the word, and I'll sing their faces off."

A bright, ear-splitting bugle flourish nearly made me jump out of my skin.

King Periclase was moving with his guards to the head of the trail, and the entire party was shifting around, ready for the procession.

Maxen linked his arm around mine and offered his other arm to Lochlyn. I tried to pull away—I didn't want to draw attention by walking on the arm of the most conspicuous New Gargoyle there, but Maxen flexed his bicep, clamping my arm against his side. He pulled us to the head of the New Gargoyle group.

I looked up to find King Periclase's gaze trained my way. I didn't like the unblinking way he watched me. I inclined my head in a tiny bow, but then looked away, hoping that someone else would draw his attention. I had a split-second of paranoia, suddenly thinking that he'd guessed I'd come to claim Nicole.

As the Duergar king turned and began leading the party down the road, I couldn't help wondering if I should have found a different way to come here. Something less conspicuous. As we began to move forward in the procession, I looked up at the hawthorn trees and spotted a camouflaged archer among the foliage.

In sharp contrast to the celebratory bugling and chatter, a knot of foreboding began to tighten in my stomach. The Duergar palace began to come into view down the road. Nicole was in there somewhere. I just needed to figure out how to find her and get the hell out.

Chapter 13

THE DUERGAR PALACE was all baroque curves and flourishes, with streamers flowing from the highest turrets and fluttering banners draping over the walls. It was made of pale-gray stone, and it seemed there was an armed sentry in every window and on every walkway. Again, the juxtaposition of guards and weaponry with cheery festivity set me on edge.

The party went up to the main entrance of the palace, where the huge steel doors were swung outward for our arrival. Inside, we passed through a courtyard with miniature hawthorn trees and pleasant fountains and went on into the central interior. The space inside was grander than the New Garg fortress—high ceilings, statuary, luxurious overstuffed furniture, and fresh flowers in giant vases.

A legion of Duergar attendants awaited us in a neat line. As soon as the entire party had gathered in the great hall, they broke formation and approached the guests they were assigned to. When a waif-like young Duergar man with shifting eyes headed my direction, Emmaline hopped around in front of me and intercepted him.

Maxen let go of my elbow. "I'll send for you after we've been shown to our rooms," he whispered in my ear.

Oh, great. That wouldn't cause any gossip at all.

He stepped away before I could reply.

Emmaline came to me brandishing her tablet. "I can take you and

Lady Tisdale to your room, now."

I glanced around, looking for the shifty-eyed Duergar attendant and spotted him sulking at the edge of the group.

"I told him we wouldn't need him until later," Emmaline said with a wan smile.

"Fine work," I said appreciatively. "Please, lead the way. I can't wait to change out of this." I plucked at the fabric of my dress.

The party began to disperse as the guests were taken to their quarters.

Emmaline consulted her tablet, which I saw had a layout of the Duergar palace, and then took us toward a doorway that led out into another courtyard. The Duergar boy trailed behind us.

"You and Lady Tisdale are sharing a suite up there," my page said. She gestured up at the second-floor balcony that ran around the rectangular courtyard. "All of the guests will be on the same floor."

We went up a staircase and around to a door with a pink flourish design molded onto it.

Once inside, I spotted our luggage and eagerly went to my trunk to pull out a blouse and a pair of riding pants. I set Mort against the wall so I could change. Emmaline closed and bolted the door before our Duergar attendant could sidle inside.

"He shouldn't expect to be let into ladies' quarters anyway," she muttered.

Lochlyn was moving around the suite, making delighted sounds at the canopied beds, the mirrored vanity, and the crystal chandelier that hung in the small sitting room. The accommodations were luxurious, to be sure, but I didn't plan to be there long enough to enjoy them.

Emmaline took my discarded dress to one of the armoires to hang it up, and I pulled out my broadsword but left the scabbard on the floor. I went to the nearest wall and started tapping Mort against it.

"What in the world are you doing?" Lochlyn demanded.

"Looking for . . . vulnerabilities," I said.

I methodically moved around the main room. When I got to the area under the window seat, the tone of the sword against the wall panels changed a bit. I knelt and ran my fingers over the panels and then searched for a way to lift the seat, thinking it might be hollow for storage. The seat tipped back, and indeed there were extra quilts piled inside. I moved the quilts and began exploring the storage space with my hands. At one end, there was a panel that seemed loose. I worked my fingertips around the edge of it and pulled, and it opened, revealing a tunnel not much bigger than an air duct.

"Ha," I said softly.

The space was tight, but big enough for a slender spy to shimmy through.

I found another hollow area near the toilet and one more in the ceiling of the closet. There was also a service panel in one bedroom that I suspected was another way into the quarters. I probably hadn't found all the secret passages, but I was satisfied I'd found enough of them. They weren't just for spies. Palaces always had hidden connections between rooms for other reasons, too—often in the name of discretion for sexual interludes. If it came down to it, I might need to use the passages to move around the palace myself.

While I'd been casing the quarters, Lochlyn had danced around humming to herself as she unpacked her things. She sat at the vanity, touching up her makeup.

I went to put on Mort's scabbard, sheathed the broadsword, and checked that my karambit, a small but wicked knife, was in its pocket on the scabbard strap. Feeling slightly guilty for destroying the stylists' fine work, I swept my hair up into a high ponytail and coiled that into a bun that was held in place by a few hairpins.

"Could I see your maps of the palace?" I asked my page.

She handed me her tablet, and I scrolled through the diagrams for a couple of minutes. The labeling was woefully sparse, only giving information about the areas where we would be attending events. The rest were big blank blocks.

"How much time did you spend here during your summers at court, Emmaline?" I asked.

"I've been here once before, the summer I was fifteen."

"If someone were held here against their will, have any guesses about where they might be housed?"

Her purple-gray gaze sharpened with interest. She put a finger to her lips and thought for a moment. "There are some quarters behind the stables, a big bunk house. I used to sneak out there with some of the other girls. Either there, or the basement. Not to sound cliché, or anything, but there is a sort of dungeon down there."

I'd take the stables over the dungeon. Periclase wanted my sister for some purpose, but I would bet that he didn't want her reporting she was mistreated too terribly at the hands of the Duergar. That would make him look bad.

"Any inconspicuous way to get to the stables from here?" I asked Emmaline.

She pointed at the map. "There's supposedly an underground tunnel that starts here, just outside the west kitchen at what looked like an old root cellar. But it was barricaded at both ends, so I never got the chance to try it."

I nodded. "Good to know. How much time do we have?"

"Another half hour until you're expected for cocktails," she said.

"Perfect." I passed her tablet back to her. "Lochlyn and I are going to do a bit of, uh, walking in the garden. We won't be long."

Before my page could protest, I grabbed Lochlyn's wrist and towed her out the door.

"You know what to do, right?" I said to her in a low voice.

She fluffed up her pink-streaked platinum hair with one hand. "You know it." Her expression turned to pure confidence.

As I'd expected, there were a couple of Duergar standing near the stairway that led down to the courtyard below. They weren't armed and plated to the teeth like King Periclase's guards, but they carried weapons and wore the vigilant expressions of men who were on duty.

Lochlyn went ahead while I hung back. The men hadn't seen me, so I pressed into a doorway to keep hidden.

They each stepped into Lochlyn's path when she went for the stairs.

"For your protection, you must stay in your quarters until your armed escort arrives," one of them said.

For protection, right. Periclase wanted to keep us contained.

Lochlyn stepped close to one of the men and placed her hand on his arm. "Oh! I'm so sorry. I just wanted to look for a place to practice. Perhaps you've heard of me? I'm Lochlyn Tisdale, world-renowned vocalist. I've been working on a new song. Maybe I could sing a little and you could tell me what you think?"

Her voice was taking on the purr of the Cait Sidhe, and she'd maneuvered around so the men were facing her with their backs to me.

She began to sing, her voice reverberating beautifully down the stairwell. I waited for a particularly powerful sustained note, took a couple of hurried steps to the balcony rail, and launched myself over it. Landing in a crouch that finished with a roll on the soft turf below, I paused just long enough to get my bearings and then ran on quiet feet to a corridor leading deeper into the palace.

The jump from the second story might have broken the ankles of another Fae, but New Gargoyles had unnatural bone strength. Plus, being smaller than most of my race, I had less body weight for the impact. I could probably have jumped from the third floor and landed without injury.

I wasn't dumb enough to gloat yet, though. I was in Unseelie territory and surely already had at least two spies tailing me. That was fine for the moment. I knew they wouldn't tattle on me yet—they'd be too interested in figuring out why I was sneaking around. When I needed to lose them, I would.

Emmaline had indicated that one end of the tunnel to the stable quarters was near one of the blank blocks on the map she remembered as a kitchen.

I was in a service hallway, but the staff I passed were casting me curious looks. I walked like I owned the place, which usually worked well to prevent anyone from questioning me, but it was only a matter of time before someone decided to notify a higher-up or I ran into a guard. I needed to get away from all of these eyeballs.

The outer perimeter of the palace was designed as a sort of squared-off U. I was still in the bottom of the U, in the section that housed my quarters. I needed to get to the area at the end of the left prong of the U. The entire structure was many times the size of the New Gargoyle fortress, and being unused to Fae palaces, I was going to have to pay attention to keep from getting turned around. My best bet was to get outside as quickly as possible.

Taking a couple of abrupt turns, I was aiming to get to an external door when I caught the unmistakable crisp linen and fresh soap smell of laundry. A laundromat would most likely be situated on an exterior wall, due to the great volume of venting required. I sped up, following my nose and the low, rhythmic rumbles of washing machines and dryers.

My hand was inches from the laundromat door when it swung inward. I was looking straight at the broad chest of a Duergar in light armor.

"Oh, shit," I said.

"Oh, shit, indeed," he replied mildly.

When I tipped my head back, I locked gazes with a pair of the most remarkable eyes I'd ever seen. Blue rings demarcated the outer iris, bleeding into gold that transitioned into grass-green around the pupil.

I had just enough time to notice that his right forearm was encased in stone armor before I whirled around, ready to dart away.

But three Duergar barreled in from the right and two more from the left. I instinctively reached back for Mort. Wrong move. They obviously took it as a threat, and a second later I was on the ground writhing as one of the guards shot me with a magi-zapper.

It seemed to go on forever, like lightning burning up my spine.

When it finally stopped, all I could do was lie there gasping like a beached fish. I watched helplessly as the one with the stone armor forearm peeled me off the floor and slung me over his shoulder like the living rag doll that I was. Still paralyzed from the zap, I tried to force the gears of my brain to grind into motion and tune into what the guards were saying.

When I caught King Periclase's and Maxen's names, I knew I was royally screwed.

Chapter 14

I HAD A pretty decent view of the ass of the guy carrying me as I hung over his shoulder like a giant sack of turnips. It was muscular. Not bad. Decent calves, too, as revealed by his tight-fitting trousers.

The feeling was beginning to return to my extremities by the time we'd gone up a couple of floors. I cleared my throat, testing my vocal chords.

"There's no reason for all of this," I said, sounding only a little hoarse. "I simply got turned around. I mean, six guards? Just for little old me? Surely that's an overreaction to a guest losing her way in an unfamiliar palace?"

I put a little extra emphasis on the word "guest."

"You didn't get turned around," said the one carrying me. Again with the mild tone, as if he was out for a stroll in the woods. He didn't even sound winded after carrying me up two flights of stairs, which I found annoying for some odd reason.

"I assure you I did," I said. I gave a self-effacing little laugh, still hoping he'd go for it and soften but getting the distinct impression he wasn't that gullible. "I have a downright atrocious sense of direction. Please, if you just put me down, I can explain."

He snorted and adjusted my weight over his shoulder. "I know who you are, Petra Maguire. And I assure *you*, you're not going to talk your way out of this."

Ire flashed through me, white-hot. I had a childish desire to try to ruffle him out of his calm tone, but given my predicament, I thought better of it.

"Well, I think you're making a huge mistake," I said pleasantly. "But since it appears we're in this together, why don't we get to know each other a little? It seems only fair that you tell me your name, seeing as how you already know mine."

He actually let out a laugh. It was deep and resonant, and I imagined those crazy eyes creasing a little at the corners.

"It's Jasper."

I frowned as the name plucked at my memory.

Oh, damn it to Maeve.

"Not Jasper, King Periclase's son?" I winced as I said it, as if the answer was going to cause me physical pain.

"See? I knew you were sharper than you were letting on." He had a very faint brogue—too subtle to tell if it was Irish or Scottish—indicating he must have spent some portion of his childhood in the Old World, unlike me. I was New World born and raised in the San Francisco-anchored fortress.

The zap wasn't wearing off as quickly as I'd hoped, and Jasper and the other guards had brought me to a wing that appeared to be offices or some other rooms where official business was conducted. The Duergar seal and colors seemed to be everywhere.

Jasper halted and rapped on a door. A moment later, I heard it unlatch.

"The others can go," said a male voice.

I tried to twist around to see who was speaking, but my torso muscles weren't up to the task yet. Jasper carried me through the doorway. When he turned to close the door, I caught an upside-down glimpse of an armored guard, like one who'd stood beside King Periclase in the forest. He was dressed differently than Jasper, who looked more like a military man than a royal guard.

With much jostling, Jasper muscled me into a chair. My head bobbed a little before I could control it, and I ground my teeth—this whole rag doll thing was not exactly putting me in a position of influence in this situation.

Jasper moved back to stand near the door. He held a magi-zapper casually at his side, and his other hand rested on the pommel of the short sword at his waist. I cast a quick look around. The room was about fifteen feet square and windowless, and I seemed to be positioned at the back of it.

When I saw that the armored guard held my scabbard, my hands twitched with the desire to snatch Mort away.

"Watch yourself," I growled at him. "That's a shadowsteel spellblade you're holding."

He didn't react but just gazed coldly at me through his barbute-style helmet, which had an open T that left his eyes, nose, the center strip of mouth, and chin exposed. Then he slowly lifted his other hand and stroked Mort's grip in a lewd gesture. Wrath and adrenaline spiked through me. There was a sharp pulse from Mort—from my own blood infused in the steel—as if the broadsword protested being touched by the brute. It was a reaction that only I could feel.

I leaned forward as if to stand. "I'm warning you, asshole."

Jasper stepped forward, his neutral expression tightening just a hair. "You're in no position to be warning anyone," he said to me. "For your own good, stay where you are."

He turned his hand, showing me the magi-zapper. At first I thought he was threatening me with it, but he was gesturing at something.

I tipped my gaze down. There were a couple of metal loops bolted to the floor. Attached to each was a short chain with a shackle. My jaw tightened as I sensed something faint but distinctly malicious emanating from those innocuous-looking lengths of metal. Sky iron. The rarest and most poisonous type of iron. This was an interrogation room. My New Garg blood was decent protection against lesser types like cold iron, but no Fae was resistant to sky iron. I suddenly became aware of the same dark impression coming from either side. I slid my eyes to the right and caught sight of a length of fine chain. More sky iron. I didn't have to look to the left to know that an identical chain hung there, too.

I only had a few seconds to contemplate the implications when the door swung open. King Periclase strode in. He was flanked by a couple of guards who were nearly identical in stature and uniform to the one who still clutched Mort in his meaty paw. The Duergar king was dressed in his courtly best. Leather trousers, a white tunic tucked in to show off his narrow waist, studded leather boots that hit just below his knees, and a cape. A floor-length fricking *cape*. It should have looked ridiculous, but somehow Periclase made it look badass.

The guards hung back while Periclase came to loom right in front of me. I planted my feet and pushed off my thighs with my hands to stand. No way I was going to sit there on my ass and look up at him, even if my muscles still felt like al dente linguine. My knees wobbled. I locked them out and leaned back just enough to brace my legs against the edge of the chair. I lifted my chin and returned his unblinking gaze. There was no way in hell I could curtsy without collapsing, but the Duergar king didn't seem to notice my violation of decorum.

Periclase tilted his head ever so slightly, regarding me. "So. Oliver's daughter. Not even here an hour, and already causing trouble."

Inside, I relaxed just a little. He was irritated but didn't seem in the mood to torture me with sky iron.

"I simply got lost, that's all, Your Majesty," I said coolly. I raised a palm to gesture at the guards. "This seems unnecessary."

He smiled, and the stone side of his face remained unmoving. There was absolutely nothing warm or friendly about his expression.

"One can't be too careful in the current political climate," Periclase said. He lifted an arm and flicked his finger, and Jasper moved to stand just behind his father. "I've spoken to Lord Lothlorien, and he agrees that we mustn't risk you losing your way again while you're here. For the remainder of your visit, my battle captain will accompany you everywhere you go."

My eyes flicked over to Jasper. He looked neither pleased nor irked with his assignment.

"Oh, I assure you it won't happen again, Your Majesty," I said. "My page has maps, and I'll make sure she's with me whenever I leave my—"

"You will have a special escort for the remainder of your visit," he repeated, cutting me off.

His voice was even, but his brows rose almost imperceptibly. I snapped my trap shut as I realized what it meant. He was challenging me to argue again. He would relish taking more severe action, and if I provoked it, he'd be able to justify it to Maxen. For once, my better judgment actually kicked in, and I restrained myself. Instead of arguing, I inclined my head.

"As you wish, Your Majesty." I nearly sounded as if I meant it.

I needed to make nice. I'd figure out how to lose Jasper later.

King Periclase turned neatly on his heel, making his cape billow out a bit, and he strode toward the door. One of his personal guards opened it for him. Suddenly feeling a whole lot steadier, I stalked toward the guy who still held Mort, ready to rip the scabbard from his hands.

Just as I reached for it, Periclase paused in the doorway and pivoted around to look at me.

"And Jasper will carry your broadsword," the Duergar king pronounced.

I saw red. It was a good thing Periclase left immediately because I couldn't contain myself. I turned my back on Jasper and Meat Hands, planted my fists on my hips, and let out a muttered string of swearing that cursed the Duergar three generations backward and forward. Then I took a deep breath and faced them.

"I'm sure my page and my roommate are wondering where I am," I said sweetly to Jasper. "Would you mind if we returned to my quarters?"

His lips twitched. "Certainly, Lady Maguire. And rest assured, I won't take you on a *single* wrong turn. Pay attention as you go, and maybe you'll become better equipped to navigate the palace."

My hands clenched into fists as Jasper took Mort from Meat Hands. My personal escort swung the strap of the scabbard over his shoulder like a bag. Having Jasper carry it was slightly less offensive, but only by a hair.

Meat Hands opened the door, and Jasper nodded at me. "After you."

I was too pissed to try to make any conversation on the way back to my quarters. I went in and slammed the door in Jasper's face. Well, I wanted to think I did. In actuality, he hadn't tried to come in.

Emmaline rushed at me. "Where have you *been?*" she demanded. "And where's your sword?" She gave me an alarmed look.

"Long story," I grumbled.

"Well, you need to change," she said. She pushed the blue dress at me. "I found out after you left that formal dress is required, and we're twenty minutes late to the cocktail reception. This is not making a good impression."

"I don't think Periclase is going to care too much about my impression at this point," I said.

With irate, sharp movements, I took off my blouse and riding pants and pulled on the dress. Having to change back into that outfit somehow added insult to injury.

Hands on hips, I stood before Emmaline two minutes later. "Okay, let's go."

"Your hair?" She gestured.

I shook my head. "Not happening."

I took a slow breath to compose myself and then pasted on the best fake smile I could manage. I opened the door. Jasper pushed away from the wall, and the faintest surprise registered in his colorful eyes as his gaze flicked down over my dress.

"Emmaline, this is Jasper," I said over my shoulder to my page with exaggerated brightness. "We're going to see a hell of a lot of him while we're here, so the two of you might as well get acquainted."

My fake smile slipped, trying to curl into an irate sneer, before I snapped it back into place.

Jasper had the audacity to let out a little chuckle. I glared at his back the whole way to the reception hall.

Chapter 15

THE RECEPTION WAS in full swing when we arrived. Jasper moved aside, allowing me to choose where I wanted to go. Suddenly Lochlyn was at my side, grasping my elbow.

"What did you do?" she whispered loudly at my ear. "Maxen has already asked me three times if I've seen you, and he's ready to spit nails."

Before I could respond or even get my bearings in the swirl of fabric, perfume, chatter, and candlelight, the milling crowd shifted and I caught sight of Maxen stalking toward us.

"Save yourself," I hissed to Lochlyn, and she let go of me and melted away into the guests.

"Lord Lothlorien," I said regally, and dropped into a deep curtsy.

"Cut that crap out right now, Maguire," he said, his voice urgent but low enough that his words wouldn't carry to anyone nearby. "You owe me an explanation. *Now.*"

I straightened and flicked a glance over at Jasper. He was watching, but was out of earshot, I was pretty sure.

"I can totally explain," I said. "I swear I didn't do anything wrong. Huge overreaction on the part of the Duergar. Huge. Seriously, so massive." I sometimes tended to backslide into adolescent-speak when I knew I was going to have to try to talk my way out of a bind.

He tipped his head, indicating we should move off to the side of the room. Jasper followed, and Emmaline hovered nearby, too. This was not at all how I imagined it would be to have my own entourage. Maxen stopped near the wall.

"What in the name of Oberon is going on?" he demanded. "I get a messenger telling me that you're in a Duergar cell and they want to accuse you of spying."

I scoffed. "We're in Unseelie territory! *Everyone* here is a spy."

His mouth drew into an angry, tight line. I shut up.

"I just went out to, you know, look around," I said pointedly. I dropped my voice to a whisper and put my hand over my mouth to keep anyone from reading my lips. "For the changeling."

I wasn't sure I'd ever seen him so tense. "You have to be more discreet, Petra. This business with the Duergar is too dire to screw around. We can't be openly pissing them off."

I blew out a frustrated breath. He was probably right. I should have been stealthier. But I was on a mission on behalf of the Stone Order, and it wasn't an easy one.

He sighed heavily and beckoned me to lean in.

"Petra, things are more escalated than I thought. If this changeling disappears while the New Gargoyle convoy is here, it will throw our talks into chaos. Periclase will think this trip was just a front for taking the changeling. I'm sorry, but I have to call it off. You can't do it. Not while we're here on a diplomatic visit. The Duergar will use it as an excuse to start a war."

"But Nicole belongs to us," I protested, my tone thick with alarm. The thought of leaving my own sister here made me feel ill. Maxen didn't know Nicole was my twin, but I couldn't help my reaction. "She's New Gargoyle, and Periclase has no right to detain her. If anything, we should be the ones initiating war against his kingdom for kidnapping one of our changelings. This should make *him* look bad, not us."

I wasn't sure exactly when I'd gotten so fully behind this rescue mission. I'd wanted to get Nicole out from the start, but I realized I also wanted to show Periclase that he couldn't screw with New Gargoyles—he couldn't screw with *me*.

Maxen pulled back a bit and closed his eyes for a beat.

"I know," he said. "Logically, you're right. But this is Faerie politics. Logic doesn't necessarily apply."

I dropped my arms to my sides and ground my teeth. I wasn't upset at him, but at the stupid politics of Faerie kingdoms.

"We can't just leave her, Maxen."

"You're right," he said. "But we can't do it like this."

I perked up at his tone. He seemed to have something in mind.

"I'm going to send you home," he said firmly.

I frowned. I'd *thought* he had something in mind. "Wait, what?"

"As far as the Duergar are concerned, you'll be going home," he said. "It would be uncouth to do it now, in the middle of a party. I'll wait until tomorrow morning, and then I'll officially dismiss you."

"But then I'll . . ." I left the question hanging, hoping he was implying what I thought he was implying.

"I'll have to figure out how to get you back in," he whispered quickly. A cloud of officials had started creeping closer and closer to us, hovering in a way that made it clear they wanted to whisk Maxen back into conversation.

He moved away, leaving me standing alone by the wall.

Jasper strolled over.

Inside, I was revved up with the prospect of what was to come, but I couldn't let on that anything was amiss. The sight of Jasper's hand wrapped around Mort's scabbard made it easy to pull a sullen face.

I crossed my arms. "Oh. It's you."

"Get a little lecture and wrist slap from the stone prince?" he asked cheerfully.

I looked off to the side, ignoring him.

"Aw, come on," he cajoled. "No need to be unfriendly."

I sighed and then slid my gaze over to glance at his forearm. The one holding my scabbard had the sleeve pulled up slightly, revealing a couple of inches of stone. "Can you form full armor? How much New Garg blood you got, anyway?"

He blinked, seeming caught off guard by my question. His hand reflexively tightened around my scabbard strap.

"Aye, I can summon full armor. As for New Garg blood, about half. Not that it really matters," he said. He pointed his thumb at his chest. "You may have heard. I'm a bastard."

It was true. Periclase was his father, but his mother wasn't the Duergar queen.

"At least you know who your parents are," I said absently. I was scanning the room for Lochlyn or Emmaline. I spotted both of them near one of the buffet tables.

"Unknown lineage?"

"Yeah, I don't know who my blood mother is," I said. I smirked at him, suddenly realizing that he and I were of similar build. "Hey, maybe we're related."

"That'd be a terrible pity."

I turned to give him a sharp look. The corners of his mouth twitched as if he held back a grin. Otherwise, his face remained stoic as he watched me with those unblinking tri-colored eyes.

Variegated eyes.

For some unknown reason, I suddenly remembered the term for Fae irises like Jasper's that displayed at least three distinct colors in a concentric pattern. They were unusual and very striking.

I dropped my arms to my sides. "If that's your idea of flirting, you're kind of shitty at it."

I turned on my heel and strode away, and his soft chuckle followed me.

Lochlyn was talking to a gray-haired Duergar official, and when she caught sight of me, she brightened and lifted a finger in a just-a-minute gesture. I grabbed a champagne flute from a server and pretended to sip it while I waited. Alcohol dulled my senses, but a drink in hand was useful for blending in.

Lochlyn hurried over. "What'd Maxen say?"

"I'll tell you later," I said with a glance over my shoulder at Jasper, who stood a couple of feet away.

"Who is that guy?" Lochlyn asked.

I blew out a breath. "My babysitter," I said grudgingly.

Her brows rose.

"I got in trouble with Periclase when I went on my little adventure earlier, so now I don't go anywhere without escort."

Approval flickered in her eyes as she gave him a long look. "Well, you could do worse. A whole lot worse."

"He's Periclase's son."

"Ah, Jasper. I remember him now from my days at court years ago. He's grown into quite a man. Those eyes," she said, her gaze still lingering on Jasper. "This throws a wrench in things, though, doesn't it?"

"Yep. But there's a plan in the works," I said under my breath. "I'm going to have to make an early departure from this realm and then figure out a way to get back in."

There was a bright flourish of horns near the main doorway, and the entire room's attention swung that way. King Periclase entered the reception hall with his wife, Courtney, on his arm. In their wake walked a few Duergar lords and ladies, plus a cadre of attendants.

Everyone bowed and curtsied as the Duergar king and queen promenaded into the room. As they passed, Periclase slid a hard glance at me, and then his eyes flicked over to Jasper. The royal couple went to sit on ornate chairs positioned on a raised platform, and a queue of people formed almost immediately.

I glanced over at Emmaline, who was standing inconspicuously off to the side with her hands clasped over her tablet. She walked over.

"We're not expected to go talk to them, are we?" I asked my page.

She shook her head. "It's not required, no. Only if you'd like to."

"Thank Oberon."

Lochlyn and I watched as Maxen spoke to the royal couple and then moved off to the side. A petite, very slim young woman with silver-blond hair approached him. She'd been standing near the royal throne as if she'd been waiting for him. There was something about her that seemed familiar.

"Who's that?" I asked Lochlyn.

"No idea," she said. "You're not jealous she's talking to Maxen, are you?"

I shot her a glare, and she snorted a laugh.

"She's King Periclase's daughter, but not Queen Courtney's," Emmaline supplied. "She's not on the royal family registry because Periclase never officially claimed her as his, but she's sworn to the Duergar kingdom. Her name's Bryna."

My pulse thumped hard in my temples. Lochlyn and I locked eyes for a second.

"Bryna, as in the Duergar-Spriggan bitch who tried to kill you?" Lochlyn hissed.

"Got to be," I said. My jaw clenched as I watched Bryna smile and chatter with Maxen. "It's probably a good thing I'm not holding Mort right now."

My muscles pulsed with the desire to do some damage to Bryna's delicately pretty face. But then I considered the situation in the larger scheme of things. I could use Bryna to prompt my early exit from the Duergar kingdom. I liked the idea of getting things rolling. I shoved my champagne flute into Lochlyn's free hand.

"Petra, wait," Lochlyn came after me as I began to stomp toward Periclase's bastard daughter. Lochlyn grabbed my arm.

"I know what I'm doing," I whispered to Lochlyn and then shook off her hand.

Chapter 16

BRYNA'S GAZE FLICKED to me as I approached, and then she did a double-take. Her eyes widened, and she stopped talking mid-sentence. I stepped in front of Maxen, so close to Bryna I could see her quickening pulse at the side of her pale neck.

"Surprised to see me here?" I asked. "Does Daddy know about your wraith? Does he know you tried to kill me? Maybe we should tell him about how you violated the sanctity of the netherwhere."

Her fingers flew to her mouth as she affected a shocked look.

"Oh! You must have the wrong person," she said loudly. Her eyelashes fluttered, and she backed up a step as she pressed her other hand to her chest. "Please, don't hurt me!"

Maxen was at my side, trying to tug at my arm. "Petra? What in Oberon's name are you doing?"

I shot him a pointed look, and he seemed to get the idea that this was part of a plan. He backed off.

"Don't you play dumb," I growled at Bryna. "I know it was you, and I've got someone who will back me up. You're going to pay for trying to murder me in the netherwhere."

She shrank away, holding up her hands as if to fend off an attack. "I don't know what you're talking about."

I knew it was an act on her part—it was on mine, too—but it was working. People were crowding around. Hands grasped my arms.

Someone hauled me backward.

Maxen kept pace with me as people inserted themselves between me and Bryna.

"Petra, get a hold of yourself, right now," he said loudly enough for his voice to carry a little. He was getting in on the act.

Maxen continued to talk to me as I was escorted out through a side doorway into a service corridor. Lochlyn, Jasper, and Maxen all stared at me. A couple of Duergar guards hovered nearby. The door to the reception hall stood open, and I could see Periclase up on his throne. He hadn't moved, but he was watching us. Jasper waved the guards back, and they retreated into the reception hall.

"What's this about?" Jasper demanded.

"She tried to kill me," I said. "She sent a wraith after me in the netherwhere. It tried to paralyze me there with cold iron; I barely made it out alive. And it came after me again." I held out my arm. "I've still got the iron burns."

They all looked at me with varying expressions of concern. Violating the netherwhere was a dishonorable and serious offense in Faerie.

"How do you know it was Bryna?" Jasper asked. His jaw clenched, and I got the brief but distinct impression that he wasn't Bryna's biggest fan.

"She's connected to a mark I was after for a Guild assignment, a drug-dealing vamp she's been escorting into Faerie. Morven identified her for me. He also named her the owner of the wraith."

Lochlyn let out a little gasp at the mention of Morven's name. Everyone in Faerie knew who he was, and Morven's word was universally trusted.

"Pursuing a problem through bureaucratic channels isn't my style, and there's nothing that requires me to do it that way," I said. "I killed the wraith. I planned to deal with Bryna after I caught the mark."

"I believe you, I do," Maxen said, playing along. "But unfortunately, that little display was the last straw as far as this trip is concerned. You can't stay here."

I huffed out a loud breath. Getting booted out of the Duergar realm was my plan. But it struck me that we hadn't gotten to the part about how I was getting back *in*.

"I know," I said. "For what it's worth, I don't blame you."

I hoped I wasn't laying it on too thick.

Emmaline had been standing in the doorway, and I beckoned her over.

"Lady Lochlyn and I will be departing this evening," I said.

"Actually, Lochlyn is scheduled to perform later," Maxen said quickly. He lifted his brows slightly, trying to signal something. He wanted Lochlyn to remain behind. Maybe he just didn't want to do anything further to irritate Periclase.

"Fine. Just me, then," I said and tried to look dejected.

Jasper was watching us, and I could almost see his brain working as he tried to read the subtext of what we said.

I caught a flash of something pass from Maxen's hand to Lochlyn's, which Jasper didn't see, and then she came over to embrace me.

"I'll be home soon," she said. I felt her slip something under my dress at my shoulder blade.

I gave a forlorn little sigh. "Don't have too much fun without me."

Maxen and Lochlyn turned to go back into the reception hall.

"Ready?" Jasper asked.

I nodded, and Emmaline walked beside me as he led us back toward my room. I could feel the small object Lochlyn had slipped to me, and I itched to see what it was. It felt like a small scrap of paper. As we walked, it started to slide lower. I was so focused on trying to surreptitiously work it to a more secure place under my bra strap at first I didn't notice the change in the air when we entered the empty courtyard at the center of the guest quarters.

The area was in shadow, with the sun having set. All of a sudden, it was like the shadows were birthing moving forms.

"What the—" Even as Jasper was voicing his confusion, he was drawing his sword from its sheath and a magi-zapper from his belt.

As soon as my eyes locked on one of the diminutive, black-clad figures, I knew what was happening.

"They're servitors," I said. "With poisoned throwing knives and daggers."

I threw myself to the ground to avoid one of said knives, which went whizzing by my temple. I hollered at Emmaline to get down and armor up, and she went sprawling behind a ball-shaped hedge.

I pulled magic, summoning my rock armor. "Jasper, my sword!"

He glanced back at me just as a servitor launched himself at Jasper with a wild yell. These servitors moved with blurring speed, much faster than the ones I'd faced before. Jasper barely managed to bat him to the side with a swing of his arm, the one that was encased in stone.

"Damn it, come *on*!" I hollered as another servitor rushed at me, brandishing a dagger in each hand.

I kicked him in the ribs and felt one knife scrape across the armor on my thigh. He didn't go down. Regaining his footing, he sprang up, reached out with the other blade, and nearly nicked my bare cheek.

"Petra!" Jasper twisted to toss my scabbard at me before whirling around to cut down two more servitors with his short sword and then kneel down to shoulder away another that dove at him. He had exceptionally quick hands, especially for a man his size.

I caught the scabbard, grabbed Mort's grip, and connected with the weapon's magic as I freed it from the sheath. Power zinged between me and my weapon as Mort seemed to relish the impending violence. Automatically moving near Jasper to fight back to back as the attackers came at us, I quickly got into a rhythm of blocking and mowing them down. They were fast, and we only just managed to hold them off. But it didn't take long for them to change their approach.

The remaining servitors retreated and formed a ring around us.

"Oh, shit," I growled.

Then, moving in unison, they began hurling their knives at us. We took cover at a huge tree trunk, but that only protected us from one angle.

I ducked and winced as one knife pinged off my shoulder and another hit my wrist.

Jasper reached around to shove something into my hand. It was a piece of his armor, a shoulder plate.

"Protect your head," he said. "They're going to run out of shit to throw at us at some point."

"Well, aren't you just cool as a cucumber on ice," I remarked, trying to match his casual tone.

Not certain whether he was capable of summoning full stone armor, I shot a glance at him to make sure he hadn't compromised his own safety by giving me some of his regular armor. He looked every bit as encased in rock as I was. Apparently, he hadn't inherited King Periclase's faulty gene.

"On the inside, I'm screaming like a pretty little princess," he said.

I cracked a grin and nearly laughed as more knives assaulted us.

"Emmaline, you okay?" I hollered.

"Thumbs up," she yelled back, sounding shaken.

"You've seen these guys before, I take it?" Jasper asked. He was using his breast plate as a shield for his head.

"Twice before. Once at a nightclub, when they seemed to be trying to take out the Spriggan king, and the other time at the stone fortress." The assault stopped, and after a moment I lowered the shoulder plate I'd been holding in front of my face. "Watch, they'll disappear."

Jasper looked around just as the servitors began to wink out of existence. First, the ones we'd killed disappeared. Then the ring of knife throwers faded out of sight.

"I heard about the assassination attempt on King Sebastian at Druid Circle. You were there for that?"

I raised a shoulder and let it drop. "Yep."

He shook his head. "Why did they come?"

For a second I debated about whether to tell him Marisol's theory but figured it wouldn't hurt to repeat it. "We believe they aren't sent for the primary objective of killing, but for some other purpose."

"What?"

"We don't know. But when they disappear, they're returning to their master, their task done."

He looked troubled.

"Creepy, eh?" I said, skirting a look around at the places where the bodies had been.

"I have to inform King Periclase." He started to stride away but then stopped and wheeled around.

I let out a withering sigh. "But you can't leave me alone."

"I'll go." Emmaline had crept out from her hiding place and was brushing off the front of her dress.

Noticing that she'd released her stone armor, I did the same. As it disappeared, the familiar ache spread over my skin. It was one of the costs of possessing such powerful magic, and all who could form the rock armor suffered it. I couldn't help wondering if the constant armor around Jasper's forearm caused him pain.

Jasper nodded. "Do you have a weapon?" he asked her.

She shook her head. He pulled out a short, curved knife and flipped it around in his palm so he could hand the hilt to her. She gave him a small, grateful smile and then hurried away, going back the way we'd come.

His gaze tipped downward, and for a moment I thought he was looking at Mort with the intent of demanding I hand over my sword.

But when I glanced down, I realized in the course of the fight I'd ripped a high slit up the center of my dress. Another couple of inches and he would have known the color of my underwear.

"It's a good modification," he said, completely straight-faced and in that mild tone of his.

I snorted a laugh in spite of myself and went to pick up my scabbard. "You're a very solid fighter," I said.

"Is that a compliment or a subtle put-down?"

I thought for a second. "Compliment. But one that implies there's room for improvement."

He chuckled, but his mirth was short-lived as we caught the sound of pounding boots. A moment later, the courtyard flooded with Duergar guards. Jasper went to talk to the one in the lead, leaving me standing there in a ripped dress, holding Mort.

I started to head to the stairs to go up to my quarters—after all, I had some packing to do—when King Periclase swept in, cape and all. His personal guards had their short swords drawn, and they moved into the space in half-crouches with their weight shifted forward, ready to fight. They all straightened when they realized the battle was done. The Duergar king scanned the courtyard, his face grimly set. But then, he always looked grim. His eyes lingered on me as Jasper went to speak to him.

I swung my scabbard over my head and settled it across my body, feeling once again whole with Mort on my back. Crossing my arms, I stayed where I was, figuring Periclase would want me questioned. Emmaline returned, slightly out of breath, and came to my side. We both watched the Duergar king.

"He say anything?" I asked her.

"Not much," she said. She glanced at me. "But he looked a little shaken."

My brows rose. The stone-faced king was rattled? I didn't really blame him. These servitor breaches were unusual. And the fact that no one seemed to know who was behind them or why they were sent was unsettling, even to a mercenary Fae who lived on the other side of the hedge.

"Are you all right, Emmaline?" I asked quietly. She'd probably never been in anything resembling a real combat situation, where she actually could have been killed.

Nodding, her face took on a fierce look, her nose creasing between her eyes as if she were looking at something far-off and she wanted to stab it through the ribs. "I just wish I would have had a sword. I hated lying there, useless and helpless."

I smiled with grim appreciation. She'd be fine.

"Good girl," I said approvingly. "I'm sure it was frustrating, but you held yourself together and you didn't die. That's always a good outcome. Next time, maybe you'll have that sword you want so much."

"You think there will be a next time?" she asked, sounding more intrigued than fearful.

I frowned. "These servitors seem to be able to go anywhere they please without permission, so until someone figures out who's commanding them, they'll likely keep cropping up."

After another couple of minutes, Jasper joined us.

"What, no inquisition?" I said, spreading my hands.

"King Periclase asked me to convey his approval for aiding me in defending the palace."

"Approval?" I snorted. "He ain't *my* daddy. I don't need his approval."

I wasn't about to admit I was relieved. After the day I'd had, a grilling from the Duergar king was the last thing I needed. I was ready to get the hell out. At least, out of all the courtly nonsense.

I tipped my head at my door on the second floor. "C'mon, let's get this eviction over with, shall we?"

Just then, Maxen and some of the New Garg dignitaries entered the courtyard. He flicked a glance at me, accompanied by a brief, relieved-looking nod, before going to Periclase.

Jasper, Emmaline, and I went upstairs. She and I went in to quickly gather the few things of mine that had been unpacked, while Jasper stood outside.

"You should stay here," I said. "You're not the one who got in trouble. You can attend to Lochlyn."

Emmaline closed the lid of my trunk. "I can't officially attend to her, since she's not New Gargoyle. But I'm sure Lord Lothlorien can find another assignment for me."

Suddenly I remembered the piece of paper Lochlyn had slid between my dress and my shoulder blade. While Emmaline was looking down at her tablet, I reached back and worked the folded scrap out but kept it concealed in my hand.

"I'm going to find someone to carry your trunk," Emmaline said and went out onto the balcony to speak to Jasper.

I turned toward a wall, and keeping the paper close to my body, I unfolded it. On it were hastily drawn marks. I recognized them immediately as sigils, the symbols which were part of the secret Fae code for using doorways. There was also a set of coordinates I recognized as being located in Duergar territory. The whole note was written in Maxen's hand. He'd slipped it to Lochlyn to get to me. I was pretty sure Maxen had given me the key to get back into the realm through a restricted doorway. How he could have come by such information, I had no idea, but maybe diplomats knew how to get through some of the more secret doorways.

I refolded the paper and tucked it into a pouch on my scabbard, behind my phone.

A sad little procession of Jasper, three Duergar guards, an attendant bearing my trunk, and Emmaline accompanied me to a doorway located under an arch of trees just outside the palace. It was dark, and there was no fanfare, only the soft cooing of night birds.

"Well, it's been . . . *interesting*, Petra Maguire," Jasper said after the attendant shoved my trunk up to the edge of the doorway.

I crooked a half-grin at him. "That it has." It suddenly struck me that Jasper seemed decidedly unlike most of the Unseelie I'd come across.

He gave me a little salute, and I turned to the arch.

I grasped a handle of the trunk and stood at the gnarled root half-buried in the dirt that marked the edge of the doorway. With my back turned, I stepped over the line as I whispered the words and used my fingers to draw the symbols that would take me back to the stone fortress. A second later, I was drifting in the void of the netherwhere.

Chapter 17

I ARRIVED IN an internal doorway of the stone fortress, one that was in a storage wing.

I dumped my trunk in a room full of unused artwork and statuary and navigated through lesser-used hallways to get back to the dressing room where I'd been primped and prepped earlier that day.

Inside, I was deeply grateful to find my ripped jeans, tank and jacket, and beat-up boots. After quickly changing and re-settling Mort's scabbard on my back, I headed to the doorway where I'd arrived. On the way, I passed a few other New Gargoyles, but no one seemed to think twice about my presence in the fortress. As long as none of them mentioned seeing me to Marisol, my untimely return shouldn't cause me any trouble.

Using Maxen's scribbled note, I traced magic-imbued symbols in the air and dissolved into the netherwhere.

When I emerged, the first thing I noticed was the smell of meat smokers. I recognized the Duergar palace not far off. I'd arrived back in the Duergar realm somewhere outside, and I stood still where I was, waiting for the chill of the void to wear off and my eyes to adjust to my dim surroundings. The smell of smoke and cooking meat made my mouth water and reminded me it'd been many hours since my last meal.

As my eyes grew accustomed to the dark, I could make out the large looming shape of the Duergar palace about a quarter mile straight ahead. In between me and the palace and off to one side were some long outbuildings. Slaughterhouses, I guessed, by the tinge of blood and other unpleasant byproducts of slaughter underlying the smoked meat aroma. Fires glowed here and there, and I spotted smaller buildings—the smokehouses. Men went in and out of them, tending to the business of converting meat into food even at this late hour. I watched them move for a few minutes as I planned my path to the palace, a route that would keep me in the shadows but take me near enough to snatch a piece of smoked meat. I was going to need some fuel to get through the night. And besides, the Duergar owed me a big, fancy court dinner. A bit of jerky was the least the palace could provide me.

As I stole from one shadow to the next, I kept to the tree line and listened to the chatter of the workers. There was a burst of ale-fueled singing from the men gathered around campfires, a group obviously off shift for the night. I tried to orient myself to which side of the palace I was facing, but the place was immense, and being unfamiliar with the landscape, I wasn't sure in the dark. My best guess was that I was at the back of the palace. I'd skirt it counterclockwise until I knew where I was.

I crept near the smokehouse that was closest to the shadows and waited. When I was sure I could get in and out without crossing paths with a worker, I darted into the weak ring of light from torches and campfires. The door to the small building swung open easily. I held my breath and ducked inside. There was a small lantern lit at the wall. Sausages as thick as my forearm hung from the ceiling like strange party decorations.

I quickly drew Mort and sliced off the end of one of the sausages. With my sword in one hand and a hunk of meat in the other, I elbowed through the door and darted back into the protection of the darkness. I ate as I walked, looking up at the windows of the palace and trying to get a glimpse of what was inside.

Another aroma began to overtake that of smoked meat. When I realized what it was, I stopped mid-chew and my boots scuffed to a halt. It was the smell of horses. Could I be near the barns and the bunkhouse Emmaline had told me about?

Yes. There was a training ring. The unmistakable smell of straw and horse dung.

And there—a lodge-like structure with no windows but skylights spaced along the roof. The bunkhouse.

There were also armed guards. Two that I could see from my vantage point.

After tossing the remaining heel of sausage into the bushes, I ran to the nearest wall of the bunkhouse. I pressed myself against it, listening. There was a door about ten feet away. I sidestepped to it and tried the latch but found it locked.

Voices sent me running across the space between the building and the forest and diving back into the darkness. I watched as a pair of guards walked around the bunkhouse, right past where I'd just been standing. It appeared there were at least two guards stationed at the main door of the building, and at least two patrolling around it. Clearly, there was something valuable in there. But the guards were moving almost casually. So that valuable person or thing, in their estimation, must not have been much of a threat for escape. Or rescue.

I was facing the short end of the bunkhouse, and presumably the front door was located on the opposite short end. With two guards there, that entrance was no good to me.

I needed to see what was inside. Tensing my muscles and taking a race-ready stance with my weight shifted to my forward foot, I waited until the patrol rounded the far corner.

I sprang from the protection of the forest, sprinting across the open space and launching myself at the drainpipe attached to the side of the building. With a quick prayer to Oberon that the pipe was firmly attached, I grasped it and started scrambling my feet to get purchase. The round faces of the logs that made up the wall provided just enough surface for toeholds. I had to make it up and out of sight before the patrol returned, and I still had about a dozen feet to go.

I pulled up, hand over hand, using the drainpipe like a mountain climber's rope. The surface of the metal flaked off in my hands, and the smell of rust rose to my nostrils. It was flimsier than I'd thought, and there was a soft whine as the top end started to pull away from the gutter it was fixed to.

"Shit," I hissed and climbed faster.

I managed to get my elbows over the rain gutter just as the pipe broke off and tipped to the ground. It landed softly in the dirt below but would be impossible to miss even in the dark.

I swung a leg up, grateful that the gutter was so solidly attached. Reaching out for a plumbing vent pipe that stuck out of the sloped roof, I got my lower body up just as the guards returned.

I heard them talking as they came upon the fallen pipe. I moved to the peak of the roof and flattened myself on it. The men would have to back up several yards to get the right angle to see me, but I'd shift my position as they moved to make sure I wasn't discovered.

For a moment I just lay there, my chest heaving from the effort of climbing and my heart tapping rapidly. About four feet away, there was a skylight glowing with very faint light from within. Staying as flat as I could, I military-crawled over to the window and peered over the edge. The glass was scratched and clouded, the frame holding it to the roof rusted even worse than the drainpipe I'd used to climb up. I probably could have pulled the whole thing off with a little effort.

Below was a room with a row of toilet stalls along one wall and a row of sinks lining the opposite wall. The bathroom itself was dark. The illumination was coming from an adjacent room, which I couldn't see into. To my right, over the peak of the roof on the other slanted face, was a somewhat brighter skylight.

The guards below were still examining the fallen pipe, but with no easy way to climb up, they seemed to be debating whether to ignore it or get a ladder to investigate further. While they argued, I scooted over to the brighter skylight.

The window revealed the sleeping part of the bunkhouse, with several bunkbeds in view. One was pushed into a corner. On the top bunk, a young woman sat with her back tucked against the right angle formed by two walls. Her knees were pulled up against her chest, and her arms were wrapped around her shins, as if she were trying to make herself as tiny as possible. She wore jeans and a sweater, and her hair was pulled up into a bun that had started to sag.

It was Nicole. I wasn't sure how I could be so positive without even seeing her face, but in my gut, I was sure.

I tapped a nail softly on the glass, and she looked up, her eyes wide with alarm. It was definitely her. I put the side of my index finger against my lips, warning her to be quiet. Like the other skylight, this one was also in disrepair. I pulled my karambit knife from its pocket on my scabbard strap and worked the point of it under the shingles that overlapped the skylight frame. Working quickly, I popped the shingles off one end of the frame and then pried up the edge of it a couple of inches.

I put my mouth next to the open space. "Nicole?" I whispered.

Her alarm morphed into confusion. "Yes?"

"I'm here to bust you out," I whispered. "My name's Petra Maguire."

The fear returned, this time mixed with suspicion. "You're one of them, aren't you? The Fae? You're all crazy. It's like I've fallen down the rabbit hole."

I could understand her confusion, but I didn't have time to convince her that it was all real, that she was, in fact, a New Garg changeling kidnapped by a Duergar Fae king and whisked away to Faerie.

"Be that as it may, I'm trying to save you. Maybe we could just focus on that for now?" I was working my knife around, prying more shingles off the skylight's frame. "You didn't swear fealty to Periclase, did you?"

"What? No! I've never *sworn fealty* to anyone in my life," she said it as if it was something I'd made up.

"Good."

"How do I know you're not just going to kidnap me, too?" she demanded.

I grunted as I pushed at the frame, forcing the opening wider. "You don't."

"Someone's coming," Nichole hissed. "And I'm going to tell them you're up there."

She scrambled to the edge of the bed and dropped her legs over the side, poised to jump down to the floor.

"Nicole, wait, don't do that!" I hissed back. "I'm your sister. Our father sent me."

Her mouth dropped open. She squinted at me.

"Give me your hand!" I shoved the skylight higher and leaned over, reaching through as far as I dared without falling into the bunkhouse.

She gave me a hard stare for a split second, and for the briefest of moments, I thought she'd refuse. But then her eyes widened almost imperceptibly, and she rose to her feet on the mattress of the top bunk. On her tiptoes, she grasped my hand with both of hers. I planted my feet and hauled back for all I was worth, dragging my long-lost changeling twin up into the night with me.

Chapter 18

NICOLE WAS LIGHT for a New Gargoyle, seemingly with none of my muscled density. She probably had about three inches on me, and by the way her form-fitting clothes looked, she was toned but slim. Runner, I guessed, as my mind processed about a dozen things at once.

There was some unavoidable noise as she scrambled through the skylight. I jumped back just as guards entered the room below, but I didn't have time to get the skylight back into place. They'd notice it any second.

"C'mon," I said to Nicole and then carefully ran across the roof to the end where I'd come up.

No easy way to climb down, with the drainpipe laying on the ground below.

"Hang off the edge to shorten the drop," I said hurriedly. "Watch what I do."

I swung my body off the roof, hanging briefly with my fingers curled over the edge of the gutter, and then let go. It was a fall that would have likely injured a human, but I landed in a crouch and then sprang up, ready to steady Nicole.

She sailed to the dirt and landed hard, touching down with both hands to catch herself, but thankfully she hadn't seemed to injure anything. Probably her latent New Garg blood that gave her bones extra strength. We ran for the cover of the forest, but by the shouts behind us, we'd been seen.

I zagged through the trees with Nicole on my heels, heading away from the bunkhouse. Suddenly something solid and very tall loomed ahead. A wall.

"Oh, damn," I ground out. I hadn't realized the palace grounds were walled on this side. I could already hear guards crashing through the forest to the left, cutting off the route back to the doorway I'd used to come here. "Okay, new plan."

I veered to the right. The doorway I'd come in through was way too far away. We were going to have to head back toward the palace. Keeping to the forest, we crashed through the brush. We were loud, but the guards were louder. I scanned the area ahead and picked the darkest point along the palace wall to aim for and then hoped to Oberon we'd find an unlocked door to slip through. Even clomping along behind us as they were, the guards would be able to tell which way we'd gone by the footprints and broken twigs we left behind.

Nicole seemed to have little trouble keeping up with me. Maybe I'd guessed right about the running.

We were close enough to the palace that I could see there was one door in the most shadowed area. Panting, I grasped the thumb-lever handle, squeezed it, and yanked back. It didn't budge. I forced more weight on the lever, but it stubbornly refused to release. Nicole continued on, looking for another way in.

"What about this?" Nicole asked. She pointed at a large grated vent about two feet square.

The guards would clear the tree line in a matter of seconds.

I knelt down in front of the metal grate, stuck my fingers through the lattice, and yanked back. Warm air blew across my face as the vent cover sprang from its frame.

"Get in," I said, keeping the grate in one hand.

She ducked inside, and I tucked in after her, pulling the grate back in place. After making sure it was secure, I shouldered past her to try to look into the vent tunnel, but it was pitch black.

"Let's go a little deeper, and then I'll get us some light," I whispered.

The shouts of the men outside had grown loud. They were passing right by where we'd escaped into the vent.

Moving in a crouch, I kept one hand lightly trailing the wall as I walked two dozen paces into almost complete darkness.

"Stay there," I said. "I need a little space."

I moved a few more steps away and then knelt on one knee so I had enough room to draw Mort. I pulled power and sent it into the sword to mingle with the blood magic it contained. A faint purple flame wrapped around the blade, giving us a bit of illumination.

Nicole was staring at Mort, blinking rapidly as if trying to be sure of what she saw. She sent a dazed look past me, peering deeper into the tunnel.

"Smells like the lint trap in my dryer," she said faintly.

She was right.

"Laundry," I said. "Good. We need to make it to the laundry room."

We continued, turning left to follow the tunnel.

"Why did you say you were my sister back there?" Nicole's whispered words floated up to me.

"Supposedly I am," I said. "That's one of the reasons I was picked to come get you."

"Who sent you?"

"My father—our father—Oliver Maguire."

"You said 'supposedly.' If you don't believe I'm your sister, why did you come for me?" she asked.

I glanced back at her over my shoulder for a second, but she was hunched over with her eyes on the ground.

"I do believe it," I said, realizing that it hadn't seemed real before, but now it did. "It was just kind of a shock, is all."

"I don't believe it," she said bluntly, her tone harder than before.

I snorted a rueful laugh. "I don't blame you."

"I'm not a Fae."

"We'll find out soon enough," I said.

The air grew warmer and more fragrant with the scent of clean laundry. The sheet metal under our feet was rumbling with the vibrations of machines nearby. We were moving past smaller inlets into the main venting artery, each of them blowing hot air against our legs as we passed.

I stopped and released my magic and angled my body so I could sheath Mort. There was light up ahead, enough to see by. The tunnel let out through a downward chute. We'd reached the end of the line.

I lay down on my stomach and peered over the edge. About three feet of conduit straight down and another grate below. Basement laundry facility. There were voices, but not many. Unfortunately, the grate was out of reach, so I couldn't try to pry it up. It looked as if it was affixed to the outer lip, anyway, which would have made it impossible to pull it inward.

Directly under the grate, there was a table with stacks of folded linens. At least we'd have a soft landing.

I waited until the room below was quiet, then shifted so my legs were dangling over the edge, and pushed off. Keeping my knees stiff and my body straight, I busted out the grate and landed on top of it and the laundry below. I scrambled in the linens as the piles toppled over, trying to scan the entire room and keep from falling uncontrollably. I rolled off the edge of the table and landed on my feet in a defensive stance, Mort already in my hand.

There was a woman across the room, standing at a rack with a steamer in one hand, but her back was turned, and she hadn't heard my descent over the loud hum of machinery. I looked up into the conduit to see Nicole's face peering down at me. I beckoned her to come down, and a split second later the grate, which rested on a precariously tipping pile of towels, began to shift. My eyes popped wide as I dove for it, but I was too late. The heavy metal lattice slid off the other edge of the table and clattered to the floor—not loudly, but with enough noise to draw attention.

The woman at the steamer stiffened and spun around, and I ducked down behind the counter. The area below the countertop was all cabinetry, so I couldn't see through to track her position. Footsteps approached, and then they stopped.

"What . . ." I heard her murmur, probably as she took in the upset piles of linens.

Some movement above caught my eye. Nicole was coming down. In the whooshing air of the duct, she probably hadn't heard the noise the grate had made. I signaled frantically, but she was positioned feet-down, ready to drop.

"Hey, Clara, can you come and help me clean up this—" the laundry woman started to holler but cut off with a squeak as Nicole dropped from above and landed on the counter.

I popped up to my feet, and the woman squeaked again, her eyes going wide and her fingers flying to her mouth.

"Party game," I said with a bright smile. Realizing I was still brandishing Mort, I lowered my sword to my side. "We're playing hide-and-seek."

The woman's eyes narrowed.

Nicole jumped down to the floor, and I grabbed her wrist.

"Let's get the hell out of here," I muttered.

Pulling Nicole along, I skirted the counter, hurried past the woman, and ran for the doorway. It led to an adjoining room with more dryers and folding counters. Half a dozen workers were busy at their tasks. A few noticed us and paused in surprise. I stopped short. There were more doorways that appeared to lead to more laundry rooms.

"See an exit?" I asked Nicole.

She pointed. "There?"

A door was swinging open, and a man pushing a cart full of white sheets was halfway into the room.

I ran for the door, yanked his cart from his hands and out of the way, and burst past him and out into the corridor.

"Petra, guards!" Nicole said behind me.

I swung my gaze to the right. There were two men barreling at us.

"Guess we go this way," I said, sprinting to the left.

As we ran, I realized I knew where we were—not far from the guest quarters—and a new plan came to life in my mind. If we could get back to my room, we might be able to disappear into one of the secret channels I'd discovered in the walls. We'd just have to elude the guards long enough to reach a doorway and get out of the Duergar realm.

Going from memory, I took Nicole up a flight of stairs and through the turns that would lead us to the courtyard below the rooms assigned to the New Gargoyle visiting party. We were running hard, and we outpaced the lumbering, armored men chasing us. Just as we took the final left turn leading to a short hallway that opened into the courtyard, a broad-shouldered figure with a short sword at his side stepped into our way ahead. I skidded to a halt, ready to backpedal, but then realized I knew who it was.

"Petra?" called the man with the ever-casual voice.

Knowing I couldn't go back the way we'd come, I jogged up to him.

"Jasper, I don't know what you've heard, but I need to get out of here," I said, speaking rapidly. "Periclase was holding this woman against her will. She's a New Gargoyle changeling."

His gold eyes flicked to Nicole and then behind us as the sounds of our pursuers grew louder.

I knew it was fruitless—I was asking him to defy his own father and sovereign—but at that point I wasn't above begging.

"Please, let us go, and I will owe you," I said quietly and urgently. "This I swear."

Something in the air seemed to crystalize as a potential oath hung between us.

He hesitated only a second. "Okay." Then he turned. "Come with me."

I barely noticed the faint tingle of magic in the air that formed a binding oath between us.

Jasper led us across the dim courtyard on a diagonal, but instead of taking us to another corridor, he stopped before a large willow tree. Reaching several inches above his head, he slammed the side of his fist on a knot in the wood where it looked like a branch had been cut off long ago. A section of bark popped away at the base of the tree. He reached down to lift it, revealing a hatch.

"Straight down and then straight ahead," he said hurriedly. "It empties out on the road you came in on with your party."

"Thank you," I breathed, and with those two words, I further sealed the favor I owed him.

I ducked under the panel and dropped down into the dark hole, not knowing how far the fall was. I thumped down awkwardly and rolled out of the way just as Nicole landed with a grunt. Drawing Mort and using magic to light the way, I ran into the narrow tunnel carved into the dirt. It was barely wider than my shoulders, and small pale roots snaked into the space from the hard-packed walls and ceiling.

My sister pounded along right behind me, until it seemed as if the tunnel would go on forever. But eventually it began to slope upward. We reached the end, with barely enough room for me to stand without hitting my head. Directly above there was a two-foot diameter hole in the dirt with a flat, rocky surface covering it. I tipped Mort against the wall and then reached up, flattened my palms, and pushed. It didn't budge. Bracing my feet more solidly, I tried again. Still no movement.

Taking a different tack, I fitted my fingers into shallow grooves and slid it instead. The slab of rock moved aside, and the night breeze washed over my face as I looked up into a canopy of tree branches and the starry sky beyond.

Chapter 19

WE FOUND OURSELVES about a third of the way down the dirt road to the clearing where I'd come into the Duergar realm earlier that day, and about twenty feet off to the side in the brush.

"Wait here," I said to Nicole, who stood panting next to me.

I went to a tree near the edge of the road and peered around it to see if anyone was pursuing us from the direction of the palace. Seeing that the road that way was empty and quiet, I let out a long breath.

I was just about to return to Nicole and suggest we make a break for it and go hard down the road, rather than keeping to the cover of the forest on either side, when I caught sight of a lone figure hurrying up the road toward us from the other direction.

I stood where I was, watching. By the light of the moon and the stars, I saw it was a woman. Something about her looked familiar. Right about the time I realized she was going to veer off the road to come my way, possibly to use the tunnel Nicole and I had just exited, I recognized her.

"Well, well, look what we have here," I murmured to myself, feeling like a cat watching an unobservant mouse.

It was Bryna, King Periclase's bastard daughter who'd sent the wraith after me, blocking me from capturing my mark.

I quietly drew Mort and then kept stone-still as I waited for Bryna to pick her way over the uneven ground. She was still in her cocktail gown and heels, so she had to go slowly. When she got within a few feet from where I stood, I stepped into her path and drew magic to light up Mort with violet flame.

"Whatcha doing out all alone, Bryna?" I growled.

I'd clearly surprised her, but she moved with unexpected quickness, and two knives appeared in her hands. She flipped one at me, and I barely dodged it, feeling the metal whir past my ear. I saw the second one coming and used Mort to deflect it. She threw two more knives, and then realizing she was out of weapons, she turned and tried to run away. I was on her in a blink, with my hand clamped around her slim upper arm.

"Not so fast," I said.

"If you harm me, King Periclase will have you executed," she spat out.

I snorted. "I doubt that. He doesn't even claim you as an official member of the royal family."

That really pissed her off. She swung out with her elbows, trying to jab me in the ribs and twist out of my grasp. With snake-quick movements, I got her in a one-armed chokehold and pulled her backward a few steps. The combo of pressure on the airway and being yanked off-balance sends most people into a mild panic.

But I'd slightly underestimated her. Keeping her cool, she turned and slipped down and out of my hold. She kneed me in the solar plexus, and I let out a grunt, bent at the middle, and sucked air. Her movements were strong and practiced. If she hadn't been wearing a dress and heels, she might have been a decent opponent in hand-to-hand combat. She tried to dart away, but I was faster.

I stomped a foot on the back of her gown that trailed on the ground. Fabric tore but didn't break free. It stopped her in her tracks for the split-second I needed to snake my arm around her neck again and pull her back against me.

"You're not going anywhere," I hissed in her ear.

I squeezed her throat and lifted Mort, bringing the blade close enough to the side of her neck that my magic licked at her skin, making tiny papercut-like slices.

She scoffed. "You're not going to kill me," she choked out.

"Not yet," I said. "Not while I still need you."

She tried to claw at my arm and twist away again. I nicked the side of her neck with my blade, and she inhaled sharply and went still.

Bryna swallowed with a dry click of her throat. "What do you want?" she asked.

"A binding promise. I want you to take me to Van Zant."

I wanted her punished for her violation of the netherwhere, but I'd survived that ordeal and could take it up again later if I felt the need. Right now, there was a vamp dealing deadly blood, and I wanted him off the streets so he couldn't endanger any more innocent people.

She started struggling again, and we fell to the ground together in a tangle. A dumb move on her part. I could have easily sliced her neck by accident.

"Oh for the—" I grumbled.

I leaned back to make a little space, lifted my sword, and smacked the flat of the blade against the side of her head, as if swatting a fly. Bryna went down in a heap.

I heard Nicole gasp behind me. "Oh my god, is she dead?"

I pressed my fingers to Bryna's carotid artery and felt a faint thump of pulse. "Nah, she'll be fine."

I quickly released my magic, sheathed Mort, and then hauled Bryna's limp body up and over my shoulder.

"We need to go before the guards think to come looking for us out here," I said.

I trotted out to the road and went at a fast clip toward the clearing. Nicole jogged along beside me.

"Who is this girl?" she asked.

"The illegitimate daughter of the man who kidnapped you," I said. "And she's the wench who sent a wraith to kill me."

"And who's the Van Zant person you mentioned?"

"My mark. He's a vamp."

"Mark?"

"I'm a freelancer with the Mercenary Guild," I explained. "Van Zant is a bounty I'm supposed to bring in. He's been a real slippery bastard. Bryna's working with him."

I glanced at Nicole. She shot worried looks at the limp girl I carried over my shoulder.

"Don't get too sympathetic," I said. "Aside from trying to murder me, she's working with a man who's selling VAMP3 blood on the black market. It turns people into murderers after a couple of highs. If Van Zant hasn't already been responsible for the deaths of innocent people, it's only a matter of time, and Bryna's trying to protect him."

"Oh," she said. "I've heard of the Guild. I didn't know about the VAMP3 blood."

We'd reached the edge of the clearing.

"There's a doorway over there," I said, nodding at a very old-looking stone arch. "It's a sort of magical portal that connects to other doorways. The three of us are going into it."

"Are you taking me back home?"

I shook my head. "We're going to the stone fortress. It's the home base for the New Gargoyle Fae."

Her brows drew down in anger, and she flicked a look back up the road. Her muscles tensed as if she were ready to spring away.

"My advice is not to run," I said, my tone heavy with warning. I really wasn't in the mood to dump Bryna to chase after Nicole. Carrying two unconscious women into the New Gargoyle stronghold, especially when one was technically one of us, would raise the kind of attention I didn't enjoy. "You're King Periclase's captive here, and Unseelie territory isn't a safe place for a changeling. It's not a particularly safe place for *anyone*. At the stone fortress, you won't be a prisoner. You're one of us, there."

Her mouth tightened into an unhappy line, but she unclenched her fists and her shoulders slumped in a posture of defeat.

I wasn't being quite a hundred percent forthcoming with her. She wouldn't be a prisoner at the fortress, that much was true, but she also wouldn't be allowed to leave right away. Once a changeling was brought into Faerie, there was a protocol to follow. It involved staying on this side of the hedge for a certain length of time before any other decisions could be made. I didn't think Nicole was in the right frame of mind for that news. But it didn't matter, anyway. We couldn't just set her free in the Earthly realm because Periclase would kidnap her again. And the next time, he'd probably make it a hell of a lot harder to bust her out.

We went up to the arch, and I shifted Bryna's weight so I had one hand free to trace the sigils in the air.

"Hold onto my arm or my shoulder," I said to Nicole. "You've got to be in contact with me to go through the doorway, since you don't know how to do it by yourself. It'll all be over in a second, so just try to relax."

She gripped my forearm that was clamped over Bryna's legs so hard I was pretty sure Nicole would leave indentations in my skin. I didn't blame her. The doorways were some freaky shit, even when you were used to them.

I drew the symbols and said the magic words, and we stepped through into the void.

We entered the stone fortress through a doorway that was near some administrative offices.

Nicole spun around, slipping a little on the marble floor. Her eyes were huge and wild, and her chest was heaving. She was on the verge of hyperventilation.

"Hey," I said softly. "It's okay. Take a breath. You made it, and you're still in one piece."

She cast me an accusing look. "Why didn't you *tell* me it was like that?"

"Would you still have gone through?"

She pressed her lips together and looked away, clearly angry. But at least her panic was subsiding.

I hiked Bryna higher on my shoulder. "Come with me to get rid of her, and then we'll get you some food and a place to rest."

It was late enough that most New Gargs were in bed at this hour, and during the short walk to the fortress holding cells, we didn't encounter anyone.

The guy on duty at intake was young, and he drew back a little when he saw me come in with a limp body slung over my shoulder.

"You want her locked up?" he asked, giving us the side-eye.

"Yep."

"Charges?" He was already tapping and swiping away at his tablet.

"She tried to kill me in the netherwhere," I said.

That made him pause. He flicked another look at Bryna.

By Faerie law, I could have her held for a day as long as the charges met certain requirements. Attempted murder definitely made the list.

"Accuser is Petra Maguire, by the way," I said.

I glanced at the nameplate—Patrick.

He spent another minute or so filling in the paperwork on the tablet and then held it out for me to sign with my finger.

"Where should I put her?" I asked.

"I need to scan her for charms first," he said.

He quickly waved a slim divining rod over Bryna, finding a ring, a necklace, a hair clip, and a brooch that were charmed. He removed all of them.

He beckoned me around the counter to the door that led to the cells and held it open for me. The lockups were all empty, their doors standing partway open down either side of the hallway. He gestured to the first cell.

I went in and dumped Bryna on the bed, which was little more than a metal pallet with a thin mattress, and Patrick closed the door and traced the sigils that sealed Bryna inside.

"I'll be back in the morning to speak with her," I said. I still needed her to get me to Van Zant.

As Nicole and I left the fortress jail, I rolled my shoulder, trying to work out the tightness and fatigue from carrying Bryna.

Nicole walked almost tentatively, swiveling her head around as if trying to look everywhere at once.

"This place is absolutely beautiful," she said quietly.

I glanced around. She was right. I often took it for granted, having grown up here, but the natural marble and other stonework throughout the fortress were exquisite.

"You can use my old room tonight," I said. "Tomorrow we'll look into getting you your own permanent quarters."

I winced as soon as the word "permanent" left my mouth.

"Why would I need my own quarters?" she said, her alarm echoing off the walls. "I don't need my own quarters here."

I waved a hand. "Oh, just so you have your own space," I said vaguely.

Eventually Nicole would have the option to go back to the other side of the hedge and renounce Faerie forever. Right then, given the choice, she certainly would. That was why the homecoming of a changeling was a process. And at the end of the process, changelings hardly ever turned their backs on their true home. It took some time, but being in Faerie seemed to unlock something buried deep within their souls, surfacing a knowledge that they didn't fully belong to the human race. It was a matter of uncovering something they'd always had but hadn't been fully aware of.

But for the moment, the fortress was the safest place for Nicole. If she went back to the Earthly realm while Periclase was still hot on the idea that she was a valuable Duergar princess, he'd have her kidnapped again. That, at least, had to be resolved. One way to settle it would be to find out that Nicole wasn't his blood daughter. Another would be to have her swear to the Stone Order.

As we walked through the hallways, I began to sense Nicole's exhaustion. Her adrenaline was probably long gone, and it was after midnight. But we had one more stop to make before I could let her rest.

When we reached Oliver's door, I knocked sharply three times. I half-expected him to be asleep, but I should have known better. He was one of those people who seemed eternally on alert. Even when I was a kid, I never remembered him being in bed. He'd always turned in after I did and rose before my alarm.

After a few seconds, I heard movement behind the door, and then it opened.

"This is Nicole," I said to him. I turned to my sister. "Nicole, this is your father, Oliver Maguire."

He blinked at her a couple of times, and his brows lifted maybe a hair, which was the equivalent of a dramatic gasp coming from anyone else. Then he swung the door wider, silently inviting us in.

As I passed him, he nodded at me. A rare expression of approval. I'd completed the task he'd given me.

"I had to tell her we're sisters," I said to him in a low voice. "She didn't want to come with me."

Oliver's eyes tightened, but he didn't say anything.

Nicole had moved into the middle of the room and was watching him, her face suspicious. It was obvious she still didn't believe she was related to me and Oliver.

He gave her an appraising once-over. "You're quite old for a changeling. Did you ever have any inkling you were Fae?"

This was a standard part of the questions she'd be answering more formally later.

She folded her arms. "None whatsoever, and I still don't." But then her brow furrowed, and she seemed to turn inward. Her face became uncertain. "If I did, I'd feel some kind of connection or . . . *known* something. Even if it was just in a dream. Right?"

Oliver's eyes gleamed a little. The fact that she was even asking, and especially the mention of dreams, meant that there was something tickling at the back of her mind. She didn't realize it yet, or if she did, she didn't want to examine it.

He tilted his head, regarding her. "Not necessarily. Especially if you're dead set against the idea." He glanced at me. "She doesn't look at all like a New Garg."

"What's that supposed to mean?" Nicole demanded.

I peered at her. I hadn't thought about it before, but Oliver was right. She didn't have the strong build or the musculature that were the hallmarks of New Garg Fae. She didn't even resemble me in particularly obvious ways. We had similar coloring and straight brows, our eyes were the same tawny color, and perhaps we had the same curve of the chin, but that was about it.

Was that why Nicole had been chosen to go to the Earthly realm and grow up as human? A simple twist of fate which gave her an appearance that would more likely fit in with human parents? I couldn't imagine not growing up Fae. Having an ordinary human life, and like the humans surrounding me, having only the vaguest awareness of Faerie. I was New Garg born and raised, even if I preferred to live and work on the other side of the hedge. My magic. The years I'd spent training with weapons. My stone armor. My shadowsteel spellblade. My very personality. They were all inherent to my identity and molded by being Fae. I couldn't imagine any alternate Petra Maguire that could exist without them.

"It just means that your—our—other blood, the part that isn't New Gargoyle, is probably more dominant in you," I said, trying to speak gently to offset some of Oliver's bluntness.

I flicked a glance at him out of the corners of my eyes. Had he been the one to choose Nicole to leave Faerie and keep me? Or had it been my mother's decision?

She sighed, slumping a little, and shook her head slowly. "I don't know what any of that means." She sounded near tears.

Oliver shifted a little.

"Why don't we let her get some sleep?" I suggested.

I thought I saw relief flash in his eyes. "Yes, it's late."

Then Oliver's face hardened, and I knew something serious was coming.

"There is one vital thing you must understand," he said, his eyes serious and his voice commanding. "You cannot, under any circumstances, reveal that you're Petra's sister or my daughter. As far as anyone else is concerned, you're a New Gargoyle changeling of unknown parentage."

She drew back a little, her eyes widening.

"Do you understand?" he asked.

She blinked and then nodded vigorously. "Yes, I won't tell anyone. I promise."

Magic tingled the air, marking the oath. He dipped his chin once, and as she turned for the door, he reached out and touched her shoulder gently, almost tentatively.

"This is a lot to take in," he said, his voice much softer than before. "It's a process, and this is just the start. Welcome home, Nicole."

I tried not to stare at him. I wasn't sure I'd ever heard him speak that way.

Nicole's lips parted, and her eyes misted with tears. Something was beginning to break within her, the barrier across a natural knowing, the mental and emotional homecoming that all changelings eventually experienced when they finally came to Faerie. But she ducked her head before her emotions could visibly develop any more.

I took her to my quarters, a sparse, tiny, little-used suite that was assigned to me. Everyone who was sworn to the Stone Order had a room in the fortress, even if they lived on the other side of the hedge like I did. It was partly for a sense of community, but also for emergencies. If the sovereignty of the Order or the fortress itself were threatened, Marisol could call in every New Gargoyle and not have to worry about where to house all of us. I suppose many people would have seen my fortress quarters as a great safety net in case my life on the other side of the hedge ran aground. But to me, living in the studio apartment would be worse than moving back into your parents' basement. My fortress quarters represented the most serious failure I could imagine— breaking promises I'd made to dedicate my life to honoring my mother by getting criminal vamps off the street. My fortress quarters also represented confinement. It was a cell in a literal jail of a building, and with it came full-time obligations to Marisol and the Order.

I told Nicole to make herself comfortable and use any of the things she found in the apartment, and she headed straight back to the bedroom. I quietly let myself out and returned to Oliver's apartment. He was waiting for me, as I knew he would be. This time, we both sat down—him on the one easy chair and me sprawled on the floor.

As I took off my scabbard and laid it down next to me, weariness began to settle deep in my bones. Oliver sat with one ankle crossed over the other knee, and his hands clasped across his stomach. I hadn't noticed it before, but his eyes were sunken and lines had settled around them. He looked every bit as tired as I felt.

"I'm still wrapping my head around all of this. Are you absolutely sure she's my sister?" I asked. "We don't look much alike, and as you said, she doesn't have New Garg features."

His face tightened slightly. "She is certainly your sister. I was there when the two of you were born. Did you have any trouble from the Duergar?"

"Technically, I was kicked out of the realm before I got a chance to grab Nicole," I said. I knew from a lifetime with my father that Oliver didn't want to hear about heroics, and he couldn't stand braggarts, so I kept it as brief as possible. "I got back in, found Nicole, and long story short, we escaped."

I licked my lips, my eyes flicking to Oliver and then away, as I remembered a little detail I'd thus far left out. The part about how Jasper had helped us escape, and as a result, there was a binding oath between us.

My father immediately recognized the look on my face. "What?" he demanded.

"One of Periclase's sons helped us get out," I said. "I owe him, now."

He'd gone tense at my confession but then relaxed slightly.

"You did what you had to do, and the oath can't be undone," he said. "You'll have to worry about that when the time comes."

He sounded annoyed, but not as pissed as I'd expected.

I was just about to change the subject and tell him about the servitor attack in the Duergar palace when there was a series of sharp, loud knocks at the door that seemed to pierce through the quiet of the apartment.

Oliver stood and strode to see who was there.

Sensing something was amiss, I rose to my feet. A page stood at the door, and his eyes were wide.

"An urgent message for you, my lord," the page said. He squinted at me, shooting me a snippy look, as if he were irritated to find me there. "I was instructed to wait while you read it."

He handed my father an envelope sealed with magic-imbued wax that would only give way under the hand of the intended recipient. If anyone else tried to open it, the whole thing would immediately incinerate. I recognized the color of the wax—Marisol's seal.

Oliver tore into the message and quickly read it. "Tell Lady Lothlorien I'll be right there."

With his back to me, I couldn't read his face, but his voice was as strained as I'd ever heard it.

He shut the door and turned to me. "King Periclase has made a formal appeal to the High Seelie King Oberon, demanding that we return Nicole to him. He's claiming that Nicole is his daughter."

Chapter 20

I BLINKED TWO or three times, unable to form a proper response, just watching Oliver as he swiftly walked into his bedroom and then emerged half a minute later wearing trousers and one of his official fortress military jackets.

"What are we going to do?" I asked finally.

"I'm not sure yet," my father said grimly. He flipped his hand. "Come with me."

I scooped up my scabbard and slung it over my head, positioning it as we hurried out of Oliver's quarters and toward the wing that housed the offices of high-ranking New Gargoyle administrators.

An official appeal to Oberon was serious. It meant Periclase wasn't bluffing. He truly thought he was Nicole's father . . . and, by extension, *my* father.

My feet stuttered as my mind reeled. I didn't realize I'd stopped until I felt Oliver's hand on my elbow.

"Periclase knows I'm Nicole's sister," I said faintly as I tried to catch my breath. "He believes he's my father."

"Shh," Oliver hissed at me. He pulled me close to speak in my ear. "He does not know you're Nicole's sister. And if he thinks he's Nicole's father, that means he believes he knows who her mother is. No one knows who *your* mother is. You've still got two layers of protection here."

He waited with surprising patience as the seconds ticked by, watching my face.

I swallowed. "Okay. Yes. He doesn't know I'm Nicole's sister. And no one knows my parentage on my mother's side."

Including me.

"Right," Oliver said. "That means Periclase can't make the connection between you and Nicole. You, Nicole, and I are the only ones who know the two of you are sisters."

"Lochlyn, too," I said. "But you know I trust her. She even insisted on swearing an oath not to tell."

The tangled web of secrets and accusations was enough to make my brain freeze up. But I understood the logic of what my father said, and that brought me some ease.

Still, as we continued to Marisol's office, my thoughts went back to Periclase's appeal and the fact that he was confident enough to tender such a request to the High King of Faerie. I couldn't quite fathom a world where the Duergar king was my father. It was just . . . absurd. And awful. Because if by some stroke of insanity he *was* my father, that meant Oliver wasn't. I stopped that train of thought right there.

I replayed what Oliver had always told me. His relationship with my mother had been brief, and he hadn't even known she was pregnant until shortly before she gave birth. She died not long after I was born. It all happened during the turbulent period after the Cataclysm, in which there was massive upheaval in Faerie as well as across the entire supernatural world. I was trying to reassure myself, but it wasn't working very well. There were an awful lot of gaps in Oliver's story.

When we neared Marisol's office, the page who'd delivered the message was waiting outside the closed door.

Oliver slowed, and I did the same. He leaned in close to speak in my ear. "If she wants to know why I brought you, it's because you're the one who rescued Nicole. Don't offer up any information unless she asks, and if you do have to answer any questions, keep it brief."

I gave a slight nod, and then we continued on.

"Lady Lothlorien wants to see you alone," the page said to Oliver. Then with a narrowing of his eyes he turned his gaze to me. "She'll have to wait in the anteroom."

Oliver brushed past the page, who went into the small sitting room outside of Marisol's office. I caught a brief glimpse of the Lady of the stone fortress as she let Oliver in. Her eyes flicked to me. Her grim expression didn't change.

The page stayed in the room with me with a look on his face like he expected me to try to swipe one of the crystal candlesticks from the mantle.

"I don't need a babysitter," I said.

"Nevertheless, I'll stay." He crossed his arms. "Lady Lothlorien wouldn't appreciate any eavesdropping from an uninvited visitor."

He placed a not-so-subtle emphasis on the word "uninvited."

"Eavesdropping? What is this, Unseelie court?" I scoffed. "I'm not trying to *eavesdrop.*"

I turned away from the page and briefly pushed the heels of my hands into my tired eyes. I wasn't even sure why I was engaging with him. It wasn't the type of thing I would normally do, but I was drained and on edge.

A moment later, the inner door to Marisol's office opened, and Oliver beckoned me inside.

Marisol was seated behind her desk, and she briefly closed her eyes and rubbed one temple with her fingertips before folding her hands on her desk and pinning me with her gaze.

"How is the girl doing?" she asked.

"She's quite shaken. It looked like she hadn't been captive on the Duergar palace grounds for long, and I think she's still in shock," I hesitated. "And, Nicole is very old for a changeling."

Marisol's forehead lined with concern. "How old?"

I shrugged a shoulder. "I didn't ask her, but she's about my age," choosing my words carefully.

I could almost sense Oliver tensing beside me.

She let out a breath. "Oh, that is *quite* old for a homecoming. Probably one of the oldest ever in Faerie. It will make the transition much more difficult."

Marisol's concern was almost maternal, but she spoke as if Nicole had already made the decision to swear to the Stone Order. That wasn't necessarily how things would play out. Nicole would be given a choice, after the requisite time period. If she chose not to swear fealty to a kingdom or the Order, she would never be allowed to return to Faerie, and she'd lose any magic she might have developed. If she did swear, she could live in Faerie or on the other side like me, but she'd be obligated to the kingdom she was sworn to just as I was obligated to the Stone Order. Nineteen times out of twenty with changelings, they chose to swear to a kingdom and embrace their Fae heritage. The one out of twenty? Those were almost always older changelings. And to us, "older" meant anyone over seventeen.

Marisol would be doing everything possible to make sure Nicole decided to become one of us in a permanent sense. Marisol needed numbers in the Order.

But first we had to contend with King Periclase's accusation.

"We need to get her magic working," Marisol said. "It will help us tremendously if she's able to demonstrate stone armor. I'll get her working with Fern right away."

Marisol made a few taps and swipes on the tablet next to her elbow.

"That's not going to prove she isn't Periclase's daughter, though," Oliver said.

"True, but without a demonstration of New Garg abilities, we have no way of claiming she's one of us," Marisol said. "And on the chance that she *is* Periclase's daughter, if she can form stone armor she can still swear fealty to the Stone Order."

Discovery of parentage worked a little differently in Faerie than on the other side of the hedge. In the human world, a simple blood test for maternity or paternity would settle questions like this one. Those tests didn't work on Fae. There *was* a magic-based test, but the only person who could perform it was nearly impossible to reach and even more difficult to persuade into actually doing it—and trying to do so was taking your life into your hands. Melusine was one of the Old Ones like Oberon, and one of very few living Fae witches, a woman with full Fae magic and full human magic.

Marisol shifted her blue gemstone eyes to me. "You will keep in contact with Nicole. It will help her to have someone around her age who's spent so much time in the Earthly realm to talk to. Plus, you're the one who rescued her."

My lips parted. It was an order from my sovereign, and I couldn't refuse it. "Of course. But there's another small matter I need to attend to immediately."

"Oh?"

I tried not to wince as I spoke. "There's a woman in our jail under my accusation. I need to question her. She's, uh, Periclase's bastard daughter."

Again, the pursed-lip look from Marisol.

"What's the charge?" she asked.

"Attempted murder. In the netherwhere."

Marisol's entire face and upper body went rigid. "She did *what?*"

"Bryna, unclaimed bastard daughter of King Periclase, sent a wraith to kill me while I was in the void," I said. "I later killed her wraith. Or destroyed it. Whatever it is you do to end wraiths."

Oliver shot me a look, and I shut up, belatedly remembering his warning to keep my answers short. I also realized he hadn't known anything about Bryna and the wraith.

Marisol took a noisy breath in through her nose. "Well, that's not going to help any negotiations with the Duergar, but that's a very serious crime. Do you plan to pursue it in the High Court?"

I managed not to snort. For the love of Oberon, *no*. Some torturously lengthy Faerie legal process was the last thing I wanted to waste my time on.

I shook my head. "Not if I can get the information I need out of her. It's related to a Guild assignment."

"Good," she said, nodding. "Your mercy in this case will make us appear generous."

I tamped down my annoyance. Everything always had to be political with Marisol. I held a neutral expression and gave a tiny inclination of my head, knowing I had to play along.

"If you can conclude your business and release her before the twenty-four-hour deadline, that would benefit the situation even more," she said.

"I will make every effort to do that. Especially knowing how much it could help our cause." I thought I managed to say it without any irony, but she gave me a look that was half-stern and half-amused.

"Finish your Guild business with Bryna and your assignment by one tomorrow afternoon." Marisol paused and glanced at her tablet. "Technically, that's *this* afternoon. Then report back here. I want you to keep close to our new changeling while she's early in her homecoming."

Irritation spiked through me again, more strongly than before. But I couldn't refuse an order that came directly from the sovereign to whom I was sworn, and this was very much an order despite the informal tag she put on it.

I had no choice. I was going to have to get Bryna to tell me where to find Van Zant, bring the vamp in for the bounty, and get back to the stone fortress. And I had less than a day to do it.

Chapter 21

I ENDED UP crashing on the sofa in my stone fortress quarters so I wouldn't have to waste any time getting back here to turn the screws on Bryna. I didn't particularly want to sleep, but I was going to turn into a stumbling mess if I didn't get at least a couple of hours of shut-eye. The door to the bedroom was closed, and as far as I could tell, Nicole didn't even know I'd come in.

Early the next morning, before I went into the bathroom for a speed shower, I called fortress food service for breakfast delivery and charged it to Nicole. I wasn't a resident of the fortress, so I didn't have the right to many of the services. I thought the person on the other end might push back, but word of Nicole's presence must have spread. Then I had to go into the bedroom for a clean shirt. My sister was curled up on her side under the covers, facing away from me.

"Nicole?" I whispered.

I had the sense that she was awake, but she didn't respond, so I let her be.

The food arrived right as I finished dressing, but it wasn't for me—I'd never been much of a breakfast person, and I'd grabbed a sandwich from Oliver's fridge before I went to sleep. I was still a little bitter I'd missed out on the fancy Duergar court dinner, after all the time and effort that had gone into getting me prettied up. I left half of the breakfast food in the fridge for my sister.

The other half I put on a plate. Then I drew my sword. I nicked the edge of my left palm on the blade and let a bead of blood grow and drip onto the metal near the grip. My broadsword vibrated in my hands as my blood connected with the magic imbued in the spellblade. I waved the sword over the food and chanted in a whisper, and violet flames of magic licked out from the metal and over the plate, coiling down into the food and disappearing, like watching steam in reverse.

I left a note for Nicole, letting her know who to call on the apartment phone if she needed anything, and that I'd be back later to check in with her. There was no danger in letting her use the phone—calls couldn't be made into the Earthly realm, or even beyond the fortress.

When I set out toward the fortress jail with the plate in hand, it was still early, but Stone Order business was getting into high gear. Pages walked the hallways with their tablets, and various other New Gargs were already engaged in their tasks for the day.

I rounded a corner and nearly rammed into Maxen.

I couldn't help my surprise. "You're back?"

He passed a hand over his eyes. "There wasn't much more to do on a diplomatic visit after Periclase's official appeal to Oberon," he said. His voice was low, with a hoarse edge. He still wore court clothing, but his shirt was untucked and the top button undone. He looked exhausted.

"I didn't exactly help matters," I said ruefully.

He lifted a shoulder and let it drop. "Honestly, in the end I don't think it mattered. The way things were going, it was all coming to a head regardless. And now with this demand that we return the changeling, well . . ." He sighed and ran a hand through his hair. "Going to Oberon is a direct shot. Diplomatic discussions are done. I, for one, am glad you got her out."

The way he spoke, with such finality, brought an uncomfortable stirring deep in my gut. I had no love for Fae diplomacy and courtly back-and-forth, but to say the time for talking was over meant things were taking a turn for the serious. Periclase had been gunning for us, trying to force the Stone Order into his kingdom, and it was escalating in a way that suddenly felt very real. And uncomfortably personal. Because somehow, I'd become entangled in all of it.

"Is Lochlyn okay?" I asked. I knew my roommate could handle herself, but I felt bad about having to leave her so abruptly.

"She's fine. She actually sang beautifully last night, and for a moment I think it distracted everyone from the tension. She said to tell you she'd see you at home whenever you make it there."

"Unfortunately, I don't think that will be any time soon," I said. "I'm heading down now to press Bryna, and then Marisol has assigned me the unofficial role of Nicole's New Garg BFF."

He shot me a look edged with confusion. "Bryna?"

"Oh damn, you probably didn't even know. Yeah, we ran into Bryna on the way out of the Duergar realm. I knocked her out and brought her here on the charge of attempted murder in the netherwhere. She's going to lead me to the vamp I've been hunting for the Guild. Marisol knows, by the way. I had the pleasure of a late-night chat with her."

"You need to hold Bryna accountable for violating the void," Maxen said sharply.

"No," I said with as much finality as I could muster. "It's my choice, and I don't want to go down that path and get tangled up in the High Court. I'll take care of it."

"Petra, you can't just let that slide."

"I'm not," I said through clenched teeth.

He held up his hands in surrender.

"Good luck with Bryna," he said. He started down the hall, walking backward so he was still facing me. "I'm glad you'll be sticking around the fortress, whatever the reason."

"Ha. That makes it all so much better," I said sarcastically, but it actually was kind of nice.

"Oh," he called from down the hall. "Jasper said to tell you hello."

My pulse bumped, and I stopped short before I could catch myself. I pivoted and looked over my shoulder, trying to play it off. "Okay, uh, good to know."

Maxen peered at me, and I couldn't quite read his expression. Curiosity, maybe?

I pushed away the mental image of the golden-eyed Duergar as I continued on to the cells. I'd hardly had a chance to think about how Jasper had aided our escape. How I'd sworn an oath, promising a favor in return. Given the current state of disintegration in the New Garg-Duergar relationship, it was unlikely we'd be crossing paths any time soon. Or, if we did, it would probably be under contentious circumstances. Unease pinged in my chest. There was a possibility that my promise could end up putting the Stone Order in a worse position with the Duergar, depending on how Jasper ended up calling it in. Nothing to do about that, though. As Oliver had so bluntly observed, I couldn't take it back. I hoped Jasper would keep the oath to himself. The last thing I needed was Periclase dictating how I'd have to make good on it. I suspected Jasper might not take that route, though. After all, he'd helped me escape.

Much as I tried to move on to other thoughts, I couldn't help recalling how Jasper and I had fought the servitors in the Duergar courtyard. He'd handled himself with practiced ease, keeping his wry humor through the whole thing. I felt a zing from Mort, as if my broadsword was also remembering the battle.

As I approached the fortress jail, I refocused my attention. I pushed through the door to the small front office and found Patrick, the same attendant, on duty. I quickly signed in. I had the right to question Bryna alone but couldn't take in any weapons. Patrick waited while I took off my scabbard. He locked my sword in the safe behind the desk. Fortunately, he didn't question the plate of food when he took me back to Bryna's cell.

Inside, Bryna was awake. Dark smudges under her lower lids and bloodshot eyes indicated she probably hadn't slept much, if at all. She was curled up in the corner of the cell on the bed, with her legs drawn up, reminding me of when I'd found Nicole. It was cool in the cell, and the skirt of Bryna's dress was pulled around her legs like a blanket. The fabric was dirty, and I could see the tear from when I'd stepped on the back of it as she'd tried to dart away. Her muddy high heels were discarded on the floor.

Her eyes narrowed as I came in, but she didn't move.

Patrick shut the door behind me, leaving me alone with the prisoner.

I went to the bed, put down the plate, and pulled off the foil. The food was still hot enough to steam, and I waved the foil a little to waft the aroma toward her before crumpling it up and tucking the aluminum ball in my pocket. I retreated to a spot near the door, folded my arms, and leaned a shoulder against the wall.

"I'm going to make this simple," I said. "Things are not good between the Duergar and the New Gargoyles. Since I brought you here, the situation has escalated. Diplomatic talks have ceased, and Maxen and the others have returned. No one's playing nice anymore. So, if you want out of here, I'm your ticket."

She just glared at me.

I waited. The food was still steaming. She didn't look at it, but when her tongue flicked out to moisten her lips, and then she swallowed, I knew she was hungry. She had to be, after all the time she'd spent running around outside the palace when the rest of the party had been dining.

"What do you want?" she asked finally.

"I already told you. I need to capture Van Zant."

"No." She folded her arms, and her eyes slid off to the side.

"You don't have any leverage here, Bryna" I said.

"You're going to have to let me go tonight. You can't hold me longer than twenty-four hours."

"I can if I submit my charges to the High Court." I really, really didn't want to do that. It would mean having legal proceedings consume my life for months. "I'm sure Oberon and the rest of Faerie would be interested in how you violated the sanctity of the netherwhere with your wraith."

One of her hands reached down to pull her skirt more tightly around her legs. She knew she'd lost. She was just being stubborn. I kind of got that.

"You're getting off really easy, Bryna," I said. "Just give me the vamp."

"In return for?"

"If your information is good and I apprehend him, I won't pursue charges in the High Court."

"If I tell you where he is, you drop the charge and let me go. Whether or not you manage to bring him in isn't my problem."

I'd purposely left her that little bit of wiggle room, and she'd taken the bait perfectly.

I let my arms drop and leaned forward, taking a couple of threatening strides toward her.

"I said you're not in a position to negotiate!" I barked the words so loudly she jumped and drew back, her eyes widening.

I gave her a steely, unblinking look of disdain and then half-turned away as I muttered a string of curses under my breath. Finally, I heaved a huge sigh.

"A compromise," I said. "I must make it through a doorway with Van Zant."

She inclined her head in acquiescence.

"Now say it."

"I pledge this promise to you. I will supply you with Van Zant and give you a way to safely leave the Duergar realm with him," she said in a grudging tone. She cast me a smirk. "Your turn."

Magic tingled like electricity in the air.

I rolled my eyes. "I pledge my promise to you. If you personally uphold your promise so pledged, I will release you from custody and will not pursue charges against you in the High Court. And so a promise is exchanged."

The air between us shivered and wavered briefly as our oath was sealed.

"I'll be back for you in twenty minutes," I said.

"Wait, I have to go with you?" she asked. "That wasn't part of the bargain!"

I shot her an incredulous look. "It wasn't *not* part of the bargain. You think I'm just going to take your information and go traipsing off to Maeve-knows-where into some trap you've set?" I lifted my chin at the plate of food. "Eat up, princess. You're gonna need the energy."

I fixed her with a hard glare, and then looked up at the closed-circuit camera, raised my arm, and flipped my fingers in a come-here motion to signal to the attendant that I was ready to leave. Patrick let me out of the cell, and I reclaimed my scabbard and sword at the front desk. In brief terms, I told Patrick about my deal with Bryna and that I'd be returning for her, so he could do whatever paperwork was required. Then I was on my way back to my quarters.

I didn't really want to waste the time leaving and coming back to the cells, but I needed Bryna to at least inhale a portion of the steam from the food or, better yet, eat a bite. Then it would take a few minutes for the spellblade blood magic to take effect. My shadowsteel broadsword contained some of my own blood, which tied us together and made certain unique magic possible. The magic I was casting on Bryna was a clever one. If she tried to resist or defy me, she'd feel the cold edge of Mort's blade pressing against her throat. The feeling was real and the threat of harm was real, but no one would see what was happening because the sword didn't have to be touching her.

Normally, most Fae had permanent protection charms against such magic, but in jail no one was allowed to keep their charms. My own anti-potion charm was a small chain I always wore around my ankle. If Bryna had been allowed to keep her charms, Mort's shadowsteel magic wouldn't have worked on her. It was shadow magic, outlawed in many kingdoms. I was willing to risk trouble to use it, though, because I had the leverage of Bryna's attack on me in the netherwhere, which was a worse offense.

I figured I'd use the few minutes I had to kill to go back and check on Nicole. But when I got near the door to my apartment, I saw that someone had beat me to it. Maxen was just raising a hand to knock. Curiosity spiked through me. Had Marisol sent her son to welcome Nicole to the Stone Order, or was he visiting of his own choice? I stopped where I was, watching as he waited. The door swung inward, and he spoke briefly before stepping inside.

"Lady Mag—I mean, Petra," someone called behind me.

I turned to find Emmaline hurrying toward me, slightly out of breath.

"I've been looking for you," she said.

I found I was genuinely pleased to see her. "Glad you made it back from the Duergar realm in one piece."

"Suffice to say, we won't be invited back any time soon," she said wryly. Then she turned all-business, holding her tablet a little tighter under her arm. "I've been assigned to accompany you when you take the Duergar woman out of the fortress."

"Wait, what? How do you even know about that?"

She held up her tablet. "It's in the system. And a prisoner may not be removed from the jail of any Faerie kingdom or Order solely in the company of his or her accuser. A sworn representative of the High Court must go, too, as a witness. I was sworn in just last month."

I pulled one hand down my cheek. "Oh, for the love of . . ." I let out a noisy, long sigh. "Okay, if that's how it has to be."

Seeing her not-quite-hidden look of disappointment, I held up a palm.

"I didn't mean you," I said. "If someone has to come with me, you're my top choice. It's just the bureaucracy of it all. I'm used to more independence. Life working for the Guild is a hell of a lot more straightforward."

That seemed to please her.

I cast another long look at the closed door to my quarters. Maxen was still in there.

"Okay, I guess we should head back to get Bryna," I said, oddly reluctant to leave without finding out what Maxen was saying to Nicole.

"So, uh, any idea of the changeling's agenda?" I asked Emmaline. "You know about her, right?"

She nodded. "Yeah, a fortress bulletin went out early this morning. Her agenda wasn't published." She peered at me for a second. "But I heard she was staying in your quarters. Wasn't that Lord Lothlorien going in there a minute ago?"

"Um, might have been." I cleared my throat.

"What was it like? Busting a changeling out of the Duergar palace?"

I cocked a grin at her, relishing the memory of the adrenaline coursing through me as Nicole and I made our escape.

"Damn fun, actually. And your info was spot on. She was being held in the bunkhouse by the stables. If not for you, I doubt I would have found her."

Emmaline returned my grin, her lavender eyes sparkling. The memory of Jasper's face just before I'd dropped into the secret passage in the tree surfaced in my mind. If not for Emmaline, I wouldn't have found Nicole. But if not for Jasper, I might not have made it out with her.

"What happened during the rest of the trip, anyway?" I asked. "You gotta tell me about dinner. Please, torture me with the details of what I missed."

"After you were . . . dismissed," she said carefully. "Things mostly returned to normal in the reception hall."

She recounted Lochlyn's singing during the pre-dinner festivities and then described every course of the meal, right up to the after-dinner aperitif selection. My stomach felt hollow all of sudden. I made a note to go all out for lunch. I planned to have Van Zant in Guild custody by then, so it would be a celebration meal.

"It wasn't until the dancing started that King Periclase got pissed and called things off," she said. "There had been people coming in to whisper in his ear like every ten minutes for a couple of hours up until then. He stopped the music and sent everyone to their quarters, and we spent the rest of the night on lockdown. We left at dawn."

"I'm surprised he stayed so cool for that long," I said. "He had to have suspected it was one of us who busted Nicole out, and at some point, I'm sure someone identified me."

"Yeah, he knows it was you," she said.

My brows lifted.

"Rumors circulate fast in the Unseelie courts, and I was seated at the back with the Duergar court underlings. They're the worst of the bunch when it comes to gossip." She slid a look at me. "Apparently King Periclase was extremely puzzled by how you managed to disappear. And very put out that you'd found a way to sneak back in in the first place."

I chuckled under my breath. Thank you, Maxen.

"Not going to spill your secrets?" she asked. "Or a hint about who might have helped you?"

"What?" I put on a look of mock outrage. "You think I needed help? That I couldn't have accomplished such badass feats on my own?"

She gave me a wry smile and a little shrug.

"Ah. Now I see how it is." I pulled a mock-sullen look, and she snorted.

My mood sobered as we arrived at the fortress jail.

Patrick was gone, replaced by a woman whose name was Nanette, according to the plaque on the desk. She had a grandmotherly appearance—soft rounded shoulders, her gray hair pulled back into a low ponytail, and readers perched on the middle of her nose. She had the crazy-long lashes of a Sylph, but otherwise looked like she had three-quarters New Garg blood, if I had to guess. I gave her a little salute.

"I'm here with my official representative of the High Court, who will accompany me with the prisoner and ensure I don't talk mean to tape kick-me signs on the back of the woman who tried to murder me in the void," I said.

Nanette raised one brow at me, apparently not amused, and peered at Emmaline over her glasses. "Your credentials, honey?"

Emmaline poked and swiped at her tablet and then turned it around so Nanette could see.

"All right, then," the jail attendant said. She moved her glasses farther up her nose, picked up a tablet, and started reading from it in a monotone.

"The prisoner Bryna no last name given is hereby released into the custody of her accuser and an official representative of the High Court for the purpose of fulfilling the oath-bound agreement between the accuser and the accused. The prisoner Bryna no last name given will be released bodily and all charges dropped upon the fulfillment of said agreement, the terms of which are known only to the accused and the accuser. Do you, the accuser, understand?"

She looked up at me. I nodded.

"Sign." She thrust the tablet at me.

I signed. A few minutes later, we were leaving the fortress jail with Bryna, who looked like a lost fairy-tale princess in her torn and stained gown, frizzed hair, and smudged makeup. She put her charmed jewelry back on as we walked. Not that they'd do any good against my shadowsteel magic. Her eyes were a little glassy, courtesy of the spell.

Bryna slowed and then stopped to lean against the wall for balance and put on her heels, which she'd been carrying. She fumbled with them a little, her fingers clumsy.

Emmaline peered at her and then shot me a sharp look. "You spelled her?" she whispered.

I lifted my hands innocently. "Is that not allowed?"

Emmaline touched the back of her hand to her forehead and then let it drop. "I'm going to have to report that."

"Do what you gotta do," I said mildly. I had no regrets about using the spell.

She let out a low sound of disapproval as she recorded something on her tablet. "What kind of magic?"

"Just a wee bit of shadowsteel blood magic." I held out my hand with my thumb and forefinger pinched together to leave only a sliver of space between them. "Teensy."

She looked up long enough to give me a withering look.

Bryna stumbled toward us like she'd had one too many drinks. When her heel slid off the side of her shoe, she nearly went down. "My shoes. They don't want to stay on my feet."

I made a strangled noise in my throat. "Okay, this isn't going to work. We need to get some real shoes for her."

Emmaline shrugged. "I can't leave the two of you alone."

I fought the temptation to yank at my hair. "I'll go get her some shoes."

I took off at a run toward my apartment. At the door, I gave a warning knock, waited a second, and then opened the door. Maxen and Nicole were sitting in the living room area, she on the sofa with her feet curled up and he in the easy chair. In spite of my warning, they both jumped about a foot when I came in.

"Just need some shoes," I said, and beelined to the bedroom. I found some of my old Chuck Taylors from when I was in high school.

"I'll check in with you later," I said to Nicole as I hurried back out the door. Her cheeks were flushed pink, and she was nervously playing with her honey-colored hair as she watched me rush in and out. I started to close the door behind me but then opened it up again and looked at Maxen. "I'll be checking in with you, too, Lord Lothlorien."

His brows rose, and he blinked a couple of times but didn't have a chance to respond before I was gone.

I caught up with Emmaline and Bryna, and as soon as our Duergar charge had my Chuck Taylors tied onto her feet, we were off again toward the nearest doorway, which was located in an interior courtyard. We stood in front of the arched alcove.

"Okay, Bryna, you're on," I said. "Where do we go to find Van Zant?"

Her face hardened, her eyes tight. She shot me an insolent look, but when she opened her mouth to speak, no words came. Instead, she gasped and her eyes widened. Her fingers flew to her neck.

I leaned in so I could speak in her ear. "I suggest you cooperate, if you enjoy having your head attached to your body."

She swallowed hard and blinked a couple of times and then drew a deep breath and let it out. The defiance had drained from her face.

"He's in my room." She turned her glassy gaze on me. "My quarters in the Duergar palace."

I smacked the heel of my hand against my forehead. Great. Back into the lion's den.

Chapter 22

"THERE'S A DOORWAY very near my quarters," Bryna said. She blinked slowly as she spoke, as if for her everything was moving in slow motion.

She kept talking, the shadowsteel magic encouraging her to offer up more information than she normally would have. "That's why I chose those rooms. I like to be able to come and go eeeasily. I do it aaall the time," she said, starting to draw out vowel sounds.

I grimaced. "I bet."

"Won't that drop us right in the middle of things?" Emmaline asked me.

"Yeah. But the alternative is wasting time trying to get in and sneak to her rooms. And at this point it's broad daylight, and I'm public enemy number one on Periclase's list. That's a bad combo for getting around unnoticed."

We both looked at Bryna.

"We need to go in without getting caught. Our oath was binding," I reminded her. "You get released only if you lead me to Van Zant and I make it through a doorway with him."

"This is the best way. Reeeally," she drawled.

I started to wonder if I'd used too much magic, and I had a bad feeling about using the doorway Bryna spoke of. But I didn't have time to waste. Marisol's deadline for turning in my mark and getting back to the fortress aligned with what my boss had told me—basically, I had a couple more hours to finish the job. If I didn't, I'd lose my chance at the Van Zant bounty and its big payout. He'd still be loose and dealing VAMP3 blood, endangering Maeve-only-knew how many people. I'd be penalized by the Guild for failing to complete an assignment on deadline, by getting slapped with at least a month-long probation—an unpaid time-out from work at the Guild—guaranteeing I'd make no bounty money for that time. The exclusive mercenary contracts with the Guild, combined with the penalty periods for failing an assignment, kept us mercs hamstrung and very motivated to do our jobs. That gap in income would sink me. I'd have to keep pursuing Van Zant if his bounty got re-assigned to another merc, just to ease my conscience, but I wasn't in a financial position to be doing charity work.

Sure, I could try to pick up other types of freelance work, but they all paid worse than Guild jobs, and most didn't offer steady employment. That was why the Guild could be so ruthless with their terms. I was already behind on my part of the rent, and Lochlyn had just lost her own job. If we got evicted, I'd have no choice. I'd have to move back into the stone fortress.

A cringing shiver worked its way up my spine at the thought of being in the fortress permanently. As a full-time, resource-consuming resident, I'd have to pull my weight. That meant doing whatever job Marisol chose to assign me. I wouldn't have time to keep up with Guild work in addition to a fortress job *and* acting as Nicole's new BFF.

But far worse than all of that, I'd betray the oath I'd made to myself. To my dead mother. I'd sworn to dedicate my life to working as a vamp hunter for the Guild. In the fortress, my vamp hunting days would come to an end.

No. Just, no.

I had to get this job done, and I had to do it before time ran out.

I gestured at Bryna. "You'll have to take us to the doorway near your quarters."

She gave a docile nod. Emmaline and I stood on either side of Bryna, each with a hand on one of her shoulders, while she traced the sigils and whispered the words to take us into the Duergar palace. Just before we went into the netherwhere, I drew Mort.

We came out into darkness, and my heart jolted with alarm. It took me a second to realize we were standing in a tiny, dark room. I lowered my sword.

"Thisss is the movie house," Bryna said, leading us out of what appeared to be an exit vestibule into a larger room.

Emmaline let out a nervous giggle at Bryna's slurring.

I could make out the faint white glow of the projection screen on the wall to the right, and the regularly-spaced lumps of theater seating to the left.

"Odd place for a doorway," I mumbled.

"Yeah." Bryna let out a sigh. "But it's good 'cause not many here know about this one."

"Which way to Van Zant?" I asked, shifting my weight to my toes, impatient to get on with it.

She lifted an arm to wave at the back of the theater. "We go that way."

She drifted ahead of us up the aisle that split the seats, but when she went to push the bar release on one double door, I grabbed her arm to stop her.

"Stay quiet," I said and moved in front of her.

I sheathed Mort. Carefully and slowly, I pushed the door open an inch and peered through the gap. A couple of Duergar guards strode by, and I froze, nearly letting the door fall shut. More Duergar passed by. I watched for a few more seconds.

I swore silently and let the door click closed. This corridor was a main thoroughfare. We couldn't just stroll out there. By now, all of the Duergar realm knew that Bryna was being held by the New Gargoyles, so they'd be sure to take notice if she suddenly appeared in the palace. And my face was probably plastered all over the palace alerts after swiping Nicole from Periclase.

"Any other way out of here?" I asked. "Maybe one that's less busy?"

"Nuh-uh," Bryna said.

"Well, how far is it?" I asked, irritated.

"Oh, 'bout a hundred feet down the hall. Then turn left. Then up the stairs. Then turn left. Then right."

"There was an exit sign back where we came in," I said. "Where does that go?"

Bryna let out a tiny, airy laugh. "Nowhere. It's just for looks."

I was about ready to punch something.

"Fine. Then we're just going to have to walk right out there and take our chances." I wrapped my hand around Bryna's elbow and squeezed.

"Ow," she protested.

"If I get caught before I can get out with Van Zant, you're screwed," I reminded her. "I'll make sure the Stone Order files charges against you in the High Court. What do you think the punishment will be for sending a wraith into the netherwhere to kill me?"

My hand was poised on the door, ready to push it open.

"Wait," Emmaline said. "Isn't there a secret passage nearby? I could swear there was a passageway near here."

Bryna stared at her dumbly for a second and then rolled her eyes with a stupid grin. "Yes! Silly me. It's across the hall in the powder room. Last stall."

All I could do was shake my head at her.

"Good work," I breathed at Emmaline.

We waited for a small gap in the corridor activity and then stole across the hallway and through the women's bathroom door and hurried to the back. Inside the stall, Bryna pressed a couple of the wall tiles and a low, narrow door with seams that had blended invisibly popped open.

She seemed to move more purposefully as she led us into the secret passage. It was a dark, narrow space in between the walls, and it broke off into branches so many times I had no idea how Bryna managed to keep us on track. We walked single file with me in the middle. I carried Mort in my hand, not that it would do much good if I actually needed to use it. The space was way too tight to wield a broadsword. Not even enough room to put it back in my scabbard.

With a glance over her shoulder at me, Bryna whispered, "We'll come out close to my front door. Just a short hop to my quarters."

She sounded confident, and I started to think we might be in the clear. That turned out to be a mistake.

We reached the end of a corridor, and Bryna stopped. There was a tiny bit of light coming from random pinholes punched in the walls. I watched as she slid her fingers over a catch I couldn't see, and there was a soft click. A narrow vertical strip of light appeared. She pushed, and the space widened another inch.

"This should be easy," she whispered. "It's just right over—"

The door jerked open suddenly, and a hand reached in and grabbed her arm, yanking her out. She shrieked and then snarled. Temporarily blinded after our journey through the dark passage, it took me a split second to realize there was a crowd of Duergar guards waiting for us. I didn't even have time to utter the curses that sprang to my mind.

My pulse jolted, and I leapt out, drawing magic and swinging Mort. It took them by surprise, and a few of them stumbled back a step or two as my violet magic licked at them like razor-edged flames.

Bryna bared her teeth and snapped at the guard holding her, the docility caused by my spell seeming to dissolve away in an instant. Her mouth came away bloody, and the guard let go of her and clamped his hand over his bloody wrist. She tried to lunge away, but another guard grabbed at her hair and caught a handful of it. She furiously twisted around and kicked at him.

I kept advancing with wide slashes, glancing out of the corner of my eye at the door Bryna had been heading toward. I wanted to look back to see if Emmaline had managed to retreat, but I couldn't give the guards the opening.

The guards were backing up and reaching for their magi-zappers. I deflected one stream of magic with Mort, the force of it traveling up into my arm and jarring me to my bones. Gritting my teeth against the foreign magic meant to incapacitate, I managed to neutralize it just as another bolt sprang at my chest. I absorbed it, too, and then whipped around to meet an attack. Mort crashed against the short sword of a guard who towered over me. When he raised his arm to try to redirect his strike, I darted under it.

I danced to the side, trying to find an opening through which I could get to Bryna. I had to hand it to her. She was doing a hell of a job fending off a couple of guards using only her teeth and claws. Perhaps because she was Periclase's daughter, they didn't turn their stunners on her. She was surely going to catch serious hell later for helping me. The guards had no problem blasting me, and my eyes were just about crossed from taking partial hits.

Emmaline had vanished, most likely having retreated back into the secret passages where she could elude the guards. She seemed to know the palace well, and I trusted she could take care of herself.

"Petra!" called Bryna, sounding strangled through the gnashing of her teeth.

I glanced over my shoulder just as she shoved her foot into a guard's groin. She whipped around and threw herself at the door. It opened under her influence, and I backed my way toward it and slipped through. She slammed it shut.

For a second or two we stood inside Bryna's quarters staring at each other, our chests heaving. The door shook as the guards pounded on it.

"They'll have to go through administrative channels to get in here, but it won't take long." The fight seemed to have sharpened Bryna's senses.

I turned a full circle. "Where the hell is Van Zant?"

Turning on her heel, she went into the bedroom, and I pulled out the bounty card with my free hand and tightened my grip on Mort.

When she came back out, she was carrying a white box with string tied around it. "Is that his box of eyeliner and cologne, or what?" I peered past her, looking for the vamp.

She held out the box. "This is Van Zant."

I stared at it and then looked up at her. "What the *fuck* are you talking about?"

"He's dead," she said. "Last night."

A strange mix of sadness and consternation passed over her face.

The pounding at the door was getting more violent.

I sheathed Mort and then shoved my fingers into my hair and yanked. Why did this shit have to happen to me? With a dead mark, I'd only get ten percent of the bounty.

"So that's—?"

"His ashes," she supplied. She thrust the box at me. "A promise is a promise. His remains don't do me any good, anyway. You can get out through the passage in my closet."

I shook my head and finally snatched the stupid box from her.

"How in the name of Oberon did this happen?" I had to know, in spite of the seconds ticking by.

She shook her head slowly. "Some kind of strange attack. Little guys with poisonous knives."

"The servitors? The same small beings that attacked me and Jasper yesterday?" I wouldn't have guessed that the ninjas' knives could take down a vamp. There wasn't much in the world that could do that.

She frowned, clearly not sure what I was talking about.

I waved a hand, brushing off her confusion. "Where did it happen?"

"Spriggan kingdom."

I filed that away. "Okay, where's my exit?"

She showed me where a panel slid away at the back of her closet.

"Keep going right and you'll end up in a hallway next to double doors. Take those and you'll be outside in front of the palace. You know the way from there."

Her stance was defeated, her voice low and hoarse. I didn't know what the nature of her relationship with Van Zant had been, but it seemed to have hit her hard.

I drew Mort and she stepped back, her eyes popping wide.

"I need to dissolve the shadowsteel spell," I said hurriedly. "Just hold still."

I whispered the words to reverse the spell, and violet vapor leaked from Bryna's mouth. It moved in a little stream to the tip of my blade, where it washed over the metal and then disappeared.

"Go, before they get in," she said.

I nodded, re-sheathed Mort, and squeezed into the compartment in her closet. I swiftly followed her directions. I was just about to get out of the secret passage when someone suddenly came up behind me.

An iron grip wrapped around my upper arm.

I let go of the box and twisted, reaching for Mort at the same time, but the space was too tight to draw my broadsword.

"Keep quiet," said a voice in my ear.

"Jasper? Were you following me?"

"I forced Bryna to tell me where you were."

My hand clenched into a fist. That little cheat. How had she slithered out of her promise? Jasper must have had held something over her.

"Petra, we can't let things escalate between the Stone Order and the Duergar," he said urgently. "There's a bigger threat to both of us. All of us."

For a moment my mission to get Van Zant's damned ashes back to the Guild faded to the background.

"What?" I asked, confused.

"Those servitors we killed weren't just assassins. They're getting into every kingdom, and that's the point."

"I don't understand."

"I don't know how, but when they breach a realm, they pick up some kind of magic that allows them to get back in. Someone out there wants access to the stronghold in every kingdom. And with each attack, the servitors are getting more powerful."

I peered up at his glinting golden eyes in the semi-dark. "How do you know this?"

"Ravens, but that's not important. My point is, I need your help. We can't get distracted by conflicts that aren't going to matter in the end."

I shook my head. Ravens? Like messenger birds? This was wasting way too much time. "I'm the wrong person to talk to. You should get in touch with Maxen. This stuff is his department."

"No," he said vehemently. "It can't be the officials. They'll make things worse."

"But why me?"

"You're the daughter of Oliver Maguire, Stone Order champion and one of Marisol's closest advisors," he said. "That means you're close enough to the decision makers, but without being a life-long diplomat. And you have no patience for bureaucracy. You can keep focused on what's important. That's exactly what's needed here."

Surprisingly insightful, and it was nice that someone in Faerie saw my loathing of red tape as a positive trait. But I wasn't interested in getting mixed up in whatever Jasper's fight was.

"Look, I appreciate your concern, but I need to get the hell out of here," I said. "I don't even live on this side of the hedge. You need someone more plugged into Faerie."

He let out an exasperated breath. His hand was still on my arm, and he yanked me close. I let him do it, a little fascinated by this different side of him.

"You're going to be involved whether you want to be or not," he said. His face was so close to mine, his strange eyes nearly filled my field of vision. "And if things go badly, you're going to *wish* the Stone Order had ended up under Duergar rule. Believe me, the alternative will be much worse."

"Why should I believe you?" I demanded.

His nostrils flared as we locked glares. "The Tuatha Dé Danann have returned. The Dullahan are with them."

A sharp laugh escaped my lips. "The Tuatha don't exist anymore, except in a few bloodlines diluted almost down to nothing. And you're seriously trying to tell me the Dullahan are coming? The Bone Warriors are a myth."

"Wrong on both counts," he said harshly.

Suddenly there was a clamoring outside the secret passage's exit.

"Shit," I hissed. I'd loitered too long.

"Come with me." Jasper pulled me away from the door, racing back the way I'd come. He had to turn his shoulders at an angle to move through the narrow space.

Seconds later, I heard the guards breaching the secret passage behind us.

Jasper let go of me and sped up, leading me through a dizzying maze of turns. We ended up at a ladder that rose into a narrow pipe-like vertical tunnel.

"Go ahead of me," he commanded.

The space where we stood was so close, we practically had to embrace in order for me to get past him. For a couple of seconds, our bodies pressed tightly against each other. I had to hold the box with Van Zant's ashes over my head, and Jasper's hand briefly touched the side of my waist as we maneuvered around to change places. If not for the light armor covering his chest, I probably would have felt his heartbeat.

I puffed out a breath, clearing my mind of such thoughts, and focused on climbing up the ladder as quickly as possible with the box under my arm. I could hear our pursuers in the passages below. A glance down showed Jasper coming up after me. The ladder seemed to go on for half a mile.

When I reached the top, I pulled a lever and the circular lid on the pipe popped open on a hinge. Squinting against the daylight, I climbed out. I was standing on one of the many tiered roofs of the Duergar palace. This one was one of the highest.

Jasper slammed the lid down on our escape hatch and then stood on it. I drew my sword.

"Okay, now what?" I asked him.

He held up a finger and with his other hand reached behind his chest armor, and then produced a small cylindrical item with a flourish. He put one end to his lips and blew into it. There was no sound, but a charge seemed to pass through the air, as if the whistle had sent out a wave of electricity.

"Watch." He pointed to the sky.

I shaded my eyes, scanning, and at first saw nothing out of the ordinary. But then in the far distance a black speck appeared over the tops of the trees forming the realm's great forest. It was heading straight for us and rapidly growing as it neared.

I spun around to face Jasper. "You're a Grand Raven Master?"

He gave me the slightest of nods. I couldn't help staring at him for a second, open-mouthed. Then I turned to watch in awe as the giant raven approached. It had a wingspan easily thirty feet across. I'd seen one in person only once at a fair when I was a child.

"This will give you away," I said, my eyes glued to the creature. I tipped my head back as it flapped overhead, its beak pointed down as its dark round eyes searched for a place to land. "They'll know you gave me an escape."

"They don't know it's my raven," Jasper said.

I swiveled around just in time to see him leap from the hatch he'd been standing on and disappear over the side of the roof. I didn't have time to run to the edge to see where he'd landed or whether he was okay. Guards were bursting through the now-freed passage.

The raven cawed at me, clearly urging me to hurry. With Mort in one hand and the box in the other, I ran at the huge feathered creature. I sheathed my broadsword and then sprang up to the raven's back, using my now-free hand to pull myself into position between its wings.

It hopped twice and then jumped off the roof and took flight. I hung on for dear life, squeezing my thighs like a bareback rider and clutching the feathers in my fist. The box was clamped under my other arm so hard I squashed the cardboard a bit. When the raven banked, I nearly tumbled off, and my heart jumped into my throat.

I chanced a look behind me and caught sight of the guards on the rooftop, and more still pouring out of the secret passage. Farther down on a lower roof, I glimpsed Jasper flattening himself against a wall, staying out of sight of the guards above. He gave me a little salute, but I couldn't let go to return the gesture.

The air whipped across my face and glossy black feathers brushed my skin as Jasper's raven carried me away from the Duergar palace.

Chapter 23

I GRINNED INTO the wind like a maniac for a few minutes, adrenaline still coursing through me from the narrow escape and the sensation of flight. The raven's powerful muscles flexed under my legs, settling into a rhythm as it traced a straight line away from the palace. After a half mile or so, it struck me that I had no idea what it planned to do with me.

"The nearest doorway would be super," I said, just in case the raven might understand.

Its sleek head twitched to the side at the sound of my voice, but it didn't change course.

We soared over forest and low rolling hills until the palace was miles behind. Then the beating of the raven's wings began to slow. The right one tipped gracefully downward, and the bird began to spiral toward the ground. It alighted in the middle of what appeared to be a circle of large and crumbling stones, but once I slid off the bird and truly looked around, I realized it was an ancient ruin. Runes carved into some of the stones were visible only by the moss that grew into the indentations.

There was an arch to my right. That was my way out.

I looked up at the great bird. It shook, its night-dark feathers shivering with the movement. With a tilt of its head, it peered at me with one great eye.

"Thank you for ferrying me to safety," I said gravely.

I wasn't sure if the words would bind me in promise to the creature, but if they did, I was okay with it. But there was no shiver of magic in the air. Regardless, the raven—and its golden-eyed master—had done me a great service.

I jogged over to the doorway, and as I stood tracing the sigils in the air, the raven took flight and soared over me.

I stepped into the void of the netherwhere and then emerged at a doorway just outside the stone fortress. I'd never been so grateful to be back in New Garg territory. Vincenzo was still parked there. I secured the box in the bin strapped behind the scooter's seat, and when I started up the engine, it felt like it had been weeks since I'd last been on my scooter.

Cursing the doorway configuration that wouldn't allow me to jump straight back home to Boise, I had to ride through the cold San Francisco drizzle to the doorway at Crossen Hall. The doorways within Faerie all connected to each other, but on the Earthly side of the hedge, the networks weren't so complete and interconnected. The restrictions sometimes made me feel as if it'd be faster to catch commercial flights. Not that I could afford air travel.

The miserable, cold ride passed in a blur. It was going to be a sprint to get Van Zant—or what was left of him—turned in for the bounty, and I had to push my speed and weave through traffic. By the time I made it back to Boise, I was stiff and travel-fatigued. The day was hot there, and when I pulled into the Guild parking lot, my hair was mostly dry and my clothes were no longer dripping.

I shoved Van Zant's box under my arm, pushed through the Guild's double-doors, and stalked through the corridors. People took one look at my face and scooted out of my way when they saw me coming.

When I reached Gus's office, I found the door cracked open. Not bothering to knock, I pushed inside, went up to his desk, and plopped the box on the open file folders he was shuffling around. His bloodshot eyes widened at the box and then shifted up to me.

I pulled out my phone to check the time. "Fourteen minutes to spare."

He pulled his chin back, making his double chin into a triple chin, and slanted a glance at the box I carried. "He's dead, I take it."

I looked down at the box. "Yup."

"You kill him?"

"Nope."

Gus sighed noisily through his nose. "Either way, the payout is only—"

"Ten percent," I cut in. "I know, I know."

I pushed my stiff hair off my forehead while he rummaged around on his desk for a tablet. He handed it to me so I could fill out the job info and sign for the completion of the assignment.

"When will the payment go into my account?" I asked as I worked my way through the forms.

"We'll have to verify this is him." Gus tapped his pen on the top of the box. "Guild rules. Can't be filing false catches."

I silently cursed. "And how long will that take?"

"Couple of weeks, if the lab mages aren't backed up."

I let my head fall back. The lab was *always* backed up.

Once I exited the Guild headquarters, my phone vibrated in its pouch on my scabbard.

I pulled it out, quickly flipped through my new assignment, and then let out a groan. It wasn't a live catch—it was for the recovery of an object. Some piece of jewelry, but it didn't really matter. Object recoveries were nearly always in a lower payout category than apprehensions of people. The payout wouldn't even cover my half of the utilities for a month. But what really stung was that it was such a low-importance job. I wanted to be hunting vamps, not tracking down Grandma's charmed locket that had most likely been swiped and pawned by hard-up Uncle Loser.

I blew out a long breath through pursed lips. I was being punished for needing an extension and then failing to bring in a live mark.

Silently fuming, I went back out into the sunshine and revved up Vincenzo. One of the reasons I'd moved from the San Francisco Bay Area to Idaho was for the lower cost of living. The area was also a hotbed of supernatural beings and activity, and one of the Guild's largest offices was located in Boise. I figured between those things I was giving myself the best chance possible at surviving independently outside the stone fortress.

But it seemed it was all going to shit. Lochlyn and I had maybe a couple of weeks at best, if we could manage to dodge our landlord for that long. Oliver would probably help if he could, but I already knew he didn't have money. Human currency wasn't much use in Faerie, and those who lived permanently on the other side of the hedge typically didn't accumulate monetary wealth. Each kingdom, or order in the case of New Gargs, had its own industries, but the money didn't trickle down much in the semi-feudal system of Faerie. It didn't really matter—I was too damn stubborn to ask for help, anyway.

I was halfway home when my phone vibrated against my chest. I pulled it out at a stoplight and saw Maxen's name on the caller ID. It was a voice message from a call I must have missed while en route.

"Petra, we need you back at the fortress right away. The Duergar are making more trouble. We've got a new situation on our hands, and it involves you. I'm going to keep calling until I get you."

That was it. I swore under my breath. Would it have killed him to give a little more detail?

My phone rang as I was staring down at it in irritation. Maxen again.

"Where are you?" he demanded, uncharacteristically terse.

"In Boise, just wrapping up my assignment. Marisol gave me until this afternoon to get back," I said. "What's the emergency?"

"Periclase has really decided to kick up some shit." Maxen rarely swore.

"What variety of shit?"

"It's better if we don't discuss it over the phone," he said.

He must have been paranoid about Unseelie spies bugging our conversation.

"Can I at least stop by home for a change of clothes?" I asked.

"We'll get anything you need here," he said. The phone sounded like it jostled a little on his end, I could hear someone trying to speak to him in the background. "I need to go."

"Wait, did Emmaline make it back okay?" I asked.

"She's here. Come back now, and find me when you arrive."

The call went dead.

I steered around, changing course and heading back to the doorway in the parking garage that would return me to the San Francisco Bay Area. I was really starting to feel like a long- distance commuter.

On the way, I tried Lochlyn.

"Are you at home?" I asked when she picked up.

"Yeah. There were like four nasty notes on our door," she said.

"Then you're not going to like what I have to tell you." I explained what happened with Van Zant and how the payout wasn't just crap, but also delayed.

She groaned. "I'll see what I can scrape together, but I'm basically tapped out unless I find another job, like, tonight."

"I know," I said. "And you already loaned me money, so this isn't on you. We'll figure it out."

We hung up, and I tucked my phone back in its pouch.

By the time I pulled up to the stone fortress, it was mid-afternoon and some of the marine layer had burned off. It'd been a dry ride from Treasure Island, thank Oberon for small favors.

I parked Vincenzo and trudged into the Stone Order's headquarters. In the lobby, pages were scurrying around. I recognized a few of the diplomats who'd gone with Maxen to the Duergar palace. They all looked harried and tense. The entire atmosphere of the place made me want to turn around and leave.

Emmaline rushed up to me. "You're here, thank the Old Ones. I'll take you to Maxen."

"Hey, Emmaline," I said mildly, trying to counteract the stress that seemed to hang in the air. "How'd you escape the Duergar?"

She slid me a sideways glance of her lavender eyes, and her lips twitched in a near-grin. "I have a pretty good memory for the passages in the palace. I used a couple of them the guards didn't know about and then ran out to the doorway in the forest where our diplomatic party came in before. Sorry I disappeared like that. I figured it would be easier that way, seeing as how I didn't have a weapon."

I nodded my approval. "That was the right decision. I knew you'd manage. We need to get you armed next time we have that kind of adventure, though."

She looked very pleased at that suggestion, but her expression quickly faded to one of serious focus.

"What's got everyone running around like scared mice?" I asked.

She shook her head. "No one in the lower ranks knows the details. Something to do with the Duergar and a new petition to the High Court."

"Petitions are usually public, aren't they?"

"Yeah, but this one is sealed."

My stomach dropped a couple of inches at that news.

"What are the possible sealed-petition scenarios?" I asked.

"It could be any number of things," she said. "Sometimes the information is sensitive and has to be discussed behind closed doors first so as not to put someone in danger or tip someone off. It might not be the Duergar who requested the seal. The High Court can seal a petition at its discretion. Maybe they need to deliberate on it and don't want to cause a stir in the meantime."

It was too late for that. Judging by the faces and energy around me, things had already been stirred.

"It could also be that a challenge was issued," Emmaline continued.

"Challenge? Like the old duels?"

Her brow knitted together. "Yeah. This is a conflict between a Seelie order and an Unseelie kingdom. In the Old World, Seelie-Unseelie disagreements were often settled with a fight between champions."

"Surely they wouldn't resort to something so arcane."

She lifted a shoulder and let it drop. "No idea."

We were in one of the corridors that housed offices and rooms for official business. She gestured to an open doorway up ahead where two pages came hurrying out and then went in different directions.

"Maxen's in there," she said. "While you're speaking with him, I'll hunt down a change of clothes for you."

She angled off down the hallway before I had a chance to respond.

I stepped into the room she'd indicated, expecting to find Maxen with his usual crowd of officials. Instead, it was just him with one assistant. As soon as he saw me, he dismissed the page and asked her to close the door as she left.

Weariness fought with apprehension, dragging at my muscles but at the same time infusing me with jittery adrenaline. Reining in the nervous energy, I lifted my scabbard over my head and set it down on the conference table that stood between us and rolled my stiff shoulders.

"What's going on, Maxen?" I asked quietly.

His sapphire eyes were unblinking and red-rimmed with fatigue.

"Periclase is livid about Nicole," he said. His chest rose as he drew a deep breath. "Taking her seems to have become the spark to the dry tinder of unrest between the Stone Order and the Duergar kingdom."

I folded my arms. "Do you know what's in the latest petition?"

He nodded. "They're asking for you."

"What do you mean?"

"Periclase is demanding you be turned over to the Duergar for whatever punishment they deem fit."

I scoffed. "They can't do that! Nicole is part New Gargoyle. She has just as much a right to be here as there, if she even is Periclase's daughter at all."

"So far, we can't prove she's New Garg. But as Periclase's petition points out, she does have clear Duergar features, even if they're not ones that make it obvious she's his blood."

I hadn't been looking for Duergar features in her face. She certainly wasn't built like them. But a case could probably be made for what Periclase claimed.

"So now what?"

"We have a chance to counter the petition," he said.

"Okay, so do it. Put in a counter-filing that says they're full of shit."

He walked around the table to stand in front of me, leaning one hip against the edge and crossing his arms in a partial imitation of my posture.

"Because their petition includes the claim that Nicole is Duergar royalty, this is very grave," he said, as if he hadn't heard my suggestion. "They're saying we kidnapped a Duergar princess."

"Um, again, he has no proof that Nicole is his daughter," I said.

"They want to execute you. That's the punishment they've put forth."

"*What?*" I barked the word so harshly my voice cracked.

He held up a hand. "It's very unlikely the High Court would see that as just. But that's Periclase's game, here. He's requesting a punishment too severe for the crime, putting us in a position of countering with something lesser, but that doesn't go *too* easy. He's trying to back us into a corner so he gets you either way."

I felt queasy. "You think he actually wants me dead?"

Maxen's face screwed up, and then he shook his head. "I don't think

215

so. But he's definitely calling you out. And he's not going to let you get off easily."

I pushed my fingers into my hair, suddenly remembering what Emmaline had mentioned. "What about a challenge of champions? Me against their champion?"

His eyes went huge. "Petra, a challenge of champions is a battle to the death. Besides, you aren't the official champion of the Stone Order."

"Who is? Do we even have one?"

"It's Oliver."

Duh, of course. "Oh, yeah. I knew that."

"But that's beside the point," Maxen said. "We couldn't put you in that kind of position."

"Why not?" I asked. "Periclase is demanding my head, even if he doesn't truly want it, and he wants me to answer for my supposed transgression."

Maxen just looked at me, his lips pressed into a tight white line.

I gave a little shrug. "I can take whoever Periclase puts up against me. Duergar are tough, but New Gargs are better swordsmen. Hell, you could probably kick their champion's ass, and you're out of practice."

A ghost of a smile passed over his face.

"Besides, Oberon can step in, end the duel, and declare a winner before anyone dies," I said, starting to dredge up bits of knowledge from my long-ago history lessons. "Isn't that what happened with the last dozen-odd challenges?"

"It is," Maxen conceded. "But that doesn't mean he'd do it this time."

"Doesn't matter, then. I'll just kill my opponent."

His eyes dropped to the floor before raising to meet mine. "I don't like that you even suggested this," he said, his voice soft.

"Why?"

"Because it might actually be the best counter-petition, and it could end in you losing your life."

"But it won't," I said. "How long can you stall before filing the counter?"

"We have twenty-four hours to answer."

"Can you put a stipulation in there that if we win the challenge they have to drop their other appeal about trying to absorb the Stone Order into their kingdom?"

His brows lifted. "I'll have to look into it, but that's a great strategy. We might just make a politician out of you yet."

I snorted. "Oh, hell no. Don't get greedy, Maxen. Okay. Here's what we do. Find every way possible to delay the process. I'll use the time to train here at the fortress, make sure I'm totally brushed up on all my moves, and do everything available to make sure my stone armor is as strong as possible. Then we do the challenge, win it, and get the Duergar assholes off our backs."

"I'll talk to Marisol," he said. "But understand that she might not go for it, and the final decision is hers."

"Hey, if she has a better idea, I'm all ears," I said, spreading my arms wide.

"I'm going to find her now," he said, already heading for the door. Before opening it, he paused and turned. "Petra . . ."

The look he gave me was so raw, my breath stilled. I saw many things in his eyes—admiration, gratitude, a little fear, and that small spark that had always burned, but that I'd always brushed away.

I waved him off. "Yeah, yeah, I know."

He gave me a slight smile and left. A moment later, Emmaline entered.

She stopped short when she saw my face. "Are you okay?"

I slowly filled my lungs and gave her a nod. "Yeah, just fine."

And I realized with a calm sense of knowing that it was true. I wanted to face the Duergar champion. I wanted the chance to get Periclase off

217

my back and show him he couldn't push us around anymore. *Us.* Maybe my connection to my people ran stronger than I'd thought.

"New clothes are in your quarters," she said. "I ordered food, too."

When I arrived in my apartment, it was empty, but there were signs of Nicole—sweatshirt thrown over the back of the sofa, half a glass of water on the counter, and an extra toothbrush next to the bathroom sink. I quickly showered and then put on the clothes Emmaline had dug up, which were admirably similar to the outfit I'd shed. She had a good sense for details.

The food she'd ordered had just arrived, and I was about to dig into a bowl of pasta when there was a knock at the door.

I opened it, and Oliver stormed in, barging past me before whirling around. My eyes popped wide. I'd never seen him look so worked up.

He flipped his hand and glanced at the door, indicating I should close it. Swallowing hard, I turned to my father.

Chapter 24

"WHAT DID YOU do?" Oliver thundered at me.

I pulled my head back and resisted the temptation to creep backward just to open up more space between us. He had a long reach, and he looked mad enough to grab me and turn me over his knee like I was seven years old and I'd been caught misbehaving at school.

"Um, could you give me some context to your outrage?" I asked, but I had a pretty good idea why he was so agitated.

He closed his eyes and pressed his thumb and forefinger over them. "Please tell me you did not volunteer to fight as the Stone Order champion against the Duergar?"

I pulled my lips in and bit down on them.

After a moment of silence, he dropped his hand and squinted at me. "Aren't you going to say anything?"

"You asked me not to tell you I volunteered to fight as the Stone Order champion. But I can't lie."

He gave me a hard, withering look.

"Don't act like a smart-ass teenager, Petra." He started pacing the tiny living room-slash-kitchen area. "How could you do this?"

I lifted my palms. "It seems like a good solution."

He kept up his restless movements for a couple seconds longer and then seemed to realize how unsatisfying it was to pace in such a small space.

He halted and huffed out a loud sigh. "So, it really was your idea," he said flatly.

I nodded. "Maxen didn't like it at first either. He doesn't want me to do it. But he sees that it's a good response to the matter. I'm not going to die, Oliver. I know I'm twice any swordsman Periclase will send as champion. They don't train the way we do. And I've got full stone armor."

"I just wish you would have talked to me first."

I raised a hand and let it drop. "I should have. But the end result would have been the same because I wouldn't have let you talk me out of it." We watched each other for a couple of breaths. "Does this mean Marisol has approved my suggestion?"

He pulled his mouth into a grim semblance of a smile. "I demanded to speak with you before she files."

"You're not going to change my mind," I said quietly.

"I know." He tipped his gaze upward, and his expression became pained. "But this is my fault, and I don't want you to pay for my decisions."

"Your fault because you sent me after Nicole?"

He nodded. He actually looked rather miserable. I averted my eyes and walked over to where my pasta was still steaming on the counter.

"I didn't know he would go after you," he said.

"Of course you didn't. You have no blame for that." I twirled my fork in the spaghetti. "And frankly, I didn't exactly make things better for myself with my little confrontation with his bastard daughter at the reception for the dignitaries. Oh, and when I knocked her out, brought her here, and put her in jail. That probably didn't help either."

I stuffed a forkful of pasta in my mouth, watching Oliver as I chewed and using the food as an excuse to stop speaking.

"You do have a way of pissing off authority figures," he said.

Moving a bit stiffly, he went to the sofa and sat down, propping his elbows on his knees and peering up at me from under his heavy brows. He still looked defeated and unhappy, but I could handle that. The pain in his eyes a moment ago had jabbed a little too deeply into my chest.

I swallowed my spaghetti. "I'm not going to die," I said again.

"You sure as hell better *not*." He straightened. "I'll help with your training."

I nodded. "Good." I forked up another bunch of pasta.

The phone on the wall rang, and every muscle in my body twanged in surprise. I was unused to the sound of old-fashioned wired phones. I got up and caught it on the third ring.

"Hello, this is Petra."

"I'm calling from the office of the Lady of the Order," an official-sounding voice said. "Is Oliver Maguire there?"

"Yep." I held the phone out to my father.

He rose and took it. "Oliver speaking. Yes, I've spoken to her. Yes." His face turned grim, and his eyes slid to me and then away.

He listened for another few seconds and gave some one-word responses before hanging up.

"That was Marisol," he said. "To make things official, she needs to knight you as the champion of the Stone Order."

I stopped chewing. "Oh. Right." I tossed him a wry look. "You pissed I'm stealing your title?"

He snorted and almost smiled.

"It needs to be done now, before she files the counter-petition."

"I'm ready." I wiped my mouth with a napkin and closed the spaghetti container. "Let's do it."

Oliver didn't say a word to me on the way to Marisol's office, but I had the sense it was important to him to escort me to this meeting. I was grateful he was there, though I knew there was very little he could do, even in the training yard, to help me prepare.

When we arrived, there was a small group waiting for us. Marisol and

Maxen, of course. Marisol's personal bodyguard Jaquard, who'd trained me in sword fighting when I was a teenager. A few Order officials.

"Let's get started," Marisol said, her voice carrying over the few quiet conversations in progress.

She lifted her hand at me, indicating I should approach. The others automatically backed off, giving us some space.

"I know I don't need to ask if you're sure," she said, her voice low and her words meant for me alone. "You're a decisive woman, and clearly a fearless one. But know I would not have made this decision if I didn't have total confidence you could prevail."

I blinked, unable to come up with a proper response to such unexpected praise.

"Now," she said a little more loudly. "You must choose a squire before we can proceed with the knighting ceremony. Who will you name?"

My brows rose, and I blinked again as my brain tried to switch gears. I knew immediately who I wanted. "My page, Emmaline."

An official hovering nearby went to a phone and began speaking into it. Meanwhile, Jaquard appeared at Marisol's side holding a long, narrow object wrapped in silky gold fabric across his arms.

Suddenly, I realized what the bundle was. "Aurora?" I looked at Jaquard and then at Marisol.

She nodded. "The sword of the Summer Court."

I had no idea how they'd managed to acquire it so quickly, but it had completely slipped my mind that I wouldn't be fighting with Mort. I was required to wield Aurora, the sword of the Seelie champion. My opponent would fight with Twilight, the sword of the Unseelie champion and representative of the Winter Court.

Jaquard let the fabric fall away, revealing a decorated leather scabbard that looked older than Faerie itself. Maybe it was. He pulled the sword from its sheath and presented the hilt to Marisol. The blade was large—maybe an inch longer than Mort and slightly wider. The metal almost appeared imbued with sunlight, as it seemed to shimmer from within with the rosy yellow light of dawn.

I loved my broadsword, but Aurora had me spellbound. My fingers twitched with the need to hold it, my arms anticipating its heft and balance, my ears the sound it would make cutting through the air.

I was so absorbed in the weapon I didn't realize Emmaline had arrived until she stood next to me, slightly out of breath. She shot me a quick look of pure delight and gratitude.

"We don't have much time," Marisol said. "We should begin."

She held the hilt with both hands. I knelt on one knee in front of her.

As she began the knighting ceremony, the words seemed to pass through me, their meaning sinking into my cells. I wasn't really listening in the normal sense. I couldn't have repeated any of it later. My attention and focus were completely absorbed by Aurora.

Marisol touched each of my shoulders with the end of the blade, said a few more words, and then asked me to rise. Laying the blade flat across her hands, she presented it to me with her head inclined.

"Petra Maguire, the champion of the Stone Order and the Summer Court."

A shiver began at the crown of my head and passed down through my body and out through my limbs. It reached my fingertips at the exact second I touched Aurora. Time seemed to pause. For a long breath, everything around me disappeared, and there was only the sensation of warm sun, the sound of summer breeze rustling leaves in the trees, and the feel of soft soil underfoot.

Then I was back in Marisol's office. People were moving and speaking. Jaquard handed me the leather scabbard, and I sheathed the sword of the Summer Court and slung the strap over my shoulder like a bag, keeping hold of it with one hand.

Maxen came forward and offered his hand in a formal congratulatory shake.

"It's done," he said, as if he didn't quite believe it. He kept hold of my hand as he gave me a long, steady gaze.

"I *will* win," I said quietly.

"I know." He gave me a firm nod, but there was apprehension in his sapphire eyes.

Emmaline came up and nodded at my hand, which was clutching the scabbard strap. She already had Mort slung across her chest.

"The sword?" she said.

"Oh, right." I reluctantly passed the scabbard to her. As my squire, she was supposed to carry all my knightly shit around.

"First, we'll go to the mineral room," she said. "You have priority access to it from now until the battle of the champions."

In a daze, I nodded, and Emmaline, Jaquard, Oliver, and a few officials herded me to the training area. From then on, it was a blur of mineral treatments, sparring, resting, and eating. My schedule was managed entirely by others, leaving me free to focus on getting ready for the fight.

Every sparring session left me exhausted, but my fatigue was swept away by the most intensive, expensive restorative treatments available. It was a strange condensed period of training, but the pure, single-minded focus of it was its own sort of ecstasy.

And wielding Aurora . . . it was better than any high I could imagine. I had a couple brief twinges of guilt when I caught sight of Mort with Emmaline on the sidelines of the training yard, as if I were cheating on my broadsword. But I knew Mort and I would reunite. Aurora was mine only for a few days—a short, passionate, wholly absorbing affair—and I let myself get swept up in the glow of it.

When the Summer Court's blade cut through the air, it felt much lighter than it appeared, almost as if it wasn't made of solid metal at all. By some magic I didn't understand, it seemed to condense its mass on impact. Light and swift as it moved, but bone-jarringly weighty when it hit. It was the most perfect weapon I'd ever touched.

"Your opponent will have a sword just as swift and powerful," Oliver said from a few feet away.

I was sparring with Jaquard, and I'd forced him back to the edge of the training field. His face dripped with sweat. Oliver kept even with us as we fought, calling out corrections to me. He'd been coordinating and overseeing my workouts for the past two and a half days.

"Get used to the weapon, but don't get overconfident," he warned.

Jaquard parried and lunged at me with movements that were so practiced they seemed more like reflexes. I sidestepped a jab and whipped Aurora up to impact Jaquard's side just below his ribs. The blade bit into his stone armor, and he winced.

We paused and Oliver came forward. The three of us watched in silence as Jaquard lifted his shirt to reveal a crack in his armor. Blood began to seep through it.

"Damn, sorry about that," I said. It wasn't the first wound Aurora had inflicted on my training opponents.

"No apologies," the expert swordsman said. "You need to see how the champion blades affect stone armor." He pointed at the crack. "This will be you if Twilight strikes you edge-on."

I nodded, flexing my jaw muscles and rolling my shoulders to try to relax my arms and neck. We'd discovered that Aurora could crack rock armor, but only with a very precise hit with the edge of the blade. The flat of the blade or even a slightly angled slice didn't seem to cause serious harm.

Oliver turned to me. "Your opponent may not know about this, but we can't assume it for sure. The Duergar have people with stone armor. If the wielder of Twilight happens to practice against one, they'll likely discover this weakness."

A New Gargoyle had never fought a battle of champions, as the last fight had taken place before the Cataclysm and the emergence of our kind.

"Get that treated, Jaquard," Oliver said. He lifted a finger at me. "And you go to the mineral sauna, and then go home for rest and food."

I released my own armor, and in its absence the familiar ache spread over my skin. Fatigue began to set in at once. I'd been working out with fully activated armor for extended periods, and it was incredibly draining. If not for the rejuvenating treatments in the mineral sauna and salt baths, I'd have been comatose.

Emmaline jumped up and trotted over to take Aurora. She accompanied me to the mineral room.

"Tired?" she asked.

I nodded, circling my dominant arm. "Nothing that can't be fixed, though."

I hadn't been in the mood for much conversation since I'd been knighted, but she got it, for which I was grateful.

When I emerged from the mineral sauna with steam clinging to my skin, Emmaline was waiting with a towel for wiping off my face and hands.

"Food's waiting, and I ordered more salts for your bath," she said with business-like efficiency.

As we passed through the corridors, eyes lingered on me. Everyone knew that I'd been knighted and would be fighting the Duergar champion.

"How'd I look out there?" I asked Emmaline, mostly as an excuse to ignore the curious looks.

"Amazing," she said, her voice edged with awe. "I can't even describe what it's like to watch Aurora in action."

"Ah, so it's not me, but the sword?" I teased.

"Well, it's both," she said. "I can't imagine two such weapons clashing. It will be like watching the gods themselves. You're going to slaughter the Duergar champion, of course," she quickly added.

At her mention of the gods, I went quiet, remembering how Jasper had sworn that the Tuatha de Danann had returned. In the whirlwind of the past few days, there hadn't been an opportunity to think much about his wild claims.

When I returned to my quarters, I found Nicole in the kitchenette. It was the first time I'd seen her in days. The Stone Order was supposed to find her an apartment of her own, but at the news of my impending battle, every New Gargoyle had flocked back to the fortress in support, and there was a bit of a housing shuffle underway.

I realized I'd hardly spoken to her since breaking her out of the Duergar kingdom.

"Hi," she said. She curiously scanned the welts on my exposed arms. "Did you get hurt?"

I shook my head. "Nah, this is just what happens after long use of stone armor."

She plopped a tea bag in the mug of steaming water she'd just pulled out of the microwave.

"They're trying to get me to summon stone armor," she said. "If I can't, the Duergar king might be able to take me again."

Her eyes were sunken with dark smudges under them. Her glance flicked to my squire, and she watched Emmaline set down my gym bag and then leave quietly with the swords.

I peeled off my sweatshirt, still damp from the mineral sauna. "Still feel like you've fallen down the rabbit hole?" I asked.

Nicole was staring over the rim of her mug at nothing. She nodded, her eyes still unfocused. "Magical rock armor, battling Fae kingdoms, champion swordfights . . . Sometimes I'm positive I'm in a coma and this is all a dream."

She'd been angry before, but in that moment she just seemed pensive. "No luck with the armor yet, huh?"

"None whatsoever. Based on what I've been told, I'm starting to think you all made a mistake about my bloodline."

"But you do believe you're Fae now?"

She sighed. "Yes. I was able to detect glamour, and I passed a couple of other minor tests."

I eased back onto the sofa, stretching out my tired legs. "It's a lot to take in," I said quietly.

Her focus sharpened, and she looked up at me. "I have to figure out the stone armor. I can't go back to the Duergar kingdom." Her face had paled. "I've learned enough about the Unseelie to know I can't end up there."

I sat up and then pushed to my feet. "I might have something to help you," I said and disappeared into my bedroom. I rummaged around in a box on the floor of the closet until my hand closed around a cool stone.

I came back to Nicole and held it up. "I used this when I was learning."

The stone, about the size of a large marble, was the soothing pale white-blue of aquamarine.

She came over to examine it, and I handed it to her.

"How does it work?" she asked.

"Use the techniques they're teaching you to summon rock armor, and keep that in your hand," I said. "Imagine you can spread the minerals from the stone like butter over your skin. There's nothing magic about it, it's just a visualization exercise. But it might help."

An almost-smile touched her lips. "Thank you," she said and then slapped her fingers over her mouth, her eyes wide. Her hand fell away. "Oh, shit. I'm not supposed to say that here."

I chuckled. "It's okay. There was no magic attached to the words, so I won't hold you to it. I'm sorry I haven't been around much. I'm supposed to be helping you adjust, and I've done a piss-poor job of that."

She lifted a shoulder and let it drop. "Eh, you've got bigger worries."

My food arrived just then, as well as her escort to another session with Fern, her magic coach of sorts. Nicole folded the aquamarine stone in her hand and tucked her fist into the pocket of her jacket, giving me a little wave with her other hand as she disappeared out the door.

I did feel bad I hadn't been more present. Nicole looked like a lost puppy. Not that I could do much for her—she'd been ripped from her life and home and thrust into a strange place that probably seemed like a fever dream. But once the battle was over, I'd make more of an effort. Most likely I was going to have to move back into the fortress, anyway, considering the way things were going on the other side of the hedge with my Guild job.

I stiffened, suddenly remembering my new assignment, and let out a string of curses. The chances of completing that job on deadline were slim to none, with my current obligation as the Stone Order's champion. After a moment, I had to laugh at myself. Was I seriously worried about some piddly lost-object assignment when I might not even survive the challenge? It was a reflex, though—keeping good on my promise to make a life away from the fortress so I could hunt vamps. And in spite of how hard I'd fought in the past ten years to make it on my own on the other side of the hedge, I'd somehow ended up right back in the stone fortress.

I planted my hands on my hips and blew out a harsh breath through pursed lips. Kind of ironic. There I was, the champion of the Stone Order and about to fight an epic battle in Faerie but on the brink of bankruptcy and eviction from my apartment on the other side of the hedge. An observer might wonder why I was trying so hard to make it out there.

But I knew why—here, in Faerie, I might be the champion of the moment, but if I stayed permanently, I'd be under Marisol's thumb. And on the other side of the hedge there would be criminal vampires on the loose, luring people in with their glamour, enticing them with the promise of VAMP3 charm, and victimizing weak and unstable people like my mother.

A rap on the door interrupted my sour thoughts.

A knot of officials, with Maxen and Oliver in the lead, stood on the other side. It was an array of tense faces and serious, unblinking eyes.

"It's set," Maxen said. "The High Court has ruled that the battle of champions will happen at dawn tomorrow."

Chapter 25

MY FIRST THOUGHT was that the timing of the battle had to be at least a symbolic decision in my favor because Aurora was the sword of the summer dawn. I decided to take it that way, even if it was an arbitrary choice. My second thought was that my training had just come to an abrupt end.

A flurry of activities happened after that. A tailor came to measure me—apparently they'd been working on a custom battle uniform for me to wear—and then I was ordered to go back to the mineral sauna. Marisol had brought out a secret healing stone for my last sauna session of the day.

Oliver and Jaquard came into the mineral room with me. They'd discovered who my opponent would be.

"Darion is King Periclase's brother," Jaquard said. "Like Periclase, he acquired spontaneous New Gargoyle blood at the Cataclysm. Unlike Periclase, Darion is able to summon full stone armor."

"Damn," I muttered. "So he's thick as an ox, and he has rock armor. What kind of training's he had?"

"Standard Duergar battle ranks," Oliver said and paused. "And he's been the master of arms for the past two decades."

Ugh. That meant he was an expert in various types of weapons, as well as various flavors of hand-to-hand combat.

I leaned back against the wall of the mineral room and folded my arms. "He may not limit himself to Twilight, then."

The two swordsmen glanced at each other.

"This is where you may have an obvious advantage," Oliver said. "He's definitely more comfortable with short swords. The only time he ever worked with a larger blade was in his early military days. He will be required to start the battle with Twilight, as is the custom, but he'll probably be looking for an excuse to go to the weapons he's comfortable with. You're each allowed an alternate weapon on your body. Two of them if they're shorter than a broadsword. Short swords or daggers, for example."

"Is he allowed to just toss Twilight at any time and pull out his short sword?" I asked.

Jaquard held up his index finger. "No, and that's the trick. He can only use an alternate weapon if you managed to knock Twilight clear of his reach."

I tilted my gaze to the floor, thinking. "Do I try to hold him to using Twilight, a weapon he's less comfortable with but that can potentially kill me much easier? Or let him go for the weapon he's more skilled with but that can't pierce my rock armor?"

"That's the question of the day," Oliver said. "Jaq and I have talked about it, and we think that's a strategic decision you're going to have to make on the battlefield."

I looked up at the two men. "It'd be nice to have that strategy hashed out beforehand, but I think you're right."

"The other thing to think about is the likelihood that Oberon will call a winner before anyone gets killed," Jaquard said. "It's happened in every champion battle in modern history."

"Why is that?" I asked.

He gave a small shake of his head. "No one knows for sure. Some think Oberon considers the traditional fight to the death too uncivilized for modern times."

"But it needs to be part of your strategy too," Oliver jumped in. "If the battle is clearly favoring either you or Darion—"

"That must factor into my decisions," I finished. "Because if Oberon calls it early, all I need to do is show that I'm the better fighter."

"Exactly."

"Any other intel about Darion's skills or weaknesses?" I asked.

"He's got a temper," Jaquard said. "He's not been known to show it on the battlefield, but he's renowned in the Duergar kingdom for his short fuse."

One side of my mouth tilted up. "I wonder how he feels about having to fight a woman."

"I think it's safe to assume his attitude is what many men's would be in this situation, if they're not familiar with your skills," my father said carefully. "Over-confidence. Arrogance. Perhaps he's even insulted on some level."

"But that's to your advantage," Jaquard said.

A cold, calculating smile spread over my face. "And you can be damn sure I'll use it."

After the mineral room, I was fitted with my battle clothing. Vera, the lead stylist who'd overseen my makeover for the trip to the Duergar kingdom, came to lend a hand.

"I didn't know battle gear was also your department," I said teasingly.

"Oh my goodness, it's not," she said. "But a warrior can still utilize style. Your opponent, and your opponent's kinsmen, will take note of your appearance. You must give the right impression."

I chuckled. "Fair enough."

My outfit was made of a thick woven material that glinted with metal threads. It wasn't quite armor—I'd never fought with the weight of true armor and didn't want to start now—but it would offer some protection. It was tight-fitting, with extra-thick layers around my torso and back and over my thighs, shoulders, and upper arms. The sleeves extended down over the tops of my hands, with loops to go around my fingers and hold the sleeves in place. Light gloves of the same metal-laced fabric would give me protection and additional grip.

An ultralight and closefitting helmet was made of a flexible alloy with interior padding. It wouldn't prevent getting my bell rung if I took a blow to the head, but it would keep a blade from slicing through my skull. An oblong oval opening allowed me to see unobstructed.

Shoes that looked like low-profile track sneakers had hidden metal plates over the arches and toes.

The whole getup was in the white-accented grays of the Stone Order, and it transformed me into a high-tech knight. Over it I added my scabbard that held Mort. The beat-up strap didn't exactly match with the rest of the outfit, but the familiar pull of it across my chest and the weight of my shadowsteel spellblade made it feel complete.

I took the battle clothing off so the tailors could make a few final adjustments, and I put my regular clothes back on. Then it was off to a dinner meeting with Maxen so he could brief me on protocol.

We met in his quarters, which was a nice change from the flurry of the public spaces. We ate standing up at his kitchen counter and looking down at the tablet where he'd pulled up some images.

"This is the stadium of Oberon's High Court," he said, pointing at the picture. "Oberon and Titania will be in the royal box with their court and any special guests on either side and behind. The New Gargoyles will be on this side, and the Duergar on that side."

"Do I get comped any tickets? Because I'd like them now so I can scalp them for rent money," I said, deadpan.

He turned his sapphire gaze on me and slowly straightened. "All you have to do is say the word and you can come back to the fortress. This is your home, Petra."

"This was my *childhood* home," I said quietly. "That's the thing. I can't save my mother. No one was able to save her. But hunting down criminal vamps feels like the only connection I have to her. The only way to do right by her. Plus, you know how I feel about being under monarch rule every waking minute. I'll do what I can for the Order—I *am* doing it—but I can't just drop my Guild work. It's important to me, too."

I expected him to try his usual persuasion, but he just nodded once and went back to the tablet. He ran through a few more details.

"You and your opponent will enter the stadium through here." He indicated a tunnel. "You'll go to the royal box and bow. Oberon will read the rules of the challenge. Then you'll separate to your marks, which will be chalked on the dirt."

"No sweat," I said. "I don't even have to try to curtsy."

He gave me a faint grin. "We've also arranged for you to stay in upgraded quarters tonight. You'll be under guard. After the servitor attack, we just want to make sure you're secure. The fortress is at your service, Petra. If there's anything at all you need, don't hesitate to ask."

With the official duties out of the way, he seemed to relax slightly. "Can you believe you're going to wield Aurora in front of Oberon tomorrow?" He shook his head slowly. "I mean, that's . . . *bad ass.*"

I grinned. "Does it make me sound insane if I say there's a part of me that can't fucking wait?"

He laughed. "I'd expect nothing less from Petra Maguire." Then he sobered somewhat. "But if anything happens to you . . ."

"I'm not going to die." It seemed like I was saying that a lot lately.

Emmaline arrived to take me to my fancy-ass quarters, where there was a fire crackling in the fireplace of the insanely huge bedroom that featured a king-sized four-poster bed. My battle clothing was hanging in an armoire.

"Anything I can do for you tonight?" she asked, her eyes big and her expression drawn.

"For one thing, relax. Your face is making me tense."

She snorted. "Sorry. I just want to do what I can to help."

I took her by the shoulders. "I'm. Not. Going. To. Die."

"No, Oberon won't let it go that far," she said firmly, and I got the feeling it was more to reassure herself than me.

"Get some sleep," I said. "It's a big day for you tomorrow, too, squire."

Emmaline left, and I lowered the lights and stretched out on the bed, staring at the fire and running through battle scenarios in my mind. Eventually, the adrenaline of anticipation gave way to fatigue, and I slipped into the hard sleep that comes after many hours of physical training.

I awoke with a start in the dark room with the smell of a log fire hanging in the air. Purplish pre-dawn light filtered through the curtains. I pushed myself up and rolled over to check the time. Ten minutes till my quarters became a whirlwind of preparation.

By the time people began arriving, I had my shower-damp hair pulled into a tight braid that ran down the middle of my back.

Emmaline came into my bedroom to help me put on the battle clothing. She was dressed in squire's clothing that matched the colors I wore. Her serious demeanor had returned, and her hands trembled just a little at first. But she held her chin up as she surveyed me in full battle dress, her lavender eyes fierce.

"You look like a legend," she said sincerely.

"Now all I have to do is fight like one."

We went out to the living room area, where it seemed like half the Order had gathered. Everyone was in formal dress, and you could practically smell the tension in the air.

The murmur of conversation went quiet as people noticed I'd emerged.

I stretched my hands in front of me, cracking my knuckles. "Seems like a good day to kick some Duergar ass," I said loud enough to carry through the room.

There were some chuckles and a few shouts of agreement, and some of the pressure in the room dissipated.

Marisol was there, looking regal as always. Her eyes were tired, though. I couldn't deny the larger implications of this battle for the Stone Order. It shone a spotlight on us, and it was a chance to show that we wouldn't be pushed around by the established kingdoms. I blew out a slow breath and began pulling in my focus. Emmaline stood at my left, and the crowd allowed us some space.

Oliver appeared at my other side. "Remember your strategy, Petra," he said to me quietly. "Remember what you talked about with me and Jaquard. Most of all, remember who you are, and know without doubt what you're capable of. You can win this. You *will* win."

I nodded, my gaze only flicking to his for a split second. I appreciated his support, but I couldn't get emotional. This was the time to go within. For all the bravado I'd displayed the past few days, I knew there was a possibility this battle would be the last thing I ever did. Darion wasn't going to take it easy on me. After all, his pride and his kingdom's honor were at stake, and Periclase had originally called for my head.

I let the others float around me like a cloud as I was led out of my quarters, through the fortress, and into the gardens. I was aware of them, and the words being spoken, but kept myself apart by my silence. We'd be using the doorway there to get to Oberon's stadium. The complete stillness of the void was a welcome though brief respite, further helping me sink into my mental preparation.

When I emerged at a doorway outside the stadium adorned with the banners of all the Fae kingdoms and orders, the New Gargoyle officials who were accompanying me lined up in formation. Emmaline went first, with me behind her and the rest marching like my own personal military.

As we filed toward the tunnel with the New Garg geometric insignia flying over it, I glanced over to see the Duergar doing the same. I caught sight of my opponent, a big man who in his battle gear appeared larger even than Periclase. Darion glowered at me. I gave him a little wink just before he disappeared from sight.

King Periclase went in right behind his brother, but not before sending me a hard, unblinking look. In the rank and file accompanying Darion, I spotted the flash of Jasper's golden eyes. Even from a distance, I could see that his face was clouded. His eyes flicked over my battle clothing, and he gave me the slightest of nods.

I wasn't sure what it meant—perhaps a wish of good luck? It didn't matter. I pulled in my focus again as we marched into the tunnel.

Horns blared flourishes. My people continued on to the right, going up a staircase that would lead them to their seats. I avoided their glances, keeping my gaze forward.

Emmaline and I stayed behind, standing alone in the dark tunnel as the first warm light of dawn began to illuminate the circular open doorway ahead that led into the arena.

I slowed my breathing and curled my hands inside my gloves.

The horns went silent and then started again. A cheer went up from the crowd. Oberon had arrived.

Chapter 26

THE NEXT FLOURISH was my signal to enter the arena. Emmaline waited for me to go and then fell into step behind me.

The sounds of the horns and the crowd seemed far away as I walked down the tunnel and out into the faint morning light. The murmur of the crowd swelled when I emerged. Darion stood fifty feet away. We both made ninety-degree turns inward and strode toward the center of the arena and then turned to face the royal box.

I looked up and then blinked, for a moment wondering if we'd come in too early or done something wrong.

Oberon's seat was empty.

Titania was there, standing with her orange-and-gold streaked hair flowing over her shoulders. There was a corona of soft light around her that was only visible when you didn't look at her quite straight-on but gave the impression she was illuminated from behind. Her perfect skin looked sun-kissed, dewy, and ageless.

But she wasn't the serene Summer Queen. Her nostrils were flared, and her eyes flashed. She looked, well, pissed.

I kept facing forward but flicked my eyes over at Darion. He shifted his weight, and his head made small back-and-forth movements as he scanned the seats, obviously also surprised by Oberon's absence.

My gut tightened as I resisted the temptation to look over at the New Gargs.

Where the hell was Oberon?

Titania looked at each of us with an expression of pointed annoyance, and I folded at the waist, bowing. Darion quickly did the same.

With a sinking feeling, I listened to the Queen of the Summer Court recite the rules of the battle. As I knew to expect, we were each allowed to carry an alternate weapon into battle. Other than that, there really weren't any rules, aside from giving the King and Queen the authority to call the battle and declare a winner at any point.

She finished and flopped into her chair, slouching over to one side and propping her cheek on her fist. She looked equally angry and bored, and as if she'd rather be anywhere else.

Fuckedy *fuck.*

I'd have bet anything that she and Oberon were in the middle of one of their legendary quarrels. Their tumultuous relationship had spanned eons, and their fights could literally last years at a time.

Normally I wouldn't care about the spats of the Old Ones, but I needed Oberon, not a bunch of petty Faerie bullshit. Because judging by Titania's face, watching someone get slaughtered in the arena might actually improve her mood. In spite of the modern trend of Oberon halting champion battles before they ended in death, the Old Ones were a violent, hot-tempered, blood-loving bunch. There was a reason the oldest Fae lore was full of pointy-toothed gore.

I went to Emmaline for my weapons.

"He's not here," she whispered, not moving her mouth, as she lifted Mort's scabbard over my head and positioned it on my shoulder.

"Nothing to be done about it now," I muttered back.

She presented Aurora, still sheathed. I withdrew the blade, and the legendary sword glinted in the morning light.

"Stay strong," Emmaline said. "Use his weaknesses against him."

I only nodded and clapped a hand on her shoulder in gratitude.

Emmaline took Aurora's empty scabbard and retreated to a box seat designated for my squire.

For a second, I closed my eyes and tightened my grip on Aurora. Then I turned, drew magic to form full rock armor under my battle gear, and walked to my chalked line to face my opponent.

Chapter 27

THE NOISE OF the crowd swelled as each side began cheering on their champion.

In the couple of seconds I had to observe Darion while we took our marks, I realized he was as not as tall as a typical New Gargoyle man, but almost as broad in the shoulder. He was powerfully muscled, a man who'd spent a lifetime working his body and wasn't afraid to use it.

His stature was intimidating, but I'd been fighting larger men and women my entire life. Size wasn't always an advantage.

The audience quieted. A short burst from the horns marked the start of the battle.

I turned my attention to Darion's blade. Twilight, the blade of the Winter Court, seemed to absorb the light around it. The sword was identical to Aurora in design, but instead of the golden glow of Aurora, Twilight shimmered deep purples and blues, colors that reminded me more of a fresh bruise than the evening sky.

I instinctively took a classic fencing stance, my body turned sideways to minimize my opponent's target, and shifted my weight slightly forward.

Darion wasted no time. With a few quick but carefully measured steps, he moved forward, swinging Twilight in an arc and twisting at the waist to add force to his blow. He was going for power right out of the gate, not bothering to protect himself much.

Anticipating a harsh impact, I gripped Aurora with both hands and braced my arms. My blade deflected his blow, interrupting the angle of his attack just enough to prevent a hit.

I swiftly switched back to a one-handed grip, danced a wide step to the side, and flicked my wrist. Darion was still off balance from his maneuver, his elbow raised to leave a small opening. Aurora glanced off his hip, and the New Garg side of the crowd roared.

I'd inflicted no damage, but even a touch would score me points if Titania decided to declare a winner before there was a fatality.

I hadn't injured Darion, but apparently I'd really pissed him off.

His lips curled into a sneer. "You're going to die, little stone girl."

With a snarl, Darion gripped Twilight in two fists, lunged at me, and brought the blade down like an ax. The edge of the sword was aiming straight for my skull. By instinct I knew there was too much power to deflect. Instead, I dove and rolled, and Twilight smacked into the hard dirt where I'd been standing a split second before.

So far, his attack was all brute force, and he was going for deadly shots. He wasn't trying to score touches, and as we circled each other, each crouched low, I wondered if he knew something I didn't. Perhaps Titania wouldn't be following Oberon's practice of calling a winner before either champion died. Or maybe brute force was just Darion's style.

He sprang again, going for a driving stab, and I darted out of the way, managing to land a solid hit against the Achilles of his rear foot as I moved. If he didn't have stone armor, I would have sliced the tendon. He barely seemed to notice the blow.

I shouldn't have gone for the touch. It kept me too close. He whipped around and landed a backhand blow on the left side of my lower back. Pain blasted outward from the impact, nearly paralyzing me for a second. Immediately after, I felt the slow ooze of wetness. He'd cracked my armor.

Clamping my teeth against the agony, I regained my balance and took a couple of shuffling side-steps to open some distance between us.

I made a few quick, puffing breaths through my lips to clear my head and refocus my awareness away from the pain. Then I let the sensation seep in, as Oliver had taught me, using the sting to fortify my resolve.

I attacked, my footwork lightning-fast and my wrist moving as if following some pre-determined choreography. It surprised Darion, throwing him back on his heels. He used his strength to fend me off, but I wasn't going for points anymore. He'd wounded me. I intended to return the favor.

I danced him backward, keeping him off balance as much as possible. Every time Aurora and Twilight clashed, there was a small spark like a flint strike.

I gripped Aurora in both hands for a moment of extra power and slashed in a tight C. I twisted at the waist, ignoring the screaming pain in my lower back and throwing all my weight and momentum into the attack. The blade sliced at the side of his knee, hitting edge-on, producing a sharp snap that was like a firecracker report.

He bellowed as his knee buckled. I'd fractured his armor.

I kept up my attack. I knew the pain he was in, and I was sure as hell going to use it.

He was partially hunched over, his non-dominant hand bracing the back of his injured knee while he defended my attack using Twilight in his other hand. He managed to swipe at my torso, gouging a line across my battle shirt and scraping a groove in my rock armor. It hurt but didn't draw blood.

His knee, meanwhile, was dripping crimson.

I increased the force and speed of my effort, trying to land a hit on his sword arm. If I could force him to switch to his non-dominant hand, I'd have a huge advantage.

Aurora and Twilight clashed together once, twice, sending out small bolts of lightning that left ozone hanging in the air. On my third try, I managed to hit the inside of Darion's wrist. It wasn't hard enough to crack his armor, but his grip reflexively loosened. Twilight flew to the side and landed with a dull clang on the dirt.

Darion gave a little chuckle as he crossed his arms low over his torso, gripped the short swords at either hip, and drew them. He was clearly delighted to be able to switch to the weapons he was comfortable with. That didn't bode well for me.

"Shit," I muttered under my breath.

Then he flew at me. His injured leg dragged behind, but his blades blurred as he worked both of them in synchronous movements. One of them jarred against my dominant shoulder, not cracking the armor, but ringing my entire body like a bell. My brain rattled, and my vision blurred.

Blinking to clear my eyes and dancing like a madwoman, I forced more speed into my movements. He was working me backward, and landing about every third hit attempt. His short swords wouldn't break my armor, but a slice to the neck or a hard enough blow to my head and I'd be finished.

Or he could just wear me down with force, as he seemed to be trying to do.

I sank even deeper into the movements, anticipating his swings and drives. After a couple minutes of straight fighting—an eternity at that level of exertion—we'd reached a sort of impasse, neither of us gaining any real ground and both of us breathing hard.

Darion swung out and caught me on the arm again and then backed off. His chest was heaving, and I was sucking wind, too. But the pause gave me a chance to see that the dirt was stained maroon where he'd been moving. He was bleeding very badly from his knee. And then it dawned on me: the Duergar didn't have a mineral sauna. It and the special salts were closely-held New Gargoyle secrets. The Duergar couldn't know as much about strengthening and healing stone armor as we did.

Darion's rock armor was weaker than mine, and I still held a weapon that could destroy his natural shield, if only I could summon the strength to do it.

My arms ached from deflecting blows, my body throbbed from the hits, and I was still out of breath, but I flew at him. His swords whirled into action again. I aimed for his armor, protecting myself only when he went for my head. He landed bone-jarring blows all over my body, but I shut out the pain. I lunged in again and again, taking hits but keeping my focus on trying to get past his defenses.

Finally, he made a mistake, leaving one side open. I swung Aurora and landed an armor-cracking blow on his thigh. He let out a low, strangled noise, his back arching in pain.

I caught him again on the elbow, and he bellowed louder. He brought his blades up again and sent them flying at me, but the one in the hand of the injured arm moved sloppily.

Still, bleeding from three different cracks didn't weaken his attack much. He came at me with fury and pain flashing in his eyes. After landing a couple of hard hits to my torso and leg, he tossed one short sword away and gripped the other in both hands. Then he began hammering at me with renewed resolve.

One blow flicked off my shoulder and caught my helmet over my ear. Pain blossomed bright and harsh. Sound faded on that side of my head. Spots swirled in my eyes.

The hit just seemed to spur him on. Growling with rage, he swung ferociously. I was quicker, but his brute strength drove me back, step by step.

I managed to smack his forearm with Aurora, but it was with the flat of the blade.

Then he lunged and shoved his foot into my diaphragm. I flew backward, landing hard on my ass and skidding a few feet. Unable to tighten up to stop my momentum, the back of my head smacked the dirt. When my vison went gray, only his enraged howl warned me to roll out of the way.

My sight returned just as he dove at me again. I curled to one side, barely avoiding the blow aimed at my head. Again, I rolled, but he was right on top of me. From my back, I wielded Aurora, barely fending off his punishing blows. He wasn't saving any strength. He was trying to end it, but not because he was overpowering me. His wounds were gushing blood, and he was getting weaker.

My mind sharpened, sensing his fading energy. I also realized Titania wasn't going to stop the battle.

He tried to fall onto me, presumably to hold me down so he could slit my throat. I scuttled backward, but not quite swiftly enough. He landed on one of my ankles, pinning it under his shin. I struggled, fending off his strikes with one hand while I tried to pull myself out from under his weight.

He straightened, wound up like a batter at the plate, and swung at my sword arm. As he did it, I saw the rage boiling in his eyes. He was hurting, he was furious, and I was suddenly positive that he didn't know how to channel pain the way I did. With his size and strength and his position in the Duergar military, he'd probably never had to.

He'd never been an underdog.

I raised my arm to protect my head. The crack of his blade against my forearm nearly made me pass out. I dropped Aurora as the nerves of my arm spasmed and screamed agony.

I couldn't look away to find my lost weapon, and I doubted I could command my spasming right hand to pick it up anyway. I reached back with my left hand and drew Mort. Magic flooded into my spellblade, lighting it in purple flames. I jabbed at Darion's face, and he lurched to one side to avoid the magic as it licked out through the air at him, forming tiny blades that would slice his skin like razors.

Finally free of his weight, I pulled my legs in. Just as he tried to lunge at me again, I rocked to my back, and then I sharply shoved my heel at the center of his face. His nose spurted blood, and his hand flew to the injury. I didn't care how badass and tough you were, a blow to the nose was enough to distract anyone for at least a second or two.

I tried to struggle to my feet, but my damaged ankle wouldn't take any weight. My right arm, the one I fought with, was still numb from the elbow down. Worse than that, injuries, exhaustion, and blows to the head had stolen my balance. The world was tilting violently, and the edges were going black. If I managed to stand, I wouldn't last long. I wouldn't last long on the ground, either.

I didn't want the battle to end with a corpse. But Darion was fighting to kill, and Titania wasn't going to call it. If the challenge was going to end in death, I sure as hell wasn't going to let it be mine.

I pushed up to one elbow, almost sitting. "Even one-handed and flat on my back, I'm bettering you," I spat at him through clenched teeth. "What kind of champion loses to a woman half his size?"

And then I laughed, a mocking, jeering laugh that carried to the crowd.

His face screwed up, and the parts I could see through the openings of his faceplate began to turn purple. Then he launched himself at me.

I watched him lift off the ground and then loom in the air over me for the briefest moment. I gripped Mort hard, the blade laying diagonally across my torso. At the last possible second, I threw up my injured arm to ward off the blow of Darion's short sword, and I flicked Mort upright, aiming the tip of my broadsword at Darion's throat and bracing the end of the hilt against the ground.

The Duergar crashed on top of me, his sword scraping off my arm like a knife across concrete. Then there was a deafening scream. He rolled off me, his sword discarded and both hands on the side of his neck. By design, I'd missed by a few inches, not quite running Mort through the middle of his throat. Blood gushed from between his fingers. He writhed, his screams dissolving into wet, bubbling noises.

My chest heaving, I watched in a daze as the blood streamed down his arm to drip in the dirt.

I could have finished him off, but there was still a chance he could be saved if there was a powerful enough healer nearby. I had no desire for his death on my hands.

I sheathed Mort and crawled over to Aurora. Then, with the legendary blade in my left hand, I forced myself to stand. My vision doubled and blurred, but I squinted and made out where the royal box was. I walked, holding back a scream each time I had to put weight on my broken ankle. With Darion's agonized gurgles at my back, I limped over to stand before Titania and looked up at her, blinking as I tried to focus. She was the only one besides the champions in the ring who could end this battle. Either she called it, or I dragged my ass back over to Darion and killed him. He was still making drowning noises behind me.

Finally, taking her sweet time, the Faerie Queen of the Summer Court stood.

"The High Court declares the winner of this battle of champions." Her voice carried through the silent stadium. She gestured at me with her open hand. "Petra Maguire of the Stone Order."

The New Gargoyle side of the arena erupted in a deafening tidal wave of noise.

I shakily went down on one knee before the Faerie Queen, bowing my head. I even managed to stand up again, using Aurora for leverage. But that was all I had left.

The last thing I remembered was Emmaline running toward me, a glimpse of Lochlyn beyond, standing up at her seat with tears running down her face, and my father vaulting out of the stands and racing after Emmaline.

Then my knees buckled, and the world dissolved into darkness.

Chapter 28

AT ONE POINT I became aware of the sensation of movement and felt that I was being carried. My eyelids cracked open, and I could have sworn I was in Oliver's arms. I wasn't sure if I was dreaming.

The next time I awoke, it was in a soft bed in a nearly dark room. There were quiet mechanical whirs. Warm humidity permeated the air, along with the damp-stone smell I associated with the mineral sauna.

I lay there, blinking in the darkness as the details of the battle slowly crept back into my mind. Overhead, I saw a canopy suspended by four posts on the corners of the bed. I recognized the bedroom where I'd spent the night before the battle.

With stiff movements, I pushed up to my elbows. I had to pee like nobody's business. My ankle had been bound and splinted, and it hurt to walk on it, but it had already healed considerably.

When I limped out of the on-suite bathroom, someone was standing in the bedroom.

"Emmaline!" I barked. "Don't be such a damn creeper!"

She rushed to my side, pulling my arm across her shoulders. "You're not supposed be up," she said with a fretting tone. "They're going to kill me for letting you walk around."

"It was that or piss the bed," I said sourly.

Since my blood was flowing and some of the fog of sleep had burned away, every fiber of my being hurt. The worst of it was centered on the left side of my lower back, where my rock armor had split under Darion's blow. It was like a line of burning needles driven bone-deep.

"Did he die?" I asked, letting her ease me back onto the bed.

"No," she said. "But he's not going into battle anytime soon."

I let out a long breath as I settled back into the pillows and then winced at the pressure on my injury. I shifted to my side. Fatigue still sat heavy in my bones.

"I should go let the others know you're awake," she said.

I mumbled something unintelligible and then gratefully sank into sleep.

The next time I woke, the curtains had been pulled back, and pale morning light glowed in the window. I moved under the covers, testing the pain of my injuries. I still felt like shit, but a little less so than before.

The bedroom door pushed open a few inches, and Oliver's face appeared.

"I thought I heard you moving," he said. He came in and sat on the edge of the bed, his eyes searching my face. "How are you feeling?"

"Like I survived a plane crash."

His head bobbed. "Sounds about right. Want food?"

Right then I realized my stomach felt as if it were trying to eat itself.

"For the love of Oberon, yes. Bring me all the food."

He left and came back with a tray piled with sandwiches. Just as I dug in, another head poked through the doorway.

"Okay if I come in?" Maxen asked.

I flipped my fingers, beckoning him inside, but didn't stop shoving food in my face.

I swallowed. "Is King Periclase backing off now, or am I going to have to kick more Duergar ass?" I asked.

He grinned and then inclined his head in a little bow. "The High Court dropped Periclase's petition on you, and even better, Nicole was able to demonstrate rock armor this morning to prove she has New Garg blood."

I let out a relieved breath. "Periclase could still be her father, though."

"Yes, but anyone able to form rock armor has enough New Garg blood to swear to the Stone Order," Maxen said. "It makes it possible for her to stay."

"What about the other stuff, Periclase trying to absorb the Stone Order into his kingdom?"

"That is still an issue of debate," he said. His expression sobered. "But no one knows where King Oberon is."

I glanced between Maxen and my father. "What do you mean?"

"He's gone. Oberon's nowhere to be found in Faerie."

I frowned. "So, what, everything going through the High Court just stalls?"

Maxen held up his palms. "Titania is apparently refusing to deal with it. She says it's his mess and she's not going to do his work for him."

I rolled my eyes. "Fricking Fae."

"That's not your problem, in any case," Maxen said. He drew a breath but didn't say anything for a moment. Then he turned to Oliver. "Would you mind giving me a moment alone with Petra?"

My brows shot up. Oliver looked a little taken aback, too, but he rose and left, closing the door behind him.

Maxen took Oliver's place on the edge of the bed. "The conflict with the Duergar isn't going to go away just because Oberon's decided to disappear. Marisol is going to be pushing harder to establish us as a kingdom, but it's going to take even more work if Oberon isn't here to make a ruling. After your victory, it would be very good for the Stone Order if you stayed here."

I frowned. "Why should my presence make any difference?"

"We need to look as unified as possible as a people," Maxen said. "Having our champion cut and run to the other side of the hedge as soon as the battle's over doesn't look very good."

A small flare of anger lit in my chest. I put my sandwich down. "Seriously, Maxen? After what I just did, you're telling me I owe *more*?"

"I know it seems unfair to ask, to pressure you like this, but this is life in Faerie. As a people, we have to give everything we have, or the New Gargoyles don't stand a chance of establishing our independence."

My mouth worked, but I didn't respond.

"I know you're out of money, Petra. And I know you're on probation with the Guild," Maxen said quietly. "Do you really have a choice?"

I looked off to the side. That stung.

"There's always a choice," I said, my voice hard. "And the thing is, even as champion, I'd have no freedom here. I'd have to quit hunting vamps. Do you understand how that would feel like a betrayal of my mother? And Marisol would tell me what to do and when to do it, and I'd have to obey her every order."

He lifted a shoulder and let it drop. "That's Faerie. That's the plight of our people. And here's the thing, something that Oliver doesn't even know yet. Marisol is going to start calling in New Gargs at the fall equinox, all the changelings and all the Order-sworn who live on the other side of the hedge. You're going to be in the first group summoned. You can wait until then if you want to, but you *will* be called back to the fortress, and you'll have to stay for as long as she wants you here. If you do it by choice before you're forced, you'll be rewarded for it. If not, you won't be happy with the result."

"Or I refuse the call," I said sullenly.

"You wouldn't."

He was right. Refusing such an order from my sovereign meant more or less giving up my magic and all my ties to Faerie. I'd be permanently exiled from this side of the hedge.

My anger flared again, but I tamped it down, keeping tight control.

I pierced him with a cold look. "You're practically blackmailing me, you and your mother. Not only that, you're doing it while I'm sitting here, unable to walk under my own power, with my wounds still fresh from the arena."

He blinked, his eyes tightening, but didn't argue. He also didn't apologize.

"I can't help the timing," he said finally.

"That's all you have to say?"

He stood slowly. I could tell he wasn't happy, but I was all out of sympathy for Maxen and his mother.

"Finish your business on the other side of the hedge," he said. "Then come home."

He turned and left.

I started to reach for my sandwich, but when I saw my own hands trembling with unspent anger, I curled my fingers into fists.

In less than a month, Marisol would summon me here and take away my freedom for as long as she wanted to. She'd force me to quit hunting vamps. And really, there wasn't a damn thing I could do. I'd have to figure out a way to ride it out. To get released from her call. But for the moment, I was too weak to do much of anything but lie there and feel pissed.

I had other visitors into the day and evening, but their congratulations were tainted by my exchange with Maxen.

As the evening gave way to night, I was surprised to see Nicole come through the door.

After asking about my injuries, we fell into awkward silence.

"Someone said you're going to be leaving?" she asked after a moment.

"I live on the other side of the hedge," I said. "I'd planned to return there, but it looks like I may not get to stay."

"Are they putting you under house arrest, too?" she asked wryly.

She was standing next to the bed, and she fidgeted, moving her feet around in different turned-out positions.

"In a manner of speaking," I said. I eyed her movements. Something about them was plucking at my memory. "Congrats on the stone armor, by the way."

She pushed her fingers though her hair in a gesture that was eerily similar to a gesture I often made. "Oh yeah, your tip helped a lot. Now I don't have to worry about going back to the Duergar, at least."

"Periclase will probably still argue that he's your father, but you're right. You can stay if you want to, now that you've shown you have sufficient New Garg blood." I looked up at her, suddenly realizing why her fidgeting seemed to have a form to it. "Were you a dancer?"

Her eyes widened slightly in surprise. "Ten years in the San Francisco Ballet. Now I'm an instructor. Or I was. You know, before I came here. I've probably lost my job by now."

I let out a short laugh. "We might have more in common than I thought."

"You have a background in dance?"

"Oh, Oberon, no. I'd look like an ox in a tutu. But I'm on the verge of losing my job, too."

"Sorry to hear that."

"Do you know what you're going to do when the time comes?" I asked. I knew it was still early in the homecoming process, but I was curious about where her mind was on the matter.

"I'm pretty sure I'll go back," she said. "Probably have to find a new apartment and a new job, but . . ." She looked around the room and shivered a little, stuffing her hands into the front pocket of her jeans. "This is all just so strange."

Pretty sure. Probably.

I hid a smile. She was going to stay. I'd bet money on it, if I had any to put down. It would be hard for her, but I could see it in her eyes. She knew this—Faerie—was the thing she'd been missing her whole life. The secret that had been whispering through her mind, but she couldn't quite hear.

If I could just come around to some of that acceptance about staying here, my life would be a hell of a lot easier.

I spent the next two days resting and healing, and by the third day, I'd had enough sitting around on my ass to last the rest of my life.

In spite of the protests of people around me, I gathered my things, hopped on Vincenzo, and made my way back to Boise.

Lochlyn had sent me notes while I was recuperating. She'd packed up all of our things, and she'd taken her stuff and moved out of our apartment. She was couch surfing with some of her nightclub friends until she found a job. My stuff was still at our old place, which I discovered had been padlocked.

I drew Mort, punched a little magic into the sword, and jabbed it into the lock. Fortunately, our landlord was a human normal with no magic ability, and he was too cheap to pay for a magic-resistant lock. The mechanism popped open, and I pulled it off and dropped it on the ground.

Inside, the place was empty except for the thrift-store furniture in my room and a couple of boxes that Lochlyn had packed for me, which I knew contained only clothes and a few toiletries. It struck me that I didn't really keep any personal things with me on this side of the hedge. Anything from my childhood was back in my tiny quarters in the fortress. Had some part of me expected I'd someday have to return to there? Maybe. But I'd always felt that getting criminal vampires off the streets was more important than Faerie politics. It was my way of paying homage to the mother I never had a chance to know, whose difficult, young life had been cut short by a vamp. I might be able to save some other kid from losing a parent the way I had.

I had no way to move the furniture, and it wasn't valuable anyway, so I left it. The two boxes got bungeed to the top of Vincenzo's cargo box.

Just as I was about to swing my leg over the seat and start up my scooter, there was a discontented yowl behind me. I turned to see Emerald sitting a couple of feet away, the end of her tail twitching and her green eyes flashing at me. I put the kickstand down and went over to her.

Squatting within arm's reach, but not too close, I reached out a hand. "Hey Emmy. I'm all out of treats, girl. Sorry about that." She moved close enough to poke her head under my outstretched hand, and I scratched her ears. "I've got to take off, but I hope I'll be back."

I straightened, and she scampered off around the corner of the building. That was the thing about cats—they didn't truly need you, so your comings and goings didn't really concern them much.

I'd only gone about two blocks when my cell phone rang. It was Gus, so I answered.

"It wasn't him." My boss made a noisy, nasally sigh.

"What wasn't who?"

"The ashes in the box," my boss said. "They aren't Van Zant's remains."

My jaw tightened. Bryna had somehow played me. How in the hell had she gotten around the promise? You couldn't lie your way through a Faerie oath. It wasn't possible.

"It's your lucky day, kid," Gus said. "You lost your other assignment, the object-find. But I pulled some strings. If you can bring the vamp in alive before midnight, you'll get the full bounty."

My pulse jumped at the challenge.

"Thanks, boss. I'm on it," I said. I hung up and stuffed my phone back in its pocket.

My mind kicked into gear and I sped up, heading to the doorway in the parking garage downtown. I knew where to look for the vamp, and I thought I even knew how Bryna had slithered her way out of our agreement. Van Zant had most likely tricked her, faking his death. Bryna had believed the remains she gave me were his.

I took Vincenzo through the doorway and emerged in the MonsterFit lobby near the Las Vegas Strip. Van Zant was likely hiding out, from Bryna and maybe from others, too. Plus, it was mid-afternoon and still broad daylight. Even daywalking vamps usually preferred to stay out of the peak sunlight hours. My mark was most likely holing up in a place where he felt comfortable and safe.

I parked near the Millennium Hotel, but instead of going through the main lobby, I went through one of the casino entrances. The place had a high-stakes poker game, and knowing Van Zant's reputation as a player, he wouldn't be able to resist. I glamoured myself into my Penelope persona and found a human bartender to chat with, a young guy who was all too happy to show off what he knew about the high-money tables in the back rooms. I nursed watered-down cocktails and spent the next hour learning where the game was held, where the players came in, and what time they usually started rolling in. Then I spent another hour scoping the place and confirming what the bartender had told me. It took some sweet-talking and maneuvering on my part, but I managed to gain access to one of the back hallways where I suspected Van Zant would go from his penthouse elevator to the high-stakes room.

In the end, Van Zant practically walked right into my arms.

The vamp and his entourage were in great spirits as they strolled toward the game. I'd been leaning against the wall, the credit-card-sized bounty certificate hidden in my hand. I pushed away from the wall, putting on a lazy smile, and strolled toward Van Zant and his crew. Several of them took notice of me, looking me up and down.

Van Zant looked scrawnier than I remembered him from the attack on the dark street in the Duergar realm, when I'd cut off his hand. In fact, he didn't look like much at all. I suddenly realized this was not the creature of my childhood nightmares. He was just some playboy poker player who thought he could make it big gambling and selling vamp blood.

"Are you professional poker players?" I asked in a sultry voice. "Because I think that's sooo hot."

"Yeah, beautiful," one of them said. "You wanna be my good luck charm?"

My eyes flicked over to Van Zant. He still sported a bandaged stump on one arm, where I'd removed his hand. "I've got my eye on that one," I crooned.

I felt the shiver of his glamour in the air as he tried to turn his charms on me, obviously not realizing I was Fae.

The group parted so I could move closer to my mark, and I pretended to be drawn in by Van Zant's mesmerization glamour. My smile widened as our eyes met. I got close to him, looking deeply into his dark eyes. Then I lifted my hand, flashing the bounty card in his face.

He looked down in confusion as the certificate lit up with yellow-orange magic that expanded toward him. It rapidly surrounded him in a cloud, and by the time he realized what was happening, it was too late. His identity was confirmed.

The magical mist blurred, shrank, and coalesced around his wrists, securing him in cuffs.

I gave him a flirtatious wink. "Gotcha."

Van Zant's entourage backed away and then split, some of them hurrying back the way they'd come, and others sidling around me and then zipping toward the poker room.

I pulled out my phone, which I'd hidden in my bra, to contact the Guild and arrange transport of the apprehended mark. I let my Penelope glamour dissolve away.

"How's that hand regenerating, Van Zant?" I asked as I raised my phone to my ear.

He sneered, his dark eyes flashing with fury.

Back in Boise, I completed the paperwork while Van Zant was

processed and then stood outside the Guild in the dark with my phone, refreshing my bank balance every few seconds.

The bounty money showed up at ten minutes to midnight. I stared at the number for a few seconds, reveling in the satisfaction of it, before stuffing my phone back into its pouch.

The money had come too late to keep the apartment, and it wouldn't have been enough to sustain me and Lochlyn for more than a couple of weeks, anyway, with what I already owed on Vincenzo's repairs and back payments on rent and utilities. In spite of the exception Gus had swung allowing me another shot at Van Zant, I was still on probation with the Guild for failing to complete the object-find assignment. That meant no real cash flow for at least a few weeks.

I saw the writing on the wall, and it said in big block letters that I was going to have to spend some time at the fortress.

It was okay. I already had the start of my nest egg that would fund my move back out of Faerie. In the meantime, there was work to be done on behalf of the New Gargs, and in my new role as the Order's champion, I had some clout. It was an important time for my people, and for the near future, I'd focus on doing some good for them—for us.

I revved Vincenzo and sped toward the doorway that would take me to San Francisco and my home-for-now in the stone fortress.

**Look for *Stone Blood Legacy* by Jayne Faith,
the next book in the Stone Blood Series!**

About the Author

Jayne Faith writes fantasy set in the real world. She's a meditator, dog lover, TV addict, clean eater, homebody, sun baby, and Sagittarius. Her superpower is her laugh. She owns way too many colored pens and pairs of jeans. Visit her website at www.jaynefaith.com, where you can sign up for her VIP list and get free books.

Also by Jayne Faith

Ella Grey Series

Demon patrol officer Ella Grey beat death after an accident on the job, but something followed her back from the grave. Will it eat her soul or become her greatest ally?

Stone Cold Magic (#1)
Dark Harvest Magic (#2)
Demon Born Magic (#3)
Blood Storm Magic (#4)

Tara Knightley Series

Between paying off a debt to a Fae mob boss, working as a professional thief, and keeping up with her busy three-generation household, Tara Knightley barely has time to eat and sleep. But now she's going to have to choose: her family, love, or her freedom.

Oath of Blood (prequel)

Edge of Magic (#1)
Echo of Bone (#2)
Trace of Fate (#3)
more to come

Stone Blood Series

When vampire hunter Petra Maguire discovers she has a secret twin who's been kidnapped, she's determined to rescue her. But it could spark a magical war.

Blood of Stone (#1)
Stone Blood Legacy (#2)
Rise of the Stone Court (#3)
Reign of the Stone Queen (#4)
War of the Fae Gods (#5)
The Oldest Changeling in Faerie (#6)

Sapient Salvation Series

An innocent young woman fighting to survive in a foreign land. A powerful overlord longing to leave his dark past behind. The moment they meet, worlds clash as forbidden love ignites.

The Selection (#1)
The Awakening (#2)
The Divining (#3)
The Claiming (#4)